GEM

M

Marie Joseph was b   educated at Blackburn High School for Girls. Before her marriage she was in the Civil Service.

She now lives in Middlesex with her husband, a Chartered Engineer, and they have two married daughters.

After a very successful career as a short story writer, Marie Joseph now writes novels set in her native Lancashire, in periods ranging from the turn of the century to the present time. No less than four of her novels have been short-listed for the Romantic Novelist's Association Award during the past few years and her many fans make any new book by Marie Joseph an immediate best-seller. She is a well known public speaker and broadcasts frequently on Radio Four and the Overseas Programmes.

Marie Joseph is also the author of ONE STEP AT A TIME, the moving and at times hilarious account of her constant battle against Rheumatoid Arthritis.

Gemini Girls

MARIE JOSEPH

ARROW BOOKS

Arrow Books Limited
17-21 Conway Street, London W1P 6JD

An imprint of the Hutchinson Publishing Group

London Melbourne Sydney Auckland
Johannesburg and agencies throughout
the world

First published 1982
Arrow edition 1983

Made and printed in Great Britain
by The Anchor Press Ltd
Tiptree, Essex

ISBN 0 09 930830 4

For Sarah and Emily,
my twin granddaughters

One

Libby Peel knew she had no right to be there. But then Libby was not over-concerned with rights and wrongs. All she knew was that on that warm summer evening her whole being throbbed with the excitement of finding herself where she was not supposed to be.

The market place of the Lancashire town that May evening in 1926, on the very eve of the General Strike, was certainly no place for a slightly built girl, her long brown hair bundled up beneath a small straw hat. But Libby felt not even the faintest twinge of fear.

Here was where she was meant to be, right here in the middle of it all, not merely sitting at home with her hands folded in her lap, waiting for things to happen. She found she was almost jumping up and down on the cobblestones as the blood pulsed through her veins with a wildness she had no desire to control.

Mr Baldwin, the Prime Minister, an obstinate, short-sighted, pig-headed little man, in Libby's opinion, had turned up his nose at the idea of any further dealings with the miners – *earthworms*, as a lady member of the aristocracy had called them.

So the strike was on . . .

Already the trains had stopped running, the town's evening newspaper had printed its last 'Special Pink', and to Libby's disgust, the government had seized the monopoly of any further news bulletins, giving of course their side of the case. Even before it had begun, the fight was unequal.

The militant speaker, balanced precariously on a makeshift platform, was a weaver from one of the town's cotton mills, possibly even from the mill owned by Libby's father. The stocky little man was waving his short arms about, yelling at the top of his voice. 'They say the weavers are in the second line. That's all. The bloody second line!' His face glistened with sweat, and his whole body seemed to swell with indignation. 'That's what they say we are!' He pointed a finger, stabbing the air to emphasize his next words. 'But *what* bloody second line? Second lines are called up second, and we are ready *now*, lads. Think on! *We're* ready now!'

The crowd surged forward roaring its approval.

'So what the 'ell are we waiting for?' The speaker put up a clenched fist as a man tried to pull him down from his perch. 'What about Chorley? Now there's a town not waiting for some bloody second line! And don't forget that Chorley's not supposed to be a trade union town. Fertile as bloody granite from a socialist point of view is Chorley, and yet their weavers are ready to walk out to a man. Aye, missus, that's right. To a woman an' all. So where does that leave us, eh?' He dropped his voice a fraction, sensing the crowd's sympathetic attention. 'I'll tell tha lot summat for nowt. The maister at my mill has a son, a great 'aporth of a son what plays golf three mornings a week when he's supposed to be working. Oh, aye, he does that. An' he's a member of the Manchester Exchange, and gets there on a railway contract paid for by the likes of us, while his father's weavers have to feed their families on bread and jam, with sixpenn'orth of fish of a Saturday night when the chip shops want to get rid. Bloody disgraceful!'

Libby stared down at the cobbles. So the man wasn't from her father's mill after all. Oliver Peel's only son, her brother Willie, had been killed in France at the very end of the war. There were no days for Willie at the Manchester Exchange. Willie's life had ended with a flash of gunfire, and life at Westerley, the big house on the outskirts of the town, had never been the same since then.

For the first time since mingling excitedly with the milling crowd, she felt apart from them, and with the feeling came the first twinge of unease. In spite of the third best coat and the plain straw hat, Libby began to realize just how conspicuous she was. She tried to move and found that she was hemmed in as surely as if she had been nailed to the ground.

'We're still a country of down to earth, moderate thinking people,' she had told her twin sister Carrie before sneaking out of the house and starting on her long walk into town. 'It's no use, Carrie, I can't, I just can't sit here at home while everything is happening. I have to be there to *see*.'

Carrie, a mirror image of her twin, had tried hard to dissuade her. Libby frowned, thinking just how conspicuous the two of them would have been standing together in the market place. Most people knew the Peel twins when they were together, even if they were sometimes unsure which was which.

'I am me!' Libby would shout in one of her childish tantrums. 'And she is her!'

Carrie was slightly smaller than her twin. Libby's small brown mole at the left side of her mouth was on the right side of Carrie's, and Libby was right-handed to Carrie's left-handed awkwardness.

Libby was outspoken and sure, while Carrie was quiet and often – very often – not so sure, but this time she had surprised her sister by her vehemence.

'Father will kill you if he finds out where you've gone. He says that dignity for the middle classes is all-important just now, and what is there dignified about going down town all alone and listening to the agitators?'

'Pooh to dignity!' Libby had said, slipping out of the side door. 'There's nothing dignified about being hungry.'

But all the same, remembering Carrie's words, her heart contracted with fear. Oliver Peel sober was a force to be reckoned with, and Oliver Peel in his cups was as bad as a raving lunatic.

'I hate him,' she thought. 'He is my own father and I loathe him.' She kicked viciously at a harmless cobblestone, then turned to apologize as her kick landed on the shin of the man standing next to her.

He stared at her with open curiosity, a tall man with black hair and a thin pale face, flushed now with an excitement to match her own.

'No place for a lass on her own.' The stranger tut-tutted in cheeky disapproval. 'And you *are* on your own, aren't you, lass?' He grinned so that the craggy seriousness of his features broke up into lines of almost boyish mischief. 'Finding out for

9

yourself what the peasants think?'

It was so near to the truth that Libby's large brown eyes fell before his steady gaze. The crowd, pressed from the back, surged forwards towards the speaker's rough platform, and at once the man took her arm and pulled her close to his side, bending down to speak into her ear. 'What the heck *are* you doing here, for heaven's sake, then? Looking for a chance to hop up there yourself and put the other side to us ignorant workers?'

Libby tried to pull away, but he held fast, and because she was privately glad of his supporting arm (although she would rather have died than admit it) she flared into instant and characteristic retaliation.

'I work too,' she told him. As the crowd swayed her hat was knocked sideways, causing the slipping bun of her long hair to wisp down her back.

'In a shop?' The stranger grinned. 'No, come off it, lass. You'll be telling me next you've been out picking coal from the surface Burnley way.' He lifted one of her gloveless hands and pursed up his lips at the sight of the engagement ring on her third finger. 'What's your man doing letting you come down here?' His eyes twinkled. 'Or doesn't he know?'

Libby blushed a fiery red as tears of humiliation pricked behind her eyes. 'I'm a teacher.' With as much dignity as was left to her, she clung to her hat with her free hand. 'And I know why I am here. *I* know.' She tilted her chin. 'There are children in my class who haven't got a pair of clogs to their name, even in the winter, and if their father is lucky enough to have an egg for his tea, they are allowed to dip a finger of toast in it.' Her eyes met his. 'I'm on *your* side, can't you see?'

Tom Silver, a compositor on the town's weekly newspaper and the youngest Father of the Chapel in the county, wrinkled his hawklike nose at her.

'All the same,' he said wickedly, 'I wouldn't mind laying bets that you have never had to queue up with your brothers and sisters for a dip in your father's soft boiled egg. That's a fact, isn't it, lass?'

Libby widened her eyes to stare furiously into the teasing, laughing face so close to her own. She was tightly pressed against his side. She could actually feel the restrained violence

10

emanating from his body. This man was making her feel ridiculous; he was enjoying himself. She did not know him at all, and yet she was being held so close to his side that they might have been lovers. She tried to turn away from him, but at once he swung her round again, and now she could see the irregularity of his front teeth, and the way his brown eyes were flecked with green. He pursed his lips into a mocking semblance of a teasing kiss, and she jerked her head backwards so that the hat slipped even farther sideways.

The part of Libby that was all Oliver Peel made her temper flare. 'If I told you who my father was you wouldn't speak to me like that, whoever you are. But I won't tell you because you wouldn't believe me!'

'Then don't bother, lass.' Tom Silver laughed outright into her upturned face. 'Tell you something, though. If you really are a teacher, I wouldn't like to be in your class.' His next words were drowned by a man built like an ox who had pushed the speaker bodily from the platform.

'This is the day we have been waiting for, lads!' The puffy face beneath the greasy cap sharpened with wild enthusiasm. 'This is the hour when the oppressed throw off their shackles and make a stand for what is theirs by right! As Mr Bevin says: "We are not declaring war on the people. War has already been declared by the Government, urged on from behind by sordid and selfish capitalism!"'

'Good man, Bevin.' Tom Silver pulled hard at Libby's arm as the crowd swayed forward dangerously. 'Come on, lass. There's going to be a free-for-all. The Bolshies want a fight. I am going to get you out of here somehow.'

But even as he turned, a tram rumbled by along the wide street flanking the market square, clearly visible to the inflamed crowd. Driven by a moustached man of immense dignity, an ex-army officer by the look of him, it stopped with a rattling shudder for the passengers to dismount.

Grasping his opportunity to incite his listeners, the speaker wheeled round and pointed an accusing finger at the man standing on the driver's platform.

'The tram men met at nine o'clock this morning, and they are out to a man,' he yelled. 'Come on, lads. Let's have 'im, the filthy scabby blackleg! Let's have them bloody whiskers out by

11

the bloody roots!'

Libby found herself swept off her feet, in spite of Tom Silver's protective arm. She watched in horror as stones were prized up by knives from the cobbled ground and hurled towards the tram. As windows shattered into a hail of splintered glass, the passengers scrambled out, a few of them mingling with the crowd as if uncertain which role would afford them the greater safety. The driver was hauled from his platform to face his accusers with the same courage he had undoubtedly shown on Flanders Field as he faced the enemy lines.

'By tomorrow,' the speaker shouted, cupping his hands to his mouth in an attempt to recapture his audience, 'over one and a half thousand looms will be stopped in this town!' His voice rose to a pitch bordering on hysteria. 'The bloody government have ignored us once too often. We've got 'em, lads, and by the time we've finished, there won't be a machine working, a train running, nor a single poor bugger eking out a miserable existence on what them in Parliament calls a living wage. Listen to me, lads! We've got 'em. I tell you, we've got 'em, and there's nowt they can do to stop us. Listen to me!'

But it was too late. The crowd, desperate now for action and not words, were fighting for the sake of fighting.

'It only takes a handful of bother-makers.' Tom Silver put both arms round Libby as stones flew like a hail of bullets.

Then someone shouted 'The police! The police are here!' and the crowd scattered. Its movement changed like a field of corn rippled by a sudden wind. For a brief moment Libby was actually lifted off her feet, so that she saw a line of policemen crossing the cobbles, truncheons raised.

Tom Silver dragged her with him to the rough platform. 'Stop there, and keep your head down. Don't run, for God's sake!' he told her, then hoisted himself up and raised both arms above his head.

'The police won't interfere!' He was yelling at the top of his voice. 'They are sympathetic, you fools! They are on our side. Drop those stones! Drop the stones, men, and they won't do a thing. Please! Listen to me!'

But again it was too late. Libby held both hands over her head in a futile gesture of protection as the missiles flew. The

12

police advanced slowly, in a determined line of dark blue, and she heard what sounded like the thud of a truncheon on a man's head.

'Run for it, love!' A woman with a brown shawl clutched beneath her chin ran past. 'They'll nab anybody, so run like 'ell.'

Libby could only stand there, transfixed with terror, as the crowd dispersed, the irons on clogged feet ringing metallically. The younger ones were laughing, the older element cursing, and a few sober-suited clerical types walked quickly away, hands in pockets, as if embarrassed by the whole situation. But the hard core of the militants lingered to hurl abuse and stones before they too melted away.

Even as Libby hesitated, a stone whizzed past her head to hit Tom Silver full in the face.

She saw it land, saw the way he put up a bewildered hand to his forehead, saw the blood gush and his features shrivel into a white mask before he fell from the platform to lie in a twisted heap on the ground.

A shout went up from the fleeing crowd. 'The police are attacking the people!'

'That's not true!' Libby heard her own voice yell back, then she knelt down by the still figure crumpled on the cobblestones.

He was quite unconscious, and she saw that the deep gash had missed his left eye by a fraction. He was a strange grey colour, and she pulled his lolling head onto her lap, trying in vain to stem the flow of blood with a white handkerchief pulled from her sleeve.

'Do you know this man, miss?'

The policeman was very young, very correct, his truncheon held almost self-consciously in his hand as he stared down at her.

Libby looked up into his round face and shook her head. 'No, I don't know him. I don't know him at all. He was just standing next to me in the crowd.' Her voice broke on the verge of lost control. 'But he wasn't doing anything wrong. He wasn't fighting. He was trying to calm them down. He *was*!' she added, as the policeman replaced his truncheon and took out his notebook.

'So the victim is unknown to you?' he asked, pencil poised.

Libby shook her head slowly from side to side. If she was watching this, she told herself, on the screen at the Olympia picture palace, she would laugh out loud and think how funny it was. It was like a Charlie Chaplin film: a man lay dying on the pavement as a policeman slowly and seriously took down the particulars in his little notebook. It was incredible, but it was happening. And the stranger, the man who had cheeked her and tried to protect her, looked terrible. He was shaking now, shivering jerkily as a thin trickle of blood oozed down his nose to mingle with the steady flow from the gaping wound so close to his eye.

The evening air was still and warm, unusually heavy for that part of Lancashire, a promise of the long hot summer to come. Libby, without stopping to think, unbuttoned her long fawn duster-coat and laid it over the still figure.

'He must be kept covered. Warm. For the shock,' she whispered, then turned startled eyes as the policeman blew his whistle in a long, piercing blast.

He nodded. 'Everything is being taken care of, miss. Now don't you fash yourself.' He licked the point of his pencil. 'May I have your own name and address, miss? I take it you was a witness to the assault?'

Libby was controlling her impatience with great difficulty. If the policeman did not put his flamin' notebook away *now*, this very minute, she would snatch it from his red hand and throw it as far as she could. But she gave him the information he wanted, unaware of the raised eyebrows as it was taken down neatly on a flipped-over page. She lifted her head and saw with surprise that the market square was now completely deserted. The large crowd had disappeared, the £5 fine for disturbing the peace a deterrent to even the most aggressive.

'What about the ambulance?' Libby's voice was sharp, but the policeman merely held up a hand as if directing the traffic.

'On its way, miss. We had it stationed down the bottom end of Victoria Street. The *motor* ambulance, miss,' he said, his voice tinged with more than a touch of pride as the newly acquired petrol-driven van chugged over the pavement and across the cobblestones.

'Thank God for that.' Libby got to her feet and watched as

14

the unconscious man was wrapped in a red blanket and laid on a stretcher.

'You coming with him, miss?'

She accepted her blood-stained coat from an outstretched hand, and shook her head. 'No. He's in good hands now, and I don't know him personally . . . it was just that – just that . . .'

But the doors were being slammed and the policeman was waving the ambulance away, directing it over the empty square with as much concentration as if streams of traffic converged from every direction.

'Wait!' Libby bent down and picked up a small leather-backed book. 'This must have fallen out of his pocket.'

She held it out in front of her, but the ambulance was already back on the road, and the policeman, his duty done to the letter, walking stolidly away in the opposite direction.

'Ah, well . . .' Libby shook her head. Then, as she pushed the book down into the deep patch-pocket of the coat over her arm, she turned and saw a familiar figure striding towards her – Harry Brandwood, the man she was to marry.

'Oh, Harry!' She tried to smile as she almost ran towards him. 'Oh, thank you for coming to find me. You've no idea! They were like wild animals . . . oh, if only you'd been a few minutes earlier, you could have done something!' She clutched his arm. 'And that policeman! He took my name and address. You don't think they'll get in touch with my father? If my father even finds out I've been down the town, he'll go mad. But I *had* to come.'

Her brown eyes were full of tears, her hair half hanging down her back, and her blood-stained coat trailing on the cobblestones. Dr Harry Brandwood loved this wayward girl with all his being, but she angered him at times with her impulsiveness, her intense way of identifying with matters beyond her experience. Had he been a violent man, he would have taken her across his knee and given her a good beating. He took Libby's hand and started to walk quickly across the square, his face set into stern lines.

He had often told himself that *Carrie* Peel was the twin he should be marrying. Carrie, with her softness, her gentle smile, her understanding. But Carrie was milk and water to Libby's full-bodied red glowing wine. Mirror images of each other they might be, but Libby's mirror was clear and sparkling where Carrie's was soft mother-of-pearl.

Already the crowd was gathering again, eager for more words, more action. The overturned platform was set right way up, and two men fought for the privilege of being the first to put his point of view.

Angrily, Harry hurried Libby along.

'I've got the car over there, down King William Street past the shops.' He was taking such long strides that Libby was forced to make small running steps to keep up with him. Now they were in for one of their frequent quarrels, and this time he didn't care. This time she had gone just too far.

'I don't suppose there's much point in asking you what you were thinking about coming down town on your own at a time like this, is there?' He opened the car door and half pushed her inside. 'And I don't want to listen to any more nonsense about you *having* to be there. You could have listened to the wireless like any other normal woman, or read the bulletins.' He ran round the car to climb in behind the wheel. 'Have you any idea what you look like? Have you any idea of what might have happened?'

He started the car and fought the gears in a fury of frustration. 'When Carrie told me where you'd gone, I could not believe it.'

Libby scrubbed at the bloodstain on her coat, making no impression at all. 'It means less than nothing to Carrie that the whole country is on the brink of revolution.'

'Revolution?' Harry's pleasant face darkened. 'What kind of Bolshie talk is that?'

'Harry Brandwood! You might have the reputation of a good doctor – for the rich of course – but you walk about with your eyes and ears closed.' Libby raised both arms to try to pin the long fall of hair back into place. 'Damn this hair! I'll have it bobbed. This week! Tomorrow!' She jammed the hat on again. 'Do you realize that in this town alone, and almost every other town in the north, come to think of it, there is a choice of three jobs for the boys coming up to school-leaving age? They can go in the mills to work for someone like my father, or they can go as railway clerks or porters, or be apprenticed if they're lucky – or they can go down the mines.'

She dropped a hairpin and scrabbled for it on the floor of the car. 'Do you know, Harry, the brightest lad in my class went as a pony drawer out Burnley way just before the lock-out? He was asthmatic and yet down he went, breathing coal dust into his lungs and crawling on his belly like a mole. You have no idea! I heard that if there's a fall the owners want the ponies out before the men. It's true!' Her eyes blazed. 'There was a girl in the top class at school – Nellie Sharp – and sharp was the right word for her. She had a mind like a razor, and yet because the money was needed at home, do you know what she is doing now? Standing by the belt at the mine and picking the coal over! I saw her once and she showed me her hands, full of blisters and going septic. She told me she has to walk to work across the fields, and it takes her half an hour each way, an' if she gets soaked then she has to stay in the same clothes all day! For seven shillings a week, Harry! And you shy away from the word revolution? You must be blind!'

Harry was bone tired. He had spent forty minutes since a hastily snatched dinner trying to convince a pampered woman there was nothing wrong with her. And above all he was a reasonable man. Struggling to keep his voice low and even, he said, 'Stop and think, darling. How can going on strike help in the long run? People like your father won't suffer, not on a day-to-day life or death basis, but his workers will. I know there *is* exploitation, and there always has been. But conditions *have* changed, and will go on changing. But not this way!'

Libby was still trying to rub at the stain on the coat held on her lap, her small face scarlet with fury. 'Oh, Harry! Can't you even *begin* to see? If the parents got living wages, then there would be no need for them to send their children out to work, *any* work, the very day they leave school. It's a vicious circle. You won't face up to reality, Harry. You never have.'

Even the patience of a man as much in love as Harry Brandwood could exhaust itself. Driving away from the centre of the town now, he turned the car into a quiet street off the main Preston road, and switched off the engine.

'But I was facing up to reality ten years ago, wasn't I, Libby?' His hands left the wheel to hold her fidgeting fingers tightly in a grip that made it impossible for her to break away.

17

He spoke softly and calmly. 'I've never been one for talking overmuch about what I went through or saw out there in France, but believe you me, I saw enough of what you call *reality* to last me a lifetime.'

His mouth set in a grim line as, just for a moment, he was back at the front again. Captain Harry Brandwood, mentioned in dispatches, twice wounded and twice returned to the front line . . . In that quiet street of respectable terraced houses, he was back in the aftermath of battle as he knelt in the Flanders mud trying to ease the last dying moments of soldiers, some of them barely old enough to be called men. Lads from his Lancashire regiment screaming for their mothers through shattered lips. In his mind he felt his feet slip from the duckboards, saw a man's open mouth as he disappeared beneath the sticky stinking mud, weighted down by the pack he had carried for two days without sleep.

'Oh, yes,' he said grimly. 'I've had my share of reality, Libby Peel.'

Libby frowned, not liking her thunder stolen in that way. She tried another tactic. 'Then why don't you take a practice in the town where folks *need* your help? Wouldn't that make more sense than blindly moving into your father's shoes when he retires? Didn't the war make you want to come home and fight for the men who were forced to return to nothing? Some of them daren't call a doctor in because they know they can't afford the shilling a week they would have to pay the doctor's man every Friday night.'

Harry let go of her hands then to stare unblinking through the windscreen. He loved this girl sitting by his side so much that he was prepared to accept the hurtful things she said. She loved him too, he knew that, but sometimes he suspected that she used him as a personal sounding board for her own ideas and emotions. Just as he needed *her* to shake him from his own admitted and sometimes deliberately self-induced complacency.

Libby was strong in both mind and body, and when they married at Christmas she would be a doctor's wife to be proud of. Once he had got her away from that mixed infants' school with its asphalt playground, once he had got her away from her friend Margaret Bottomley with her half-baked socialist

18

ideas, Libby would conform.

Or would she? Harry sighed. 'Remember, Libby, love. The world is made up of winners and losers, and always will be.' He started the car. 'And another thing. The rich can suffer too.' They were on the main road again now. 'This morning I stood by the bed of a child dying of diptheria. I was helpless to do more than watch.' His face crumpled into sadness. 'That child's father owns enough shops to line the Arcade twice over. But no power on earth and no medicine we know could have prevented that child choking to death on its own spittle. So don't get too carried away, Libby. I do sometimes come face to face with what you call realism. Even if my patients do pay through the nose for the privilege of seeing their loved ones die.'

Libby had nothing more to say for the moment. Now that they were getting nearer to home she was forgetting wider issues for the time being. At Westerley her father was waiting. Somehow he would be sure to have found out where she had been. Libby chewed at her bottom lip. Her father could sit at his desk in the billiard room all evening, and still know exactly what was going on everywhere else in the house.

And oh, dear God, if he had drunk too much whisky then his anger could leap and crackle like a fire out of control. Libby closed her eyes, seeing it all . . .

Her mother would cry and clutch her heart, but Carrie would defend her twin even if her body shook with terror. It was all so petty, so shameful, so degrading to have to stand there like a child instead of a grown woman of twenty-two, listening to her father's bigoted, sarcastic flow of invective that made her suspect at times that he might be going mad. Like his sister before him, ending her days in a private clinic, plucking with nervous fingers at the bedclothes as she tried in vain to remember who she was.

Libby sat up straight, tilting her chin defiantly, and when Harry risked a sideways glance he saw that her eyes were as bleak and hard as moorland stones.

'Let's hope the *maister* has drunk enough whisky to soak up most of his temper,' she said without much hope.

*

Oliver Peel had been born in 1862. His grandfather had built Bridge Mill, a four-storey building with a vast weaving shed. A self-made man rather than an established landowner, Abraham Peel had been a weaver himself, had stood at his looms with the noise deafening him, vowing that someday he would move on to what he called 'better things'.

He had achieved this by marrying into money, and from then it was all plain sailing. A fair-minded man, he had given birth to a fair-minded son, Benjamin, who in his turn had fathered Oliver. But with the death of Willie Peel, Oliver's only son, in France, the fair-mindedness had ended.

Westerley was built in Georgian style. There were five wide steps up to the front door leading into a mosaic tiled hall. In the dining room hung an enormous crystal candelabra, and the lounge at the front was liberally dotted with potted ferns. On the first floor were the main bedrooms, with boxlike rooms for the servants at the top of the house, and though Libby on entering the house glanced longingly at the wide staircase, Harry urged her towards the drawing room door.

'You may not have been missed,' he whispered, but in that first quick glance Libby knew the worst had happened.

Her mother, Ettie Peel, cowered like a small pale ghost in the corner of the chesterfield, with Sarah Batt, Ettie's maid and companion, positioned behind her mistress, hands clasped together beneath her high pouter-pigeon bosom. Carrie stood over by the window, her brown eyes wide and anxious as she tried to send out a message of unspoken sympathy and apology for giving the game away. And last but not, dear God, least, Oliver.

He stood in front of the fireplace, legs straddled wide apart, black eyebrows drawn together over the high ridge of the distinctive Peel nose, his glance sliding over Libby as if she did not exist.

'Ah, Harry, lad.' He nodded into the fold of his treble chin. 'There's been a message for you. Over the telephone. Urgent. It was a Mr Bebbington.'

'Oh Lord, I know what that means.' Harry took an instinctive step backwards. 'But her baby's not due until the end of the month.'

Oliver nodded. 'So he said. But it seems her time's come on

sudden like, and she won't see nobody but you, not even your father.' His loud voice boomed in anger as he shot a venomous glance at Libby. 'And if you hadn't had to go traipsing after that one there you'd have been here to take the message a good half hour ago. As it is you'd best be off.'

Libby swivelled her eyes sideways and saw the expression on her fiancé's face – a farmer's face, she often thought. It was a mixture of indecision, anxiety and a professional obedience to his calling. 'I have to go,' the expression said. 'Please try to understand, sweetheart.'

'Yes, you must go at once, Harry.' Libby made no move to go into the hall with him as, reddening uncomfortably, he made his excuses and left, leaving behind him a silence that grew and lengthened, lasting until the sound of the car's wheels on the gravel path outside died away.

And all the time Oliver's dark eyes never left his daughter's face. He was drunk enough to sound sober, but too drunk to sound reasonable, Libby calculated. Trying hard to meet his gaze, she felt her legs tremble and her heart begin to race and she despised herself for her weakness.

She was twenty-two years old, she reminded herself silently. A qualified teacher, engaged to be married to the son of the town's most distinguished doctor. She could walk out of this house and never come back, without taking a thing with her. Harry would marry her next week if she asked him to. They could be married quietly, and his mother and father could retire to their bungalow waiting for them at Lytham St Annes. And she need never set eyes on her father again.

Libby held her head up high, as the silence in the room grew even more menacing. Oh, no, she would never do that, not to her little mother sitting there quietly, nor to Carrie, the sister who was more than a sister. She would stay and stand her ground.

At last Oliver spoke. 'All right then. Now tell me where you've been. Take it slowly, then I can take it in, because when your mother told me I couldn't rightly believe it.'

'He got it out of me love.' Ettie's voice was a whimper. 'And don't go blaming Carrie. She only told *me* to set my mind at rest.'

'You *know* where I've been.' Libby heard the tinkle of a

21

hairpin as it escaped her slipping bun to fall on the polished surround where she stood by the door.

'I would like to hear it from your own mouth.' Oliver was using his voice now to full dramatic advantage, so that it hissed like a whiplash.

Suddenly Libby could bear it no more. 'Oh, Father!' she burst out. 'Please don't make such an issue out of nothing. I only went down the town to see for myself what was going on. I knew there would be speakers on the market place, and I wanted to hear what they had to say. Father! They were decent, hard-working men in the main, and they are fighting for their very existence. I'm a *teacher*, for heaven's sake. Isn't it right that a teacher should know both sides of things?' She glanced round her wildly. 'All I see here, in this house, is *one* side, and I've got to see both. Can't you understand?'

'The miners should have learned their lesson five years ago. Or *last* year, come to that, when Baldwin settled things down.' Oliver's face was now dangerously quiet. 'What I want to know is, were there any of my weavers there? Because if there were . . .' He rolled his big head from side to side. 'They don't know which side their bread's buttered on. It only needs *one* man, one ignorant bother-maker to shout the odds, and they'll all be following him, like sheep. There's only half of them turned up today, and tomorrow, if I know owt, I'll be faced with idle looms, and three bloody contracts unfulfilled. I could tell you summat about strikes, lass, if you asked me. *And* about the unions. Do you know how much the union spent way back in 1896 to keep that strike going?' Clasping the lapels of his smoking jacket with both hands he rose up onto his toes. 'Eight hundred and fifty pounds a week! So how much do you think they've got in the kitty now?' He snorted. 'Enough to put me out of business if it goes on long enough, and you, *you* have the effrontery to creep from the house to side with them!'

'No!' Libby took a step forward. 'No, that's where you're wrong, Father. I didn't go down to take anybody's side. I went because I wanted to listen to what they had to say. I have a right to know, to make up my own mind.'

Oliver's florid face turned purple. 'Right? Did you say *right*? Let me tell you something, lass. As long as you live under my roof you have *no* rights. If you'd been born sooner you'd have

22

been like them daft women chaining themselves to railings for the vote. And for what? To vote for something they know nowt about!' He raised a clenched fist. 'One son. One son was all I had, and he had to go and get himself killed, leaving me here in a house full of women, with even the cat a bloody female!'

'Oliver . . .' Ettie Peel made an involuntary movement as if to get up. 'Please don't bring Willie into it. You know how it upsets me.' She laid a hand over her heart. 'It's not my fault, and it's not Libby's fault she's not a man. She's high-spirited, that's all. No harm's been done.'

'No harm?' Oliver turned on his wife. 'No harm for a daughter of this town's best-known mill owner to be seen mingling with the scum of the earth, down on the market of an evening looking like a night woman? What did you do down there, Libby Peel? Jump on a soapbox and encourage that rabble to walk out on their wicked employers? I must be the laughing stock of the whole town. "How can he control his workers when he can't control his own daughter?" That's what they'll be saying over their ale. Oh, aye, they can always find the money for ale even when their families are supposed to be starving.'

'Some of their children *are* nearly starving, Father.' Libby spoke quietly. 'There are a dozen children in my class alone with rickets, and that is a direct result of not getting proper food. Half of them with head lice, and not because they're dirty, but because they have to sleep four and sometimes five to a bed.' Forgetting all self-control, Libby raised her voice. 'It's *time* they rebelled. And I'll tell you something else. I hope they all come out, and I hope they stay out long enough to make you and your like see sense! That's what I hope!'

One minute Oliver was standing, back to the fire, then the next, without seeming to move, he shot out a big hand and struck Libby hard across the face.

Too shocked to retaliate, Libby felt tears of outrage and shame fill her eyes, and saw in the same moment her mother crumple forward, to be saved from falling to the carpet by the swift action of Sarah Blatt who, moving like lightning, came from behind the chesterfield to take her mistress in her arms.

'I am all right.' Ettie spoke in a whisper, her face white as chalk, her lips a strange blue colour. 'I never thought to see the

23

day when in my own house . . .' Her voice faltered as Sarah, helped by Carrie, led the trembling woman from the room.

Oliver stood irresolute for a moment. Before Libby too turned to follow the little procession upstairs their eyes met, and the glance was shot through with mutual dislike, a hatred that was almost tangible.

'Go and see to your mother,' he muttered before striding into the hall and flinging open the door of the billiard room opposite. 'And just keep out of my sight for a bit, that's all.'

For as long as Libby could remember her mother and father had slept in separate rooms. The carrying of twins and their difficult birth had left Ettie a semi-invalid. Libby could never remember a time when, bursting in from school full of the day's doings, she had not been shushed into silence by the frail little woman half lying on the chesterfield in the big front room.

Now Ettie was drooping, ashen-faced, as between them Sarah Batt and Carrie helped her to undress and got her into bed.

'Shall I send for Dr Brandwood?' Libby hovered, helpless, one side of her face scarlet, the tears of humiliation still prickling behind her eyes.

Sarah shook her head. 'I don't think so, miss. She's just upset, that's all. It affects her like this. I'll go down and fetch some hot milk. It usually settles her off nicely.'

Neither Libby nor Carrie thought there was anything unusual in Sarah talking to them over her mother's head as if Ettie was not only blind and deaf but mentally retarded as well. Sarah's devotion to her mistress was complete, and although the reason was never mentioned it was fully understood.

At twenty-six, Sarah Batt had the figure of a young matron and the face of a twelve-year-old child. Hair as red as a lick of flame sprang from her childish forehead above eyes as blue and shining as bluebells. Coming to the family straight from school, she had disgraced herself by having a baby in 1918, fathered, it was understood, by a soldier who had had his way with her on one of her rare evenings off. The child, a boy, was being brought up by Sarah's parents in a village five miles the other side of the town, and in deference to Sarah's sensitivity the matter was never referred to. The entire episode had warranted a mere five months' absence by Sarah from Westerley, and if Sarah pined for the boy she saw only once a month on her weekend off, the longing was never expressed, not even by a sudden unexplained clouding of the blue eyes or a droop of the wide smiling mouth.

When Sarah came back upstairs bearing a tray with hot milk in a glass and a couple of water biscuits on a tray, Ettie was being ministered to by a twin on either side of her bed, one patting her hand and the other smoothing her brow.

'You must try and understand your father better,' she was telling Libby in a weak voice. 'It's not just this strike upsetting him. He's not a young man, and with Willie gone . . .' Her lip trembled. 'With Willie gone there's nobody to take over.' She sighed at the skin forming on the top of the hot milk, only to have the offending layer spooned away by Sarah Batt before the sigh was over. Tears formed in her eyes, and as if following an unseen signal Libby and Carrie nodded to each other, leaned over to kiss their mother good night and left the room.

There was a dividing door between the twin's bedrooms, usually left open so that they could call out to each other, but conferences, shared secrets, long unrewarding discussions about their parents – 'Was Mother really as ill as all that?' and 'How much longer could Libby stand being in the same house as her father?' – always took place in Libby's room.

'That's it! Finished!' Libby declared the minute the door onto the wide landing was closed. 'If it hadn't been for Mother I would have left, for good!' She threw herself down on her bed, twisting round so she could see her reflection in the dressing-table mirror. 'I can't stay here now until the wedding at Christmas. He might have reduced Mother to a nothing, but he's not doing it to me.' She touched her cheek as if still feeling the flat-handed slap. 'He's mad, that's what he is, and it's no use blaming Willie's death for his behaviour. It's eight years since it happened. Eight years since the war ended, and I am sick and tired of being blamed for not being a boy to take over at the mill.' She sat up suddenly. 'How does he know that Willie would have wanted to, anyway? He hadn't shown much aptitude for it when he rushed off to enlist. Why should his being killed have suddenly turned him into a plaster saint?'

Carrie sat down on the dressing-table stool. 'Nobody knows how Willie would have turned out. But he was special, you know that.' She picked up a small leather-framed photograph of a fair young man in army officer's uniform gazing seriously into the camera. 'He only went into the mill for Mother's sake, because that was what was expected of him, and because he knew Father would have created. It was his *kindness* I remember best. Do you remember the time he talked Father into letting us ride bicycles? And how nice he was to Sarah? I think she had a bit of a crush on him. I've seen her blush sometimes when his name is mentioned.'

Libby wasn't really listening. She was still shaking inside from the aftermath of the scene downstairs. It was all very well for Carrie to sit there, calm and reasonable so that it was impossible to know what she was really thinking. Carrie was *too* calm and reasonable, especially lately. It seemed at times as if she was away in some far-off place, dreaming her own dreams, thinking her own thoughts, so that nothing happening around her really touched her. She would come home each day from the private school by the park where she taught History and French, to sit with her sewing, going occasionally to concerts in the town with a friend who still wore black for her sweetheart who had been killed at the front. Carrie, in her twin's opinion, was halfway to being a spinster herself. And she didn't seem to care, which was worse.

'What will you do here when I'm married?' Libby heard herself ask the question suddenly.

'What do you mean? What will I do?' Carrie stared down at the pink flowers blooming on the carpet. 'Stay here, of course. What else could I do? I like my job, and I've got my friends and my music, and you're not exactly going to the other side of the world. Not even to the other side of the town.'

For a long moment the sisters stared at each other, a look compounded of a love that was closer than any mere affinity. Libby, perhaps for the first time, was seeing clearly how it would be for Carrie when she had gone. How it would be for herself, too.

No more bedroom conferences, no more shared amusement at mealtimes when their eyes would meet in silent laughter.

No Carrie to run to when she was mixed up and frustrated. No Carrie for Libby to lead, sure that her sister would follow.

'Oh, I *wish* Harry had fallen in love with you instead of with me!' Libby kicked off her shoes. 'You would make a much better doctor's wife that I can ever hope to be. You *tolerate* fools, Carrie, where I . . . where I want to spit in their eye.'

'If you really wish that, then you don't love him.' Carrie went to pick up the scattered shoes, laying them neatly side by side. 'You're not marrying Harry just to get away from Father, are you? Because if you are, that's despicable. He's far too nice for that.'

'I think you love him more than a little yourself,' the demon on Libby's shoulder prodded her to say. 'All right, then, you can have him. I hand him over to you, as of now.'

To her astonishment, instead of flaring up in indignation, Carrie went as pink as the carpet flowers. Turning her back and sitting sideways so that all Libby could see was her straight back and her brown hair twisted into a knot at the nape of her neck, she whispered, 'Suppose you fell in love . . . oh, what I mean is, suppose, just for the sake of supposing, you fell in love with someone not at all suitable – what would you do?'

'Marry him,' Libby said promptly. 'If he wanted me, that is. But then I would never fall in love with anyone who didn't love me. It would be a waste of time.' She started to unpin the heavy weight of her hair, too self-obsessed to realize that her twin was in real distress, that Carrie's fingers were twisting together in an agony of despair. 'I happen to love Harry, not because he is a good doctor with a thriving practice to take on when his father retires, but because I enjoy being made love to by him, especially when he is angry with me. His kisses are exciting when I know he really wants to hit me, like Father hit me downstairs.' She took her brush from the dressing table and began to sweep it through her hair. 'I'm longing to know what it's *really* like when you're married. Aren't you? I wonder if it's as wonderful as it says in books?'

But Carrie, her shoulders heaving, got up suddenly from the stool and rushed through into her own room, closing the dividing door behind her with a soft click.

As she was standing right behind the door, Libby could

hear her crying as she turned the door handle, only to realize that the bolt had been shot into place on the other side. With the width of the oak-panelled door between them Libby spoke softly, urgently. 'Carrie! Open the door! Come on. Stop being silly.' She pushed as if by sheer strength she could force her way through into the other room. 'Carrie! I had no idea. I didn't know . . . look, we have to *talk*. I always knew you liked Harry, but I never dreamed . . .'

'It's not Harry.' The whispered words sounded as though they were hurting Carrie to say them. 'Please go away, Libby. I can't talk to you. Not just now. Tomorrow perhaps, but not tonight. There's been enough.' There was a slight pause. 'When Father hit you it was as though he was hitting me, and in a strange way it hurt me more than I think it hurt you. I just want to be alone. *Please*, Libby.'

Libby rattled the door handle in a last protest, then stepped back. What Carrie had just said made indisputable sense. To chastize one twin was to chastize the other, to hit one twin was exactly the same as hitting the other. It had always been so, and always would be, because the bond between them was stronger than could be explained rationally. It was probably the only inexplicable fact that Libby could accept.

But who? When? Where? She tried to bring to mind half a dozen of Carrie's admirers, dismissing each one with a shake of her head. Carrie had never been serious about any man. Libby knew her through and through. Sometimes the ten minutes' difference in their ages stretched into years as far as worldliness and experience went. And yet . . . She moved to the door again.

'You're all right? I won't go to bed till I know you're all right.'

'I'm all right. Truly.' Carrie's voice was weary, but she had stopped crying. Knowing for once when she was beaten, Libby began to pull the stockinette blouse over her head. It was nothing. Probably some man had stared at Carrie on the tram on the way to school, and, knowing her sister's romantic turn of mind, Libby assumed she had blown it up into a grand passion, fired now by the distressing scene downstairs. Libby raised her voice. 'Meet me after school down town tomorrow and we'll have our hair cut off, shall we? I dare you.'

'Without telling Father?'

Libby sighed with relief at the normality of her twin's breathless voice.

'Without telling Father. He can't stick it back on again once we've done it.'

'Maybe.' Libby saw the door handle begin to turn, held her breath, then sighed as Carrie changed her mind. She rubbed at the beginning of a headache throbbing between her eyes. Enough was enough for tonight. Too much had happened in too short a time. Now she was alone for the first time since coming back home, she could hear the shouts and angry voices of the men down on the market place. She saw the tall, thin man with black hair fall from the platform, his face as grey as dust, the blood running down his cheeks from the wound on his forehead.

'Oh, God. My coat!' She looked wildly round for a second, then remembered dropping the fawn duster-coat on a chair in the hall as she came in with Harry. The bloodstains down the front would be the start of another violent inquisition by her father if he found it.

Pulling the loose blouse over her head again she opened the door quietly. If she could creep downstairs without being seen she would be safe. She hesitated, peering through the crack in the door.

The house was quiet. Sarah Batt would be in her own room, the little room at the end of the landing, once used as a sewing room but now given over to Sarah so that she could be as near as possible to her mistress. Mrs Edwards, the live-in cook, as deaf as a post, would be snoring her head off in her room on the upper floor, and Martha Cardwell, the maid of all work, had gone to bed long ago to read one of the new confession magazines to which she was addicted. And Oliver . . . he was still downstairs in the billiard room. Libby knew that because the hall light was still on. If she went down now, if she crept down, picked up the coat and ran back, all would be well. Libby bit her lip. It was possible that Oliver would never see it, but then Sarah Batt or Martha might pick it up early in the morning, see the mud and the bloodstains on it, and oh, dear God, she was in no mood for explanations. She moved to open the door, then stepped back quickly as the light streamed out from the billiard room into the hall with its shaded wall fixtures.

Oliver Peel was coming up to bed.

Still as a mouse, Libby waited until she heard his unsteady progress up the stairway, heard him stumble past her door. Opening it a crack she saw him turn, not into his own room at the end of the landing, but towards the shorter flight of stairs to the upper floor, pulling himself up by the banister rail, unfastening his waistcoat buttons as he went.

There was no mistaking it. No mistaking where he was going. Libby put a hand over her mouth. Her heart was beating rapidly as if she had run a race, and she felt sick. She could have been sick right there.

Instead she tiptoed to the foot of the short flight of stairs, heard the click of a door – but whose door? Mrs Edwards, a thin sparse widow of at least forty-five, hiding her deafness with wild and mostly inaccurate guesses at what was said to her? Or little Martha Cardwell, sixteen, no more, with her giggles and her pathetic efforts to please?

Was she pleasing Oliver Peel this minute, sitting up in her narrow bed in her nightdress, waiting for him to come to her?

But her father was *old*. He was . . . he was . . . Libby ran downstairs, making no sound, needing to run somewhere, even if it was only to fetch the coat, which now seemed less important.

Back in her room she sat on the edge of her bed, holding the coat pressed to her cheek, rocking backwards and forwards, trying to come to terms with what she had just seen. Oliver Peel was a strong, virile man, with a full-blooded man's appetite. As his wife had lived the life of a semi-invalid since the birth of her daughters, it followed that what he needed he must find. Libby stopped the rocking and let the coat drop to the floor.

With trembling fingers she began to undress, kicking the coat to one side and dislodging the little leather-backed book from the pocket. It meant nothing to her at that moment, but when she was in bed and before she had put out the light, she opened it at random.

'My heart leaps up when I behold a rainbow in the sky; So was it when my life began; so is it now I am a man.'

Libby rippled the closely written pages and read on:

'The day is placid in its going, to a lingering motion bound, like the river in its flowing; Can there be a softer sound?'

Then scribbled at the bottom of the page; 'Wordsworth's poems, each time I read them, seem to be so simple, so fresh, it is as though the dew were still on them . . .'

The book lay on the coverlet as Libby put both hands to her face to feel the tears slipping down her cheeks. Had he copied them out, the tall thin man, at a time when he felt unhappy? And had they helped him, as they were undoubtedly helping Libby now, to release the tensions of an emotion-filled hour with the comfort of tears?

Two

The lane leading to the main road from Westerley was May green, fields glittering yellow with buttercups stretching away to one side, flanked on the other by the dark brown of ploughed earth. In the soft spill of sunshine the air was scented with hawthorns, and the horse-chesnut tree on the corner had patterned the grass verge with pink petals.

It was a morning for slow lingering, but both girls pedalled away furiously, the wheels of their bicycles turning in unison. Carrie's face was pale beneath the upturned brim of her hat, and Libby was unusually silent.

'Thank goodness Father got away before we came down to breakfast. I couldn't have borne a scene before breakfast.'

Libby put up a hand to hold onto her hat, dislodged by a sudden gust of wind, and the bicycle veered dangerously close to her sister's front wheel.

'I'm not afraid of Father,' she shouted. 'I admit I might have been at times, but not any more.'

She pressed her lips tightly together at the memory of him creeping soft-footed up the stairs to the upper floor, her concentration slipping again.

'Careful!' Carrie wobbled towards the kerb. 'See, there's no tram there. We were right to get our bicycles out. The men *must* have come out on strike.'

'They've got pickets down at the depot.' Libby started to freewheel as the road sloped downwards. 'They're to get seventeen shillings and sixpence strike pay. How about us going into the recruiting station at the Public Hall and volunteering as conductors? It would be a bit of a lark, wouldn't it?'

'Whose side *are* you on?' Carrie shouted the words back over her shoulder. 'Last night you were talking Bolshie, now you're on the other side. Come on, our Libby. Whose side are you on, really?'

'Both, I suppose.' Libby was loftily unperturbed. 'I was talking to a man on the market place last night. He wasn't a Bolshie, but he knew the miners couldn't go on and on talking. After five years of trying they've had enough!'

For the next mile or so they pedalled on in silence. Carrie was busy with her own tremulous thoughts. Soon she would leave Libby to turn into the rhododendron-fringed drive of the Park School. Already pupils wearing the scarlet blazers and caps with black velvet trimmings were hurrying in twos and threes along the wide pavements. The majority of them were girls from the big houses on the outskirts of the town, their fathers the businessmen, lawyers, bankers and professional men who could afford the fees to have their children privately educated. Soon she would wheel her bicycle into the shed at the back, hurry through the back door of the red-brick building and up the wide oak-panelled staircase to the staff room, taking off her hat as she went, her heart beating in anticipation and hope that Mungo McDermot, the English master, would be there alone. Anticipating the smile on his lean face as he turned and saw her.

When it actually happened it was almost like the re-run of a film, except that this morning he broke their rigid rule to take her in his arms and kiss her mouth.

It was not a very long kiss, and, terrified of being caught, Carrie did not respond. Instead she pushed him away and went to stand at the other side of the room with the width of a table between them.

'You mustn't do that here! You promised!' Her face was full of fretting anxiety. 'I passed Mr Eccles on the stairs, and Miss Clayton has arrived. I saw her bicycle in the shed. I came on mine,' she added desperately, trying to channel the conversation into some sort of normality. Mr Eccles, the headmaster, had once sacked a woman teacher on the spot for coming to school in too short a dress, only to have her reinstated the week after by the intervention of her father who was on the board of governors. Besides, Carrie knew she was no Libby, defiant just for the sake of being defiant. What was happening between her

33

and Mungo McDermot sent the blood flowing nervously through her body with an emotion that was half fear and half thwarted passion. She steeled herself against the slumbering desire in his eyes, making a determined effort to change the subject.

'Isn't the strike awful? Libby went down to hear the speakers on the market place last night, and she says it will go on for months. Father's workers are joining in unofficially before they are even called out. Libby says she doesn't blame them.'

Mungo wasn't in the least interested in the strike or in what Libby Peel might say or think. Ever since the day he had seen the two sisters together, walking home from church in the dusk, and had raised his trilby hat to one of them without being completely sure it was Carrie, he had disliked intensely the inescapable fact that she was an identical twin.

To Mungo, Carrie Peel was unique – she had to be. He felt the familiar stirring of desire as he watched her take off her short jacket and saw the high swell of her breasts straining against the button fastening of her cotton dress. His Carrie was as clean and fresh as bleached linen, and when he held her close she smelt of sun-warmed apricots. He took a step forward, only to see her back away as she picked up a blue-covered register and held it in front of her like a shield.

'I hate it when the evenings grow lighter,' he whispered with one eye on the door. 'But I have to see you alone. Meet me after school.'

There was no need to tell her where. As the long cold winter had turned into spring they had found a place and made it all their own. It was an old summer house, nestling behind a high brick wall in the grounds of an eighteenth-century manor house, too neglected and overgrown with ivy and trailing weeds to be of interest even to stone-throwing boys. There had been talk for years of turning the manor into a school or a nursing home, but with every passing year it grew more derelict, seeming to sink deeper into its shroud of ivy.

There was an inside bolt on the door of the tiny summer house, an ancient bamboo lounging chair, a relic of glories long since past, and two small windows over which Mungo sometimes fastened pieces of corrugated paper. Once through the rusty gate and inside the summer house they were totally private and excitingly alone. As it was no more than a quarter of a mile from Westerley, and as no one ever thought to query the time a teacher stayed late after school, it was the perfect rendezvous.

'I can't meet you today,' she whispered frantically. 'I'm meeting Libby in town.' She put up a hand to the tidy bun at the nape of her neck. 'We are going to have our hair cut short.'

'Oh, no!' Mungo forgot to be circumspect, raising his voice as he leaned across the table. 'I won't allow it! Not your beautiful hair!' He had noticed the way she had said 'our' hair, not 'my' hair, and his hands clenched into fists as he thumped them on the table. 'Let your sister do as she likes, but you stay the way you are.'

'Then I will never again mistake one of you for the other,' was what he really meant. 'Tomorrow then,' he whispered as Miss Clayton, the gym mistress, burst into the room, bouncing on her crêpe-soled plimsolls, her shiny face eager with suspicion as she darted quick glances from one to the other.

'Good morning, Miss Peel. Good morning, Mr McDermot.' She walked over to the cupboard, her shoes making little sucking noises on the parquet floor. 'What's the matter with *him*? He looks as if he's lost half a crown and found a sixpence.' She stared at the door as it closed behind Mungo. 'Bit shirty, is he, because we teachers haven't struck?'

'He isn't always very well, Miss Clayton.' Carrie walked towards the door with the register, deciding to tell Libby she had changed her mind about her hair, yet knowing that when the time came she would follow her sister and submit to the scissors like a sheep submitting to the shears.

In the mean streets surrounding Libby's school no birds sang. There was no rhododendron-fringed drive leading to the squat two-storey building, its grey stones weathered with grime, just a square asphalt playground penned in from the street by iron railings. The children wore mostly hand-me-downs, and the only sport was drill, with the pupils marching round and round the playground, swinging their arms to the shouted instructions of whichever teacher happened to be on duty at the time.

The three classes for the younger children were held in one big room, split into sections by sliding glass doors, and because Libby's class of seven- to eight-year-olds was at the far end it could only be approached through the two outer rooms.

Margaret Bottomley, the infants' teacher, was already at her desk, sorting through a pile of grey colouring paper, her neat head with its two earphones of plaited hair bent industriously over her task.

'Well, did you go?' She pulled at the drooping skirt of her brown jumper suit, torn between the desire to look modern and the shame of showing her fat knees. 'I heard there was a bit of a to-do. You would have been far better coming with me to the Labour meeting. They let us in with the men. You'd be surprised how much money they've collected from their ha'penny a week door-to-door collections. We're going to win, Libby, make no mistake, this time we're going to win.' She lowered her voice. 'There's a rumour that Ellen Wilkinson might be coming up to give us a talk, and you know what they say about her? She's a woman for women all right.'

Libby wrinkled her nose at the sour smell which always seemed to be at its worst in the infants' classroom. It was the smell of neglect, of ammonia, of clothes not washed often enough, and made worse by a flannel of cress growing sourly from one of the high window ledges.

'I can't join, Margaret, not while I'm living at home.' She rubbed the side of her face reflectively, remembering with shame the sharp sting of her father's flat-handed slap. 'I'm with you all right, but I can't openly flaunt my faith.' She stared down at the bare boards of the classroom's slightly sloping floor. 'It's different for you. You're independent.'

'You mean I live at home with a mother who couldn't care less? You mean I haven't got a man? Not a father nor a fiancé to keep me in line?' Margaret Bottomley's thick neck flushed an unbecoming red. 'Especially a father who is a capitalist.' She glared at Libby with an expression of contempt. '*You* are only playing at it, Libby Peel! You think you can identify, but you can't. *You* didn't have to leave school at thirteen, then work in a factory by day and swot at nights for years and years to get your place at college. Then when you were there you didn't have to exist on a grant so small you were patching the inside of your shoes with cardboard. Libby Peel, it took me six years to be a teacher, so no wonder I am *independent*!'

She banged the register down on her desk, and made no attempt to pick up a pen when it rolled to the floor. 'You should be thinking of joining the Conservative Club, not the Labour movement. Stanley Baldwin's more of a Labourite than you!'

'Have you heard of a man called Tom Silver?'

Libby had no idea what had made her say that. All she knew was that somehow she had to put a stop to her friend's chip-on-the-shoulder tirade. She liked and admired Margaret Bottomley, knew that her life was drab, her out-of-school activities given over to caring for a querulous invalid mother and her newly found burning enthusiasm for the women's section of the Labour Party. But the flushed quivering face with its thin tight lips filled her with distaste.

'I met him last night,' she went on miserably. 'He was hit by a flying cobblestone, and I thought that as he seemed to be . . . as he was so obviously wrapped up in the cause . . .' Her voice trailed away.

'Tom Silver? Tom Silver?' Miss Bottomley pursed her top lip so that her incipient moustache darkened into ugly prominence. 'I should think I do know him. He's been victimized twice for what he believes. He'd die for his members, Tom Silver would. He's a Father of the Chapel, and turned down the offer of a job as Secretary of the Trades and Labour Council not long ago. Was *he* speaking, then?'

'No.' Libby turned her head towards the windows as the playground bell clanged out. She was furious with herself for mentioning the name she had seen written inside the front cover of the small notebook, and could not think why it had just popped out like that. Now Margaret Bottomley would worry at it like a puppy with an old slipper until she found out more. For someone who boasted she could get along without a man, thank you very much, Margaret took a marked interest in them, Libby thought uncharitably. She imparted a bit more information with an obvious show of reluctance.

'I don't think he was too badly hurt, though he looked awful. He was knocked unconscious, and his face was bleeding.' Her eyes half closed at the disturbing memory of that grey

37

face and the blood trickling down the side of his nose. 'He dropped a book. I've got it at home as a matter of fact.' She sighed. 'His name and address were in the front.'

The children were marching into their classrooms now, to stand by their desks for morning prayers before the slides were dragged across by the boy monitors from the top class. Miss Thomson, a large John Bull type woman, was easing her ample behind onto the piano stool, but Margaret would have her say, and Libby knew it.

'Bring the book tomorrow.' The pale eyes shone with eagerness. 'I have to go up to the infirmary in the evening to visit a friend. I'll take it off your hands, find Tom Silver and explain. Save you posting it on.'

'I hadn't quite decided . . .' Libby turned away, knowing that as far as Margaret was concerned the matter was settled. She moved through into her own classroom.

She paid no attention at all to the religious doctrine gabbled by the children. She sang 'Fight the Good Fight' with her head held high, her lips moving without any sound coming from them. Damn and blast Margaret Bottomley with her interfering nosiness! Libby closed her eyes as the morning prayer washed over her. She hadn't even finished reading the poems penned in that neat firm handwriting. And the ones she had read seemed to be such an antithesis of the man himself. She remembered his teasing laughter, his scorn of her middle-class ignorance and all he thought she stood for, and she remembered the feel of his arm holding her in tight protection against the swaying crowd. She had thought . . . she must have thought subconsciously that she would return the book herself. To thank him, that was all, merely to thank him for helping her, and maybe to show him that she was serious in her need to identify with the strikers. It didn't matter, of course, what he thought of her, one way or the other, but it would have been – it might have been interesting, at least.

'Amen,' intoned the headmistress, and Libby went to take her place on the raised dais which supported her desk. She waited until the children were seated, hands on heads, patiently obedient.

'Take out your arithmetic exercise books.'

As the dividing glass slides were dragged back into the

closed position, thirty-eight children banged back their desk lids. Libby began to set out the sums on the blackboard while the ink monitor, a smug boy wearing round spectacles and an air of gloating power, walked round the desks with a tray, dropping the grey inkpots into their waiting wells.

The squeaking of the chalk on a greasy patch of blackboard set Libby's jangled nerves quivering. She felt suddenly penned in, trapped, as if out there through the high windows things were happening, wonderful, terrible things that could change the course of the country's history. She made a mistake and rubbed at it furiously with the board duster. Banners were being paraded, open-air meetings held, blacklegs routed, picketing organized, collections raised for those without a few pennies put by. Miners, railwaymen, transport workers, engineers, weavers and spinners, all united in the common cause.

And the only futile pathetic gesture of defiance she, Libby Peel, was going to make that day was to have her hair cut short at half past four . . . She pressed too hard on the chalk and it broke into two pieces in her fingers, causing her to whip round in anger at the girl in the front row who had dared to laugh.

'Do you two know what you look like?' Oliver Peel's lips curled with sarcasm, and his words had a slurred edge to them.

He had been drinking before dinner, Libby concluded, shutting himself away in the billiard room straight from his return from the mill, scarlet-faced and glowering. Carrie shot her a warning glance, so with difficulty Libby held her tongue.

Because each twin possessed an identical unruly cowlick at the hairline, Libby's on the right and Carrie's on the left, the hairdresser had trimmed the front of their glossy hair into fringes, club-cutting the rest to jaw length so that it swung forward onto their cheeks.

Mesmerized by the two faces staring at him from the long mirror, he had snipped away, first at one head then the other, matching each snip so that the end result had been to make the two girls look even more alike than when they had first walked into the newly thriving salon in the town's main street.

'Like two bloody peas in two bloody pods,' he was to tell his wife that night. 'Till the cheeky one smiled, then you could tell the difference. But before that there *were* no difference!'

Now Oliver faced them across the dining table, with Martha Cardwell serving the roast lamb in her usual fluttery manner, her movements jerky and disconnected. Had a glance passed between the peak-nosed girl and Oliver as she hovered by his shoulder with the jug of mint sauce? Libby shivered with distaste. Or was Mrs Edwards, out in the kitchen sliding the milk jelly onto a platter, counting the hours till her maister crept up the stairs again? Disgust sharpened her voice so that Carrie looked up in dismay.

'What *do* you think we look like, Father?' Calmly Libby passed the dish of chopped carrots to her sister, ignoring Carrie's eye signals. 'At least it won't take hours to dry now. When we went up to Mother's room she said she thought it looked rather nice.'

'Then your mother's a fool!' Oliver tucked a white linen napkin into the front of his waistcoat, threading it between two buttonholes, then picked up his knife and fork. 'Right then, Libby Peel. Since you ask me I will tell you what you look like.' He pointed his knife at each twin in turn. 'You look like a couple of street women! A pair of whores. All you need is a feather boa apiece, stuff on your faces and your skirts even shorter than what they are. And I'll tell you something else. You wouldn't get past the Town Hall without being picked up by two men who have nowt else to do at the moment but roam the town looking for trouble!'

'Father!' Carrie blushed bright red, but Libby waited until Martha had walked out of the dining room. Turning her head to make sure the door was safely closed, she leaned forward and said softly, 'Martha Cardwell has her hair cut short, Father. Even shorter than ours. Do you think of her like that? Does Martha look like a whore, Father? Is that why the word came to your mind?'

Carrie gave a little gasp, but Libby kept her gaze steady on her father's face. For a moment their eyes locked, then Oliver was the first to turn away. His high colour deepened to purple and his left eyelid began to twitch. For a startled moment Libby was sure he was going to hurl the contents of the gravy boat straight at her.

40

'Get on with your dinner.' He was blustering and she knew it. 'There's been enough bother down at the mill today without you riling me. You'd be smirking the other side of your face if you knew how many contracts I stand to lose. Aye, and it would be jam butties for your dinner, not roast lamb. You'd soon lose them Bolshie ideas if you had to get your snouts in the trough along with the rest of them. I've had enough, more than enough, for one day.'

As the meal continued in uneasy silence, Libby knew she had guessed right. It was to Martha's bed her father crept at night when the house was shrouded in darkness and his family slept.

Triumphantly she speared a sliver of lamb on the prongs of her fork, telling herself that never again would she walk in terror of this man, this shouting bully of a man who just happened to be her father. She watched him carefully as he gulped his food without chewing, controlling his emotions with difficulty. Refusing the Lancashire cheese which followed the pudding, he threw down his napkin with an obvious gesture of relief and walked quickly to the door, slamming it behind him. The slam was echoed by the banging of the door of the billiard room.

Libby smiled at her sister. 'Well, that wasn't too bad, was it?' She pulled a dark wing of hair forward, laughed as it barely reached her nose, then squinted down at it. 'The only way to defend oneself against a bully is to *attack*. I'm always telling you that, Carrie.'

'All the same, I wish you hadn't said that.' Carrie rolled up her napkin and slid it tidily into the silver ring marked with her initial. 'Father will never forgive you. He's not stupid, you know.'

'Aren't you going to have any cheese?' Libby helped herself to a crumbly wedge, then stretched out a hand to the bowl of fruit. 'It shut him up, anyway.'

'It wasn't just an innocent remark, though, was it?'

Libby froze with a grape halfway to her mouth. Oliver's reaction to her words had in no way spoilt her enjoyment of her meal, but what Carrie had just said, and the *way* she had said it, made her push her plate aside, her appetite gone.

'I don't quite know what you mean.'

41

'Oh, yes, you do.' Carrie's eyes were downcast. 'I saw the way you watched Martha when she was serving Father, and I guessed what was going on in your mind.' She twisted the rolled napkin round and round in her fingers. 'I've known for a long time what was going on. My bedroom is directly underneath Martha's, and Father's voice and laugh aren't exactly on the quiet side.' She breathed on the silver ring and rubbed at it with her fist. 'So you see,' she added softly.

'But you never said!' Libby stared at her twin in disbelief. 'You kept it all to yourself!' She twisted round in her high-backed chair. 'Why? I thought we always told each other things. Especially anything as important as that.'

Carrie shook her head. 'Not always we don't, Libby. And besides . . .' She glanced over her shoulder towards the door. 'I don't think it *is* all that important, if you must know.'

'Not important?' Libby forgot to keep her voice down. 'Not *important*? Our father making love to the housemaid? A girl young enough to be his daughter, his granddaughter, even! You must be mad!'

Carrie put a finger to her lips as the door opened to reveal Martha Cardwell, cap awry, tripping over what could only have been the pattern in the carpet as she came forward with a tray to clear away.

'Mind if I side the pots now?' She hovered uncertainly. 'I've been a bit run off me feet all day with Mrs Peel having all her meals in her room along with Sarah, and Mrs Edwards getting off early to the second house pictures. She's gone to see Zazu Pitts at the Olympia.'

'That's all right, Martha.'

It was Carrie who smiled at the tall clumsy girl, Carrie who led the way down the hall and into the big front lounge, there to carry on the conversation as if they had never been interrupted.

'Listen, Libby. Our mother has been an invalid since we were born. That is over twenty years ago, and in all that time – for as long as we can remember, anyway – Father has seen to it she's been taken care of. He even let Sarah come back after she'd had her baby because he knew how fond of her Mother was.' She patted the cushions on the chesterfield for a bemused Libby to sit down beside her. 'Think, Libby. Father

42

used to be a keen Rotarian and a Mason, but he seemed to lose interest in them after Willie got killed in France. Do you ever stop to think what it's like for him down at the mill? Father isn't a man who can easily trust, so he takes on far too much, and it's sometimes as hard being a boss as a worker, you know.'

'Hah! Talk about middle-class righteousness!' Libby's voice rang with scorn. 'I suppose you'll be saying next that Father's workers have a struggle to keep fed because of their own inadequacy? Bosses have been saying that for hundreds of years. Anyway, what has all that got to do with. . . ?'

'Everything. You know as well as I do that the boom in cotton didn't last long after the war. Father was a broken man because of Willie, and Mother being the way she was, and it was only natural that his weavers turned against him when he had to reduce their wages by forty per cent four years ago. Of course they were bitter, so they set against him.' She patted Libby's hand. 'Father is an anti-union boss, so they are only loyal to him for fear of losing their jobs. It's clear to me. Six of one and half a dozen of the other, so why can't you make allowances for him?'

'Allowances for that?' Libby jerked her head upwards. 'And why tell me what I know already? Father tells us often enough, but a lot of it is his own fault. Father treats his workers as if they were the scum of the earth. No wonder they hate and loathe him. He treats you and me and Mother as if we were the scum of the earth, too, just because we're women. His sun rose and set with Willie, and just because he hasn't a son to follow him into the mill he takes it out on us.'

Carrie agreed. 'But have you ever stopped to think how lonely he is? He needs comfort. All men do, even the toughest of them. Can he turn to Mother? To you and me?' Her cheeks grew pink. 'He is a *man*, Libby. A strong normal man, and he has to get it – affection, love, softness – from somewhere.'

'You mean lust.' Libby hardly knew how to contain herself. Carrie was so serious, so intense, pointing out the reason for things as if she were ten years older and not ten minutes younger. She got up to stand in front of the fireplace. 'You'll be saying next that they are in love! Our father and that – that unfinished girl who started as one of his weavers. He brought

43

her here, Carrie, I distinctly remember him bringing her here himself and telling Mother she was half-starved and having to sleep four to a bed at home. The great philanthropist! Him! Our father treats his weavers as if they were mere extensions of their machines. They're not even human beings to him! And now he's using Martha, that's all. *Using* her, Carrie. So how can you defend him? What's got into you, for heaven's sake? And, oh God, don't cry, please don't do that.'

Libby went to sit beside her sister, her own throat tightening. It had always been the same. If one twin cried then the other followed suit. She placed an arm round Carrie's shaking shoulders and drew her close.

'You're not upset just because of Father, are you?' She whispered as she had whispered through the closed dividing door between their rooms the night before. 'What is it, Carrie? Is there someone – some man you are trying to tell me about? Someone at the tennis club? The church?' Her darting mind considered one acquaintance after another, dismissing every one as impossible. So many of the boys they had known had gone straight to France from university, never to return. And those who had come back seemed remote and strangely indifferent, as if what they had seen had marked them for ever. Libby frowned. There was more here than met even her penetrating eye. She had seen nothing, suspected nothing – she had dismissed Carrie's strange behaviour of the night before as trivial.

'It's not a married man, is it, Carrie? You wouldn't be such a fool as that?'

Carrie raised a face stiff with pain. 'Being a fool doesn't come into it. Not when you love someone as I love him.' Tears rolled down her cheeks as she groped in her pocket for a handkerchief. 'His wife has no feeling for him. None at all. She is unbalanced, Libby. Insane.' Her voice broke on a sob. 'Sometimes he has bruises on his face, and once his eye was closed right up. She *attacks* him, Libby, and he is so gentle, so sensitive, he just has to take it. He didn't go to the war because he . . . because his beliefs wouldn't let him fight back. He just lets her scream at him. Oh, Libby, it's so awful.'

'You mean he was a conchie?'

Carrie bit her lip and nodded. 'Yes, he was, but what he had

44

to face took as much courage as if he had rushed out of the trenches with a fixed bayonet. For what he believed to be right he went to *prison*, Libby. And now that dreadful so-called wife of his keeps reminding him of it, taunting him. The war has been over for eight years, but she will never let him forget that he stayed at home. They were newly married and she *wanted* him to go. Imagine.'

'And he stands there and lets her hit him? Oh, my sainted aunt!' Libby opened her eyes wide in disbelief. 'What kind of a man is he, for heaven's sake?'

'He's good. That's what he is.' Carrie jumped up from where she sat, twisting the handkerchief round and round in her fingers as she had twisted the napkin ring not ten minutes before. Now there was a desperate pleading in her voice. 'Try to understand, Libby. At least *try* to understand. He has no one, not one person in the world to turn to.'

'Only you.'

'Only me. She has even tried to turn his son against him, a boy who was born at the end of the war, deaf and dumb, as if fate hadn't been cruel enough.'

'I thought you said he was in prison?'

Carrie flapped a hand from side to side impatiently. 'He was sent home because of his health. His lungs. He had a mild form of consumption, and he's so thin and so pale. Oh, Libby, you don't know. You just don't know. His wife sleeps in a separate room, and he told me once that if only he could wake up one morning and see the face of a woman who loved him on the pillow beside him, he would think he had died and was in heaven.'

'*Your* face?' Libby found she was holding her breath. 'You're not . . .' She hardly knew how to go on. 'You wouldn't be such a fool as to . . . oh, Carrie, you wouldn't?'

'I don't know!' Carrie's voice rose to a wail. 'He needs me so much!'

'And like Father, he's only human?'

Libby was so angry she wanted to grab her sister by the shoulders and shake her until her teeth rattled. 'Oh, Carrie, you silly, stupid – I don't know what !' For once words failed her. 'Do you want to end up like Sarah, with an illegitimate child? Do you? Because that's what will happen if you let him,

45

whoever he is, have his way with you. If he can't control his own wife, then he'll hardly be able to control himself any other way.' She fought the blush rising to her cheeks. 'Oh, Carrie, I'm engaged to be married. Harry . . . we're getting married at Christmas, and he . . . we want it to be the first time for, well, for *me*. Harry was in the army and, well, it's different for a man. Biologically different.' She gave up, and threw up both hands in a wild gesture of exasperation. 'Besides, where would you go? Not to his house, I'm sure. In the back of a car?'

'Stop it!' Carrie backed away as if physically trying to ward off anything else her sister might say. 'You're so – so *clinical*. You don't know what loving means, to talk like that. You might be going to get married, but you don't know! Oh, I wish I'd never told you.'

As the door bell rang she was running upstairs to shut herself in her bedroom, and when Harry Brandwood was let in by a dishevelled Martha with a dish towel over her arm, Libby was waiting for him in the lounge with hands outstretched in a dramatic greeting.

'Oh, Harry. I can't tell you how glad I am to see you.' She turned her face into the comforting smell of his tweed jacket. 'Father slapped my face last night, and now I've quarrelled with Carrie. She looked at me just now as if she hated me, and I can't tell you anything about it because it's a secret, a terrible, terrible secret.'

Harry, an expression of resignation on his round ruddy face, held her close and stroked her hair. 'Now then, love. You've quarrelled with Carrie before, but you know the arguments between the two of you never last. What were you doing? Waving the red flag at her? You know Carrie has no social conscience, and I told you last night the strike will succeed or it will fail, and there's nothing you can do about it.' He smiled into her hair. 'And if your father slapped you I'm sure it was only a little smack and you must have provoked him.' Suddenly his voice trailed away as he realized something about his beloved was very different. Gently he pushed her away. 'Libby! You've had your hair cut off!' His blue eyes twinkled. 'It's lovely, darling. Absolutely lovely. Spiffing. You look about seventeen years old.'

Libby put up a hand and touched the swing of her cropped

hair. The appeal to her vanity and the admiration in his eyes steadied her as nothing else at that particular moment could have done.

'Do you really like it?' She gave him a trembling smile. 'I wasn't sure . . .'

'I like it and I love you, and I wish I could take you out somewhere so that I could show you off, but I'm on my way to see yet another patient with strike fever.'

'Strike fever?' Libby widened her eyes, then snuggled close again.

Harry's voice was teasing. 'Remember last night when you told me it was only the downtrodden poor who suffered? Well, it seems you were wrong, Libby Peel. I can't speak for the majority of the rich bossmen in this town, but one coal owner who shall be nameless worked himself up into a mild heart attack this afternoon. One of his miners actually stormed his way into the pit office and declared that the outcome of this strike would be the nationalization of the whole of the coal industry. Result – one poor downtrodden boss practically foaming at the mouth, in need of urgent medical attention.' He put up a finger. 'No, not a word. I haven't finished yet. And I'm off now to minister to Mrs Amos Birtwistle at Gawley Hall, prostrate with a migraine because her dress for the tennis party on Saturday is holed up somewhere in a siding, and likely to remain there till the railways start running again. So you see.'

He was so solid, so reassuring, such a comfort that Libby actually smiled properly before surrendering to one of his pleasantly thorough kisses.

Harry relaxed. His Libby wasn't always as easily calmed down as this, and she had seemed to be genuinely upset. He surfaced for a moment, then bent his head to kiss her again. And Carrie with a terrible secret! Docile, gentle Carrie with a secret too terrible to be told – how Libby liked to dramatize everything! Her twin was as open as a spring-lit day, so passive as to be merely a shaded echo of her sister. He touched the tip of Libby's nose with his finger.

'I think Mrs Amos Birtwistle is quite taken with me, especially when I assured her that with her grace and charm she was bound to be the belle of the tennis court with or without the missing dress. If she invites us to the party on Saturday, shall I accept? I'm free after lunch. I hope.'

Libby walked with him to the door. 'Oh, yes, please Harry. I've never been to Gawley Hall, and we haven't worn our new tennis dresses yet.' She patted the new fringe. 'They are an exact copy of Suzanne Lenglen's, with orange bandeaux to go with them.'

'We?' Even as he asked the question Harry knew what the answer would be.

'Me and Carrie, of course. You'll wangle an invitation for her as well, won't you darling? It's just what she needs.'

Harry ran down the steps to his waiting car, seeing himself for one slightly hysterical moment arriving at Gawley Hall with two Libbys in tow, identical in white dresses with orange bandeaux round their short dark hair.

'Love me, love my sister,' he muttered good humouredly, then turned to wave before driving back down the drive and heading the car towards the road leading away from the town.

As soon as Libby went back into the house she remembered her intention of going down to the tram depot at the weekend to volunteer as a driver. She started upstairs, then hesitated for a second with one hand on the banister rail. Ah, well . . . She tossed her head, enjoying the feel of her hair bouncing freely. It had been a crazy notion anyway, especially in view of the fact that she was on the side of the strikers. And she was. Most definitely. She was thinking about them at that very moment, walking with earnest workworn faces to their meetings, tightening their belts in determined preparation for the long weeks and months of struggle to come. Oh yes, there would be lots of ways she could help, she decided vaguely. If the teachers remained uncommitted she could drive a tram during the long summer holiday, in an impartial way of course, not really identifying with either side. And besides, going to Mrs Amos Birtwistle's party wasn't going to influence the outcome of the struggle one way or the other. And the orange bandeau might need a tuck in the back now that her hair was short.

When she saw Tom Silver's notebook lying on her dressing table where she had left it before going down to dinner she picked it up, held it for a moment while running her fingers over the binding, then almost without volition pushed it deep into her school purse. Margaret Bottomley would take it to him at the infirmary tomorrow, report on his progress, and that would be that.

Tom Silver, tall and dark with his teasing eyes and strong arms . . . he had thought her beliefs shallow. He had openly laughed at her, and made a kissing movement at her with his lips. She felt her cheeks grow pink at the memory And if he *had* copied out bits of poetry, bits that reached out for rainbows and soothing comfort, then it didn't make him anything out of the ordinary. He probably only did it for effect anyway, like a lot of working-class men who fancied themselves as amateur botanists, going on hikes into the country on Sundays with shabby haversacks on their backs.

Libby opened a drawer and, taking out a strip of brightly coloured material, slipped it over her head so that it covered the fringe and showed her eyes in the mirror, bleak with surprising despair.

Snatching it off she threw it from her, then stared down at the purse with its bulge showing where the notebook lay.

He was rude and mocking and arrogant, and she would never see him again. And she didn't care. . . . Well, of *course* she didn't care. For heaven's sake, why should she?

Three

It was very hot in the summer house in the late afternoon. Mungo had taken off his tie, and was feverishly trying to unbutton the front of Carrie's cotton dress even as she pushed at his hands, begging him to stop.

She wanted him to; at least part of her wanted him to, but he was, as usual, in too much of a hurry. She needed, first of all, to be reassured that what they were doing was right, wanted to hear him saying once again that as neither of them was hurting anyone, where was the harm?

'She isn't getting suspicious about you having to stay late at school? Surely she must be?' Carrie always referred to Mungo's wife, Beatrice, as 'she', finding herself unable to say the name. Her eyes clouded over with worry.

Mungo's mouth fastened hungrily on her own, forcing her lips apart. Then when he surfaced he said bitterly, 'She wouldn't give a damn if I never went home again.' His hand slid inside Carrie's dress as he pulled down the strap of her underskirt. 'Oh, God, how I love you, sweetheart!'

With a frantic determination Carrie tried to stop thinking about the wife whose existence she had never really admitted to the reasoning part of her mind. There was an ache deep inside her, a quivering, burning sensation, but when Mungo's hand crept lower she pushed him away and sat up, hot and distressed. She pulled the ribbon strap over her shoulder.

Groaning, he pulled her close again. 'I *have* to, darling. You can't keep tormenting me like this. Nothing will go wrong. I *promise*. I give you my word.' He closed his eyes so that she saw the long eyelashes fan out on his cheek above what looked like a recent scar.

'She did that?' Carrie's fingers were gentle as she traced the tiny half-moon shape.

'Yes. And this.' He turned his head so that she saw a scratch running down from beneath his left ear. 'She wasn't quite drunk enough last night. Properly drunk she has no fight in her, but halfway gone she can fight like a hell-cat.'

'Have you ever tried hitting her back?'

'The boy,' he said softly. 'I have to endure in silence because of the boy.'

'But he's deaf!'

Mungo shook his head sadly. 'I did retaliate once, and she ran into the boy's room and showed him the marks on her wrist, faint marks which faded while he was staring at them in horror.' His head drooped, and when he raised his eyes Carrie was dismayed to see that they swam with tears. 'She pointed at her wrist, then at me, then she clung to the boy as if he were the only thing standing between her and a further attack. And Edwin suddenly rolled on his back making terrible noises. It was dreadful. I sometimes catch him watching me warily as if he were just waiting for me to turn violent again.'

Carrie put her arms tight round him then and rocked him as she would a child, pity welling inside her. 'Oh, my love . . . oh, my love,' she whispered.

Mungo relaxed against her with a sigh. 'So you see, for Edwin's sake, I have to endure. Because he can't hear or speak it's impossible to know what he's thinking, but he watches me. I feel his eyes watching me.'

'And you would never leave her?'

It was a question to which Carrie knew the answer. This lonely man could never bring himself to desert a handicapped child. And his wife would never leave her home and give up the husband who was no more to her than a meal ticket.

Carrie pressed her lips close together in an attempt to hold back her own tears. Being in love, she had always believed, was meant to be a joyous thing; a meeting of eyes, a sharing of private jokes, laughter on a summer's day.

She remembered Libby coming into the house wearing her engagement ring for the first time. Holding out her hand, turning it so that the light caught the three diamonds, whirling round the room, skirts flying, hugging her twin, shouting 'You

51

next, Carrie! You next!'

But *this* love, this powerful overwhelming obsession, weighed on her like a spreading net, enmeshing her in strands of despair. Mungo was there in her thoughts from the moment she opened her eyes in the morning. She would sit with her mother in the evenings and imagine he was there sitting in a chair, smiling at her, telling her of his love in his beautiful voice.

Sometimes she would try to tell herself it was hopeless. She would steel herself to tell him the same. Then the next day, at school, she would see him, brown hair waving back from his high forehead, shoulders stooped, and she would be engulfed in a wave of tenderness so great that she would have to hold herself back from running to him.

'We can't go on meeting like this without something happening,' he was saying now, making no attempt to touch her again. 'I tell you, Carrie, the way I want you is killing me. And being alone like this, in our own little hideaway, I – I haven't got that much control, sweetheart.' He ran a finger round his unbuttoned stiff collar as if he were choking. 'A more ruthless man would insist, but I'm not like that. I love you so much I'm prepared to wait for you to come to me.' His smile was tinged with sadness. 'I'm a very patient man, Carrie. A deeply frustrated man, but a patient one.'

Carrie felt as if she were choking too, but her emotion stemmed not from frustration, but because she knew Mungo was waiting for her to make up her mind. The heat inside the tiny building was sticky; she could feel the perspiration sliding down her sides. And they had been there for longer than usual – the light had shifted as it seeped through the cardboard shutters. She sighed. Ironically it was Mungo's very restraint that made her hesitate. If he had taken her forcibly, *made* her give in by bruising her mouth with kisses, she would have . . . oh, God, at least she *thought* she might have . . .

Slowly she began to button up her dress. It could never happen like this – with Mungo waiting patiently for her to decide. She didn't want to decide; she wanted the decision to be taken from her, and now he was going to be angry again. She could see his face working as though he had a tic.

'But I will,' she whispered as he buried his face against her.

'It's just that, just that . . .' Her voice tailed away as she remembered.

She could still recall the look on Sarah Batt's face on the day she had admitted she was going to have a baby. A shy schoolgirl of fourteen, Carrie had come into the kitchen at Westerley to see Sarah sobbing uncontrollably, trying to hide her rounded stomach by holding her clasped hands over it, then running upstairs to pack her bag and leave Westerley. True, Sarah came back, but her child was being brought up by his grandmother and only visited by his mother once a month. And Sarah was so ashamed of her past that she flatly refused to talk about her son. It was as though what she had done in a moment of passion eight, nine years ago had filled her with a shame that would linger for the rest of her life. Carrie shivered.

'What are you thinking about, darling?' Mungo's voice was gentle, and though normally Carrie would tell him exactly what she was thinking, this time she shook her head.

Just how did you tell a man as unworldly, as sensitive as Mungo that every time he wanted to make love to her *properly* she became a fourteen-year-old schoolgirl again? A girl in a pudding-basin hat gazing in horror, pity and fascination at a housemaid with tears running down her cheeks and her arms wrapped round her swollen stomach.

'I think we must go soon,' she whispered. 'It must be very late.'

'To hell with time,' Mungo muttered, taking her into his arms again.

They were eating earlier than usual that evening at Westerley because Oliver had to go down to the mill again.

'They should rechristen Bridge Mill,' he thundered, striding into the house around six o'clock. 'Moscow Mill it should be called.' Then he shouted through the swinging door leading to the kitchen, 'Look sharp with it, you two lasses. I want to be away in half an hour at the most.'

'Where's Carrie?' He came into the lounge with a glass of whisky in his hand, then he narrowed his eyes at Libby. 'I can't make out why she's always stopping on late. You can get home in good time, it seems.' He jerked his chin upwards. 'Is

53

your mother coming down for her dinner tonight?'

'Why don't you go up and ask her yourself?' was what Libby wanted to say, but the most important thing was to stop him going on about Carrie. So she took a deep breath and let it out again with a sigh. If her father found out that Carrie was meeting a married man after school, a man who had stayed at home during the war instead of going out to France and being killed like Willie, then murder would be done. Libby was sure of it.

'Why have you to go back to the mill, Father?' She assumed a bright expression. 'Is the strike affecting you badly?'

Oliver swilled the whisky round and round in his glass, then took a deep swallow. His ill-humour was such that Libby guessed he was prepared to release his frustration, even to the extent of discussing the situation with her.

'If I have to fill the mill with tramp weavers I'll keep those looms running,' he almost growled. 'And if I have to run the place without tacklers, then I'll do just that.' He went to refill his glass. 'They reckon there'll be well over a thousand looms stopped as a result of the strike whichever way it goes. But what can you expect when the union representative's a damn Bolshie? This strike is right up his street, isn't it? He hasn't got enough up top to remember that his bloody union has fought and lost two strikes in the last year against necessary wage cuts. Don't the stupid fools realize we're in a period of economic chaos, and that cotton exports are one of the hardest hit? Haven't they the sense to see that the cotton which used to go to India is either produced there, or got from Japan?'

He went to stand with his back to the fire. 'It's like what it was at the beginning of the war. Then everybody got excited and jumped about, desperate to do something. It's a sort of hysteria. Why, one of my tacklers told me his wife has started her own soup kitchen already, making broth and getting cheap offal from the butcher. All her neighbours are collecting coppers for her, and they've got enough to take round to the co-op bank.' He snorted. 'And they have the nerve to say they are starving!'

Oliver patted his stomach. 'Where the devil has Carrie got to? We'll have to start without her if I'm to get back. I'll have a word with Joe Postlethwaite next time I see him.'

'Joe Postlethwaite?' Libby was still stalling for time 'I've never heard you mention that name before, Father.'

'On the board of governors at Carrie's school. I'll have it out with him about the extra hours his teachers have to work. Teachers' hours are supposed to be civilized, they're not miners or factory workers. Go into the kitchen, Libby, and tell them we want to start. I can't hang about like this another minute.'

'They're not miners or factory workers! Oh, dear God . .' Libby was muttering to herself as she walked down the long passage to the door leading to the kitchen. 'Oh, Carrie, why do you have to be so stupid? Why? And where *are* you?'

'Miss Carrie's just wheeled her bike round the back. She says she had a puncture and had to walk all the way home with it.'

Mrs Edwards was putting the finishing touches to a pink blancmange, and Libby was sure the look she gave her was knowing. 'I'll go upstairs and tell Mother,' she said, and left the kitchen before any more could be said.

'Carrie's just come in,' she told Ettie, and saw the relief on her mother's face as she got up from her dressing table.

'I'm much better today, dear,' Ettie said wistfully. 'I am so glad we will all be sitting down to a meal together. Your father is so busy, and Carrie has so much extra work to do at school these days, then you are often out with Harry . . .' She pulled at the strands of faded hair covering her forehead. 'I sometimes feel that you have all made separate lives for yourselves, and just come home to eat and sleep.' She smiled at Sarah hovering in the doorway. 'I can manage the stairs myself, Sarah. I mustn't let people think I am an invalid.' She left the room.

Libby sat down on the edge of the bed, her hands for once still in her lap. Then suddenly her mood changed as she watched Sarah pick the hairs from Ettie's tortoiseshell brush and stow them away in the hair-tidy on the dressing table. With her head on one side, her restless mind ticking over, she studied the matronly solid figure through narrowed eyes.

'How can you stand it, Sarah? I mean having to be with Mother all day long? It would kill me. Do you never feel you want to break away to go and do something quite different?'

55

'Oh, no, Miss Libby. I'm right fond of your mother and I like looking after her. We have a nice understanding, me and your mother,' Sarah bustled forward to strip the green satin cover from the bed, twitching at it in a pointed way so that Libby was forced to stand up.

It was an unspoken rule that Sarah's 'trouble' of eight years ago was never referred to, but now the worry of Carrie's behaviour filled her twin with an anxiety that bordered on a terrible half-acknowledged fear. Surely Carrie wasn't going to make the same mistake that Sarah had made all those years ago?

'How is your little boy, Sarah?' Libby asked the question, not quite admitting the association of ideas, even as she told herself that Carrie would never . . . not with a married man. Not out in the fields . . . she shuddered. 'We never hear anything about your son. How old is he now, Sarah?'

'Eight, Miss, coming up.' Sarah had her back turned as she shook out her mistress's nightgown and laid its crêpe-de-Chine folds over the top sheet.

Libby persisted. 'What does he look like? Is he dark? Red-haired like you? Small for his age? Big for his age?' She smiled. 'I know. Why don't I get the doctor to drive me over to your parents' cottage on one of your weekends off, so you can introduce him? It seems so silly that none of us have seen him. There's no shame, Sarah, not to my mind, anyway. You mustn't feel there is.'

'No!'

Libby blinked as Sarah turned round, her face contorted with what seemed to be fear. 'He's to be let be. He's happy as he is with his grandma and grandpa, and me going home regularly. I won't have him *shown*! I won't!' She gripped a corner of her apron in both hands and twisted it round. 'An' if you insist I will give up me job, and then where will your poor mother be without me?' The blue eyes filled with tears. 'There's only me what cares about her, really. *He* doesn't . . .' – this with a jerk of her head towards the door – 'an' you and Miss Carrie, you're so full of each other you don't need nobody else.'

She started to back out of the room. 'In all this time your mother has never once asked me a thing like that. She knows

56

when to let be. She cares about folks' feelings, while you . . .'
Overcome, Sarah rushed out of the door, leaving it wide open behind her.

'Oh, my sainted aunt!' Libby opened her eyes wide at her reflections in the tripled mirror over Ettie's dressing table, then, shrugging her shoulders, she went out onto the landing.

There she bumped into Carrie, warm and pink, with hastily brushed hair, and verging on hysteria in her twin's opinion.

For a second they stared at each other; in another second they would have had their arms round each other as Carrie's obvious distress communicated itself to her sister. But Oliver's loud voice boomed up the stairs.

'Will somebody tell me what you two are doing up there? The soup is on the table, though why anybody wants soup on a warm evening like this I don't know!'

'And I heard you come in, Carrie,' he added, as soon as they were all seated round the big dining table. 'Teachers are supposed to finish at four o'clock, aren't they?'

Silently, with head bowed, Carrie spooned her soup. Silently Libby watched her, noticing the way her twin swallowed with difficulty, left hand trembling as she lifted the spoon to her mouth.

'I'm sorry, Father.' Carrie dabbed at her mouth with the large damask napkin. 'We had a meeting and I couldn't get away.'

'Meeting?' Oliver hacked away at the joint of beef placed in front of him by the young maid, Martha Cardwell. 'Don't tell me the teachers are going to be the next to come out on strike?' He passed a plate over to his wife, then went on carving. 'There's bound to be Labourites amongst your lot. You know what will happen if you come out, don't you? If I know Joe Postlethwaite and his committee, he'll have the bloody school closed, and there won't be a job to go back to when this lot's finished. Joe won't have any truck with sympathy strikes. The miners might have a grievance, a slight one at that, but nothing that can't be settled with negotiation. God damn it, you don't know when you're born!'

'It was nothing like that, Father.'

Libby held her breath as she calculated that Carrie was close to breaking down. And if she did, if she were foolish

57

enough to burst out crying and rush from the room, then God help her. Even Oliver's preoccupation with the strike and his worries about the mill wouldn't stop him from rushing after her and shaking the truth out of her.

Quickly she came to one of her swift decisions. Drawing Oliver's fire to herself, she said, 'Maybe if you hadn't put your weavers working on piece rates at a lower return last year, they would have been content to stay at their looms. They are bound to make comparisons when the rates vary from mill to mill. Now they could be grasping their chance to show their disapproval, wouldn't you say, Father?'

When Oliver dropped the lid of the vegetable tureen onto the table with a clatter, widening his eyes before letting fly with a spate of angry words, Libby knew her ploy had worked.

'It's all right now,' her eyes signalled Carrie. 'He'll be on his way out down to the mill soon, then you can give way.'

'But not before,' she prayed silently. 'Dear God, not before!'

Tom Silver, sitting up in his high bed in the long ward of the town's infirmary, saw Margaret Bottomley the minute she came through the doors, but couldn't quite place her. Her face, with its eager, thrusting jaw, was familiar, but he couldn't for the life of him put a name to it, so he leaned his head back against the piled pillows and closed his eyes.

'Mr Silver?'

He opened them again to see her standing by his bed, pale eyes shining, her upper lip with its shadowy moustache quivering with enthusiasm.

'Yes?' He sighed. Now he had placed her. She was one of the band of supposedly liberated women who tried to talk like men. And this one even looked like a man. Peevishly, because his head was aching and he had been told that morning that his immediate discharge was out of the question, he sucked in his bottom lip and tried to look even more ill than he felt.

But Margaret pulled up a little hard chair and sat down, pulling her skirt over her knees. As if he wanted to stare at her legs, Tom thought with distaste, then widened his eyes as she opened her purse and took out the little brown leather book. Forgetting his act of invalidism, he sat bolt upright.

'How the. . . ? Where on earth. . . ?' He held out his hand, only to have his wrist tapped playfully.

'Don't say you hadn't missed it, Mr Silver?'

Women with faces like that shouldn't try to look coy, he thought uncharitably, shrinking away from her unwelcome touch.

Margaret wrinkled her nose. 'Your little scribblings are safe with me, Mr Silver. I guessed the book meant a lot to you, so at the first opportunity I have returned it to you.' She tapped the book with a gloved finger. 'It was handed to me, so I thought it was the least I could do.' She smiled. 'I must say you look in better shape than I expected you to. My . . . my informant told me that the last sight she had of you was when you were stretcher-bound, being handed into an ambulance.'

Tom put a hand up to his bandaged head. 'Oh, yes. The market square. It must have dropped out of my pocket.' He winced with the effort of sitting upright, and sagged down against the pillows again. 'The crowd got a bit out of hand and decided to use me for target practice, and the next thing I knew was when I woke up in this bed. The damnable thing is I can't find out what's going on.' A sudden stab of pain drained the colour from his already pale cheeks. 'I have been trying to get hold of the reports from union headquarters, but from what I hear even the reports contradict each other.' He frowned, then winced as the frown pulled at the stitches in his forehead. 'My lads will be counting on me. They'll be at sixes and sevens without me there. And there's nothing I can do, lying here like a wet lettuce.'

He suddenly looked much older than his years, as if the whole responsibility of running the strike had been his alone. 'Those men throwing stones, they weren't helping. If we succeed, and we *have* to succeed, it has to be done through patience, not by force. Violence never gets anyone anywhere.'

'Oh, I do agree.' Margaret was too insensitive to realize that the grey-faced man was talking more to himself than to her. She beamed. 'They say Ellen Wilkinson could be paying us a visit up here. Imagine! She's a real fiery speaker, and she knows what she's on about when she talks about the injustices done to the workers. There'll certainly be a full house if she does come. I know I'll be there, that's for sure.'

59

Tom was very tired. He did not feel like talking politics with this woman. He reminded himself that she had brought the book back out of kindness, so, speaking slowly as if every word pained him, he thanked her, closed his eyes and waited for her to go.

'It wasn't exactly me who rescued your book, Mr Silver.'

Margaret did not want such an interesting encounter to end like this. It was a long time since she had talked so intimately with a good-looking man like Tom Silver. He was a real charmer, in a masculine way of course. There was a touch of the Byron in the way his hair fell forward over his forehead like that, and his eyes were the most unusual shade of grey. Not flint grey, or steel grey, but a soft gentle grey, like rain clouds.

With difficulty, because her plump knees were already touching the bed, she moved forward. It was growing dark outside, and because the trams were so unreliable she would have a long walk home. She sighed. The very minute she turned her key in the door her mother would call out, 'Margaret? Is that you?'

As if it would or could be anyone else! She would have to take her mother's nightly cup of cocoa upstairs, then help her out of bed and onto the commode, averting her eyes from the yellowed toenails and the stick-thin legs. And oh, how she hated the lack of modesty that seemed to have afflicted her mother in her old age. Sometimes Margaret saw in the little body slumped on the commode a picture of how it would be with *her* one day, except that she, Margaret Bottomley, who had never known a man's touch, would be all alone.

'It was Miss Peel – Libby Peel, who asked me to bring your book back,' she said, not quite truthfully, and was rewarded by a sudden flash of interest in the grey eyes, and the semblance of a smile.

'Ah, yes, the teacher who wanted to see how the other half lived, all fierce and unenlightened. She got home safe then? I've wondered about her.' He kept his eyes tight shut, but this time he was not escaping. Instead he was recalling the small girl with the silly straw hat. He was remembering the earnest way she listened to the speakers, and the softness of her, small-boned and somehow fragile, as he held her tight against him when the crowd swayed and the stones began to fly.

'She teaches at the same school as me. Her father owns Bridge Mill.' Margaret gave the information reluctantly, sensing that her captive audience had somehow dismissed her more surely than if she had got up and walked away down the ward. It was always happening. A pretty face, a shapely leg, and she, Margaret Bottomley, might as well not exist.

She hurried on with a bit more information. 'Libby, Miss Peel, is getting married at Christmas to a doctor. Dr Harry Brandwood, in practice with his father up Park Road.' She laughed a trill laugh at variance with her bulk. 'I know exactly what you mean about Miss Peel being unenlightened, Mr Silver. It would be impossible for the likes of her to understand the present conflict, or the needs of the workers. The Peels of this town won't go short of a bob or two, no matter how long this struggle lasts. *Her* family have never known what it is to want. It's still Them and Us, Mr Silver, and always will be. When the likes of you and me say we are hard up we mean we are *hungry*. When Libby Peel thinks she is hard up she means she has spent her monthly dress allowance in the first two weeks. *She's* never had to turn a skirt, nor steam a hat to stop the brim from curling, and she's never had to be the sole support of her mother from the day she left college.'

It was with a deep sigh of relief that Tom heard the bell clang out heralding the end of visiting time. He knew he should have been feeling pity for the sallow-faced woman now gathering gloves and bag together, because a lot of what she had just said was right. It *was* still Them and Us, and as far as identifying with hardship and poverty went, well, he had no difficulty there, God knew. But he hoped, oh, he hoped most fervently that he would never spit out his grievances with his lips twisted into a bitter line. His mission, if mission was the right word, was to improve the lot of his men, to help lift the lower-paid workers from despair, not sink them down into a sea of envy and spite against those who had more.

And now the ache in his head was worse. There was a sour taste in his mouth as the depression closed down on him again. The pudding-faced lass, she was looking for justice, and he could have told her that justice was merely a word. Because if things were just and fair and the scales of fortune balanced out the bad with the good, how was it that he had come back from

France unscathed? And why had his young wife, the girl he had married on his last leave, been blown to pieces in an explosion at the grey spread of munition factory buildings where she worked?

No, there hadn't been much justice there, by all that was holy.

And yet, at that very moment, what wouldn't he have given to be sitting at the wheel of a car, the kind of car Libby's fiancé was sure to own, with her by his side, the wind loosening that brown hair of hers, blowing it across her eyes as she laughed and pleaded with him not to drive so fast? If that was envy, then he was guilty of it all right.

Reaching for the little brown book, he opened it at random and read:

'How pleasant as the yellowing sun declines, and with long rays shades the landscape to mark the birches' stems all golden light, that lit the dark slant woods with silvery white. . . .'

And was comforted.

Four

'Forget the past; look to the future,' the King said when the strike was called off on 12 May 1926.

'GREAT WORKERS' VICTORY' the *Daily Herald* declared with banner headlines, but Libby was not too sure about that.

'So much for your revolution,' Harry had teased. 'Now, if there really had been a revolution, a real Lenin-flavoured uprising, then the government would have completely lost control. And far from doing that, the government were in control all the time, from start to finish. He smiled. 'The bluff failed dismally, Libby. You must agree there.'

'The miners haven't given in. They never will give in,' Libby had retorted, but some of the fire had gone from her in the past few days. Carrie's refusal to go to the tennis party and her subsequent moping about the house with a white face and haunted expression had, of course, affected her twin. Harry knew this, but was determined not to probe. His beloved would tell him all about it, whatever it was, in her own good time.

He was, above all, a patient man.

Far more patient than Mungo McDermot, who at every opportunity tried to catch a few minutes alone with Carrie at school.

'Why won't you meet me in the summer house?' His face was lean with suffering. 'I can't go on like this.'

'I've told you why!' Carrie, with one eye on the door of the staff room, put the width of the table between herself and Mungo's wandering hands. She blushed and hung her head so that all he could see was the parting in her shiny brown hair.

'That last time we nearly . . . we almost . . .'

The break in her voice told him that tears were not far off, and his own voice was suddenly hoarse. 'But we didn't, did we? We stopped just in time.'

'What we did was just as bad.' Carrie felt a hot flush of shame wash over her as she remembered the urgency of his hands, the weight of his body, the searching open-mouthed kisses, and her own frantic struggles. 'The next time I might give in, and oh, Mungo . . . I must never give in. It's wrong, and besides, I'm so scared, so terribly frightened.'

'I would never hurt you, darling, in any way.'

He was saying that just as the door opened and Carrie, blushing scarlet, made a pretence of collecting books together. She reached for her register with a trembling hand. Then, as Miss Clayton, walking as though her heels were sprung, bounced into the room, Mungo walked out, his thin shoulders drooping in the jacket that always seemed too big for him, a neglected, lonely-looking man, with brown hair straggling over his collar.

'I wonder if his wife will come to Open Day?' Miss Clayton, cold eyes shrewd beneath the cap of her Eton-cropped hair, flopped down in a chair. She produced a packet of cigarettes and a box of matches from the leg of her knicker elastic and blew a perfect smoke ring into the air. 'Have you ever met her, by the way?'

'No, I've never met her.' Carrie longed to escape, but knew that if she did so it would only arouse suspicion. No teacher worth her salt ever emerged from the staff room unless she was on mid-morning duty at the drinks table set out in the hall if it was raining and outside if it was fine. So she compromised by walking over to the window and staring out.

Under the long verandah pupils were queueing at a trestle table for mugs of cocoa, hot or cold milk, still lemonade and biscuits. She saw Mungo, head bowed, standing behind the table, supposedly checking that each pupil dropped two pennies into the round tin provided. But it was obvious that his mind was in some faraway place as he stared down, then lifted his head as if he sensed she might be watching him.

'She's a lot older than him.' Miss Clayton addressed Carrie's unresponsive back. 'And she wears the trousers, from what I've heard. Though I believe she's good to that poor little lad of theirs.' Carrie heard the clatter of a tin ashtray falling from the table to the floor. 'She won't let him go into an institution anyway, so she can't have much of a life cooped up with a child like that all day. Not much fun for her.'

'Nor for him,' Carrie said, then bit her lip as if she wished the words unsaid.

'For old McDermot?'

'He isn't old.' Carrie turned round, knowing she was saying too much, but powerless to stop.

'Our Mr McDermot is nearly forty, if he's a day.' Miss Clayton flicked ash in the vague direction of the ashtray. 'He gives me the creeps, but then maybe he's your type?' She narrowed her eyes. 'I must say you seem to be pretty thick with him, but he looks to me as if he'd been grown in the dark. Like a mushroom, with a big white head and wobbly legs. How he ever had the nerve to stand up and be counted and declare he was a conchie during the war I just can't think. I wouldn't have thought his guts were as strong as my garters.' The cropped head went to one side. 'Wasn't your brother killed in France?'

Carrie nodded.

'Then how *can* you be so friendly with a little squirt like that? Maybe you're sweet on him? Is that it?'

Carrie felt her face flame, and knew that she had gone scarlet. 'I am not sweet on him! What a thing to say! I just feel pity for him, that's all.'

'And pity is akin to love, so they say.' Miss Clayton stretched out her legs in their black lisle stockings and checked that the seams were straight. 'Good God, Carrie, there's no need to look so flummoxed. Your murky secret is safe with little Angela.' Smiling, she licked a finger and made the sign of the cross on her throat. 'But I'd watch out for that wife of his, if I were you. God, I wouldn't like to meet her up an alley on a dark night. She's a fat woman with a face like the back of a fish cart, and shoulders on her like an ox. Get the wrong side of *her*, and she'd flatten you as soon as look at you.'

She sat up suddenly as Carrie moved blindly towards the door. 'Where are you off to in such a hurry? Our cocoa will be here soon. Steady on! The fire bell hasn't rung, has it?'

But Carrie, the small heels of her court shoes tapping on the

65

wide polished stair treads, was flying as if pursued by devils. The monitress, on her way up with the tray, had to step quickly to one side to avoid being knocked over. Her face was a study as she watched the quiet Miss Peel hurtle past her.

Carrie hesitated by the door leading out to the playing fields; then she turned left into the corridor leading to her form room, her heart beating like a drum.

Angela Clayton *knew*. That blab-mouth had guessed, so it followed that the rest of the staff knew too, and oh, dear God, if it ever got to the ears of the headmaster then heaven help both her and Mungo.

Sitting down, she stared at the rows of desks and at the far wall with the map of the world with the Empire filled in with red crayons. Soon it would be Empire Day. The Union Jack would be flown from the flagpole in the grounds, and the children would be decked out in costumes representing the various countries. They would march round the field singing 'Land of Hope and Glory', and Mungo would recite a patriotic poem in his beautiful voice. She would be expected to play her part, and the truth was she did not care. The sun could set on the Empire, never to rise again, and she wouldn't give a damn. At the moment Carrie could not see an inch farther than the horizon of her own immediate distress. She shivered. It would have to be left to people like Libby to worry about the Empire, and the miners and their lock-out, and the men who would lose their jobs as a result of the strike.

Libby never got involved in anything over which she could not retain absolute control. Libby had fallen in love suitably, she would marry Harry, stop work and throw herself whole-heartedly into the role of doctor's wife, while she Carrie, would still be making up her mind whether to share her life completely with the man she loved. And if she did surrender, she would have to forget that he had a wife and a handicapped son, and she would have to live in monthly terror in case anything had gone wrong.

Burying her face in her hands, Carrie tried to face up to a future as bleak and grey as the gathering clouds outside.

Libby, at that very moment, was opening and reading the

letter which had arrived at Westerley by the morning post. She had seen it on the hall table when she came down for breakfast, recognized the handwriting immediately, and pushed it deep into the pocket of her skirt. Surprised at the way her heart beats had quickened, she had said nothing to Carrie. If her twin could have secrets, then so could she.

'I will never be another Sarah!' Carrie had said through clenched teeth the last time Libby had tried to question her. 'But I can't talk about it. This is something I have to solve for myself, Libby. Can't you see?'

But no, Libby could not see, and when Harry had told her to leave her sister to get on with her own life, she had turned on him in fury.

'So you think I should just sit back and let Carrie make a mess of her life! Is that it?'

'Yes.' Harry had been adamant. 'You can't live your sister's life, and she cannot live yours. Some time the division has to come.'

'But how is it possible to divide two halves that are really one person?' Libby asked that in all seriousness, leaving Harry shaking his head in honest bewilderment.

'A pity I'm not marrying both of you.' He had pushed out both elbows, moving his head from side to side as if he were glancing from one bride to another. 'I take thee, Libby and Carrie Peel,' he had said, and the comical expression on his ruddy face had forced a smile to her lips.

Now she was furtively hiding the letter beneath the covers of a book as she sat alone at her desk during the mid-morning break. Outside the children were chanting their games in the square of concrete playground beyond the tall windows.

'The big ship sailed through the Alley-alley O, the Alley-alley O . . .'

Libby smiled to herself. All through prayers and the first lessons, she had been acutely aware of the letter in her pocket. Through the glass partition she had seen Margaret Bottomley standing on her raised platform beating time as her class sing-songed their way through their multiplication tables. And she had felt a strange sense of triumph that he had written, not to Margaret, but to her.

Taking out the single sheet of paper, she read:

Dear Miss Peel, I would like to thank you for returning my notebook by one of your teaching colleagues. It used to be a habit of mine to copy out verses of poems which appealed to me, and the book is doubly precious because I had it with me in France. As you can imagine, the words flowed like honey through a mind distracted by so much that was distinctly unpoetic. I am afraid I haven't written in the book lately. I am distressed by the premature ending of the strike and afraid for the miners in their determination to go on fighting. It will be a long and bitter struggle for them, and who knows what hardships their families will have to face? Yours sincerely, Tom Silver.

There was a PS at the end. 'One good thing came out of the strike, due to the suspension of the press. Six hundred and ninety-seven extra books were issued from the public library. Somehow that is a cheering thought, *n'est-ce-pas?*'

Libby read it quickly, then again more slowly. She looked at the address. Number 14, Meadow Street. She sighed. What a name for a street where no grass grew, a street backed by the tall menacing chimney of her father's mill. A street of Victorian houses, left to rot and grow shabby as their original owners moved out to the semidetached villas spreading from the centre of the town. Lodging houses, let off into rooms. . . . With a quick decisive movement Libby reached for the register with the list of addresses at the back.

Yes, she was right. Meadow Street was where most of the 'theatricals' lodged. Two of the children in her class were living there temporarily at number 20, and attending the school whilst their Troupe of Tiny Tappers played in the *Paint Box Revue* at the Palace Theatre. They were undersized girls, with straight hair club-cut into fringes, and were the envy of the rest of the class in their black patent-leather bar-strap shoes and their short white socks. Frowning, Libby folded the letter and pushed it back into her pocket. Then for the rest of the long day she imagined him, tall and thin, coming home from work to one of those shabby houses set in a street where babies played bare-bottomed in the gutter, and housewives gossiped on unwashed doorsteps, arms folded across their pinnies.

No wonder he scribbled verses in his little brown book, verses about streams where fish darted like pins spilled from a paper, where birds sang, and green fields starred with daisies stretched as far as the eye could see.

'What's been eating you all day?' Margaret Bottomley was waiting for Libby at the school gate at the end of an afternoon which had seemed endless. 'You've had your lot sitting with their hands on their heads at least twice. Have you had a row with the doctor, then?'

Libby smiled sweetly. 'Harry and I are always agreeing to differ, if that's what you mean, but we don't count them as rows. He likes me to have a mind of my own.'

'He's an unusual bloke then.' Margaret sniffed. 'I went to a meeting in King George's Hall last night. Councillor Smith was talking about the lock-out. He seemed to think they had a first-rate organization going for them. He actually gave it out that any man in dire need could go to the public office for assistance if needs be. Then he urged them to put their pride in their pockets and think of their children. A real stirring speech it was. You should have been there.'

Libby shook her head. 'You know I can't go to Labour meetings, not while I'm still living at home. Harry might be tolerant, but my father certainly is not.' She glanced up at the sky. 'I'm only putting up with it until I get married at Christmas. Father lost a big contract on account of the transport difficulties in the second week of the strike, and we are all having to suffer for it.' She started to walk away. 'I'm with you in principle, Margaret, you know that, but I'm either too much of a coward, or too canny, to flaunt my beliefs openly at the moment. It just isn't worth it.'

Margaret felt suddenly very cross as she mentally calculated the cost of Libby's simple dress and coat. The plain tailored lines set off her figure to perfection, and the fawn leather of bag and shoes picked up the narrow binding round the neck of the navy blue linen outfit. Not for Libby Peel the necessity to keep a dress and coat like that for best. *Her* wages did not go to pay the rent and the coal bill, or to keep a sick mother on the tasty foods her delicate stomach craved. Mrs

Peel was an invalid too, but she was waited on hand and foot by a maid. And it wasn't fair. Nothing in this rotten world was fair.

'Tom Silver got his cards when he went back to work after coming out of the infirmary,' Margaret said. 'The management said it was because the compositors and the machine minders were going to have to go on short time anyway. But it's obvious that Tom Silver was victimized. He knows it, and they know it.' The expression on the plain face darkened with disgust. 'The worst thing is that it's doubtful whether any other paper will take him on. The bosses don't like troublemakers, especially now when things are going from bad to worse. Mr Silver was there at the meeting last night, looking absolutely awful. He never spoke, just sat there, quiet and on his own. They say his nerves have been shot ever since he came back from the war. So where's the justice? I ask you, Libby! Out there in France, fighting for his country, losing his wife, and now this.'

She was talking quickly as they walked down the street, head jutting forward oblivious of the effect her words were having on Libby. When she turned at last and saw the expression on Libby's face, noticing how she had paled beneath the brim of her neat straw hat, she stopped dead on the pavement. 'You all right?'

Libby took a deep breath as her hand went instinctively over her bag where the letter was now hidden away. Oh, that proud man! He had written to thank her for the book, and he hadn't said a word about losing his job. Not a word. 'But he wasn't like the others.' Her voice came out hoarse. 'He was just standing there, Margaret, that night, listening quietly. He tried to stop them rioting. He wasn't there to make trouble. It wasn't like that at all.'

Margaret's pale blue eyes were fishlike in their curiosity. So there was something that could ruffle Libby Peel. 'Nobody said Mr Silver had got the sack because of that night, Libby. They've been laying off men from the compositors' room for a while now, and they say the rest will be going on short time. No, it was because he was the Father of the Chapel, and a troublemaker in their eyes. Now the strike's over I bet their next union man will be a little chap without the strength to waft a fly off his rice pudding.'

'The management don't choose.'

'Hah! But they have ways and means. I'll tell you something for nothing, Libby. This strike has done the workers more harm than good, you'll see. They are back where they started, and probably farther back than that.'

Margaret was on her orange box again, stabbing the air with a finger and for once Libby made no attempt to interrupt. She was back in control of her emotions, and now she was asking herself why the news of Tom Silver's dismissal had affected her as if she had been dealt a blow to the stomach. He was just a stranger, and yet when he had made that cheeky kissing movement with his lips she had wondered how it would be if he had really been making love to her. Oh yes, she had thought about it often. In the middle of the night, lying awake, she had imagined it. . . . He had come into her life briefly, and she had thought that was the end of it, but now, hearing that he was in trouble, Libby knew she would have to see him again. 'I'll leave you now, Margaret,' she said, and walked away, her feet dragging and her thoughts awhirl.

Libby's opportunity came on 23 May, the day before the Empire Day celebrations at the school.

With a little moan, Britannia fainted over her trident at the dress rehearsal as she was being wheeled round the play-ground in a go-cart trimmed with flags and flowers made of crêpe paper. The part had been given to one of the two theatrical girls working in the town that week and attending Libby's class, a girl who had a loud, carrying voice and an air of dramatic confidence which gave her speech a weighty significance.

After lessons were over and when the girl came to, the headmistress beckoned Libby over.

'Would you mind taking her home, Miss Peel? She lodges at number twenty, Meadow Street. I don't think there's much wrong with her but overtiredness.' She shook her gunmetal-grey head. 'You know my feelings about these half-timers, but I suppose their parents think they know what they are doing.' She stared with distaste at the patent-leather shoes. 'I suppose pushing them on the stage does guarantee that they are dressed well and eat three meals a day, but what they can ever hope to achieve in the way of a good education beats me.' She smiled her watery smile. 'Meadow Street is near your father's mill, isn't it? Maybe you can get a lift back home with him?'

Libby nodded. The headmistress had obviously never heard that Oliver Peel *walked* to and from his mill – never realized that the family did not own a car, only hired one when circumstances necessitated such extravagance.

'Of course I'll take her home,' she said, and in the cloak-room she pushed the child's arms into the sleeves of a blazer and pulled on a panama hat, adjusting the elastic underneath the trembling chin.

'Right then, Amy. Off we go.' And taking the small hand tightly in her own she set off down the sloping street.

In that particular part of the town well over six thousand houses had been built in the period from 1878 to 1918. They were terraced houses, spotlessly clean in the main, a semicircle of mopped flagstone in front of each door, with a step and window bottom edged with a flourish of cream or yellow stone.

But Meadow Street was different. At one time the three-storeyed houses had been lived in by professional gentlemen. There was a flight of steps up to the front door, and a basement kitchen where maids had once worked. Now the original owners had moved to new houses on the outskirts of the town, leaving the street to fall into shabby disrepair, the houses let off into single rooms with the landlady and her family occupying the ground floor.

Libby handed over the white-faced child to a middle-aged woman who answered the door of number 20. She told her, in her teacher's voice, that on no account must Amy be sent back to school until she was feeling better.

'I think she may be sickening for something,' Libby said, then before she could give herself time to think she turned and walked quickly back down the street to number 14.

This time the woman who answered her knock was wiping her hands on her apron, red puffy hands that looked as if they had been immersed in soap and water for a long time. Her eyebrows flew up towards the scragged-back hairline of her greying hair as she stared at the well-dressed young woman

72

standing on her door step. Her mouth dropped open in a round 'O' of surprise as she waited for Libby to speak.

'Mr Tom Silver?' Libby's recently authoritative manner deserted her completely as she spoke his name. 'Is he in, do you know?'

The woman nodded. 'Aye, he's in. Top floor, the door opposite t'stairs.' She stood back, mouth still agape, as Libby thanked her and climbed quickly up the uncarpeted stairs, wrinkling her nose at the smell of stale cooking and a sweeter smell she failed to recognize.

She was horrified. The house was worse than anything she had expected, far worse. Brown paint peeled off doors, and the banister rail felt greasy to her touch. Heart thudding now like a drum in her chest, she knocked at the door across the top landing and waited.

When it opened almost immediately and she saw Tom Silver standing there, she put a hand to her mouth. The man was ill. He had been discharged from the hospital, but the line of purple stitch marks on his forehead stood out like swollen veins against the pallor of his skin.

His surprise was as great as that of the blowsy woman downstairs, and all the more apparent because he tried to conceal it.

'Well, well! Miss Peel?' He pretended to look round. 'Where's the basket?'

Libby blushed. 'Basket? What basket?'

He put a hand as if to support himself against the door frame. 'The basket of goodies brought by the lady of the manor to succour the starving poor. That's what you've come for, isn't it, to dispense a little charity?'

Libby's blush deepened. 'As a matter of fact I *had* to come this way. A few doors down the street. A child in my class was taken ill at school and I have just brought her home, and I thought . . . I thought that as I was so near I would call and see how you were.' She was gabbling, unsure of herself for once. 'I got your letter last week, but you didn't say . . . you never mentioned losing your job.' A door opened along the landing and a tousled curious head peered out. 'I just wanted to say how sorry I was,' she finished desperately, 'and to say that if it was because of what happened that night I am willing to write

73

to your editor . . . to your manager and explain. May I come in?' she added, with a sideways glance along the landing at the half-open door.

'Welcome to my humble abode.' Tom Silver held the door back for her to enter. Then with an exaggerated gesture he took a handkerchief from his pocket and dusted off a chair. 'I'm right out of sherry unfortunately, but I can offer you a cup of tea if you don't mind it being in a mug.'

'Stop it!' Libby sat down gratefully, trying to still the trembling of her legs. 'Why must you always mock me?' She lifted her chin. 'I bet you didn't mock Margaret Bottomley when she brought the book back to you. I know you didn't because she was full of it.'

'Full of what?' Tom sat down opposite her and raised a quizzical eyebrow. 'You're trying to tell me she was impressed by my charm? Sorry, love, but if you've come on her behalf then you're wasting your time. Miss Bottomley is just not my type.'

Libby clenched her hands into fists. She glanced round the room, at the single bed in the corner, the tiny fireplace, the round table covered by a skimpy cloth, the rows of bookshelves, and the curtain concealing what was a makeshift wardrobe. 'Look, Mr Silver, I'll say what I have to say, then I'll go.' She bit her lip. 'You are obviously far from well. That cut on your head might be healing, but you were concussed, and concussion can do funny things. You're depressed and bitter, and I want to help if I can. It was awful, your coming out of the infirmary to find your job had gone. You didn't deserve that. It wasn't fair.'

'But life isn't fair, is it, Miss Peel?' He smiled. 'You've had your hair cut. Take off your hat and let me see.'

Mesmerized by the steady gaze of the dark eyes Libby did as she was told.

'It's lovely,' he said at last. 'It suits you. Before, it swamped your face, now it shows up your bone structure. You will never look old with cheekbones like that.

His eyes were the strangest eyes she had ever seen. Piercing, dark and yet kind. She shifted in her chair. This interview was not going at all the way she had planned it should. She had expected him to be, well, *grateful* for her concern and offer of help, and instead he was so much in command of the situation that she felt about eighteen, being interviewed for a place at teaching college. She coughed nervously.

'With your permission I will go and see your boss at the *Weekly Times*. If he did what he did because he thought you were behaving in an unseemly manner that evening . . .' Her voice tailed away at the sound of her stilted phrases. Oh, God, what a mess she was making of things . . . she could see his face darkening in anger.

'You will do no such thing, Miss Peel! I absolutely forbid you to go to my place of work. My recent place of work.' He slapped his knee hard with the flat of his hand. '*I* could have gone cap in hand if I had wanted to. I could have told them things they don't know. Things *you* don't know.' He waved a hand to encompass the shabby room. 'God knows I wasn't earning much, but when I was on full time it paid the rent of this room, and I was able to send fifteen shillings a week to my late wife's mother.' He nodded. 'So you know about my wife, then? I'm not surprised. I don't suppose there's much your Miss Bottomley doesn't ferret out.'

He leaned back, closing his eyes for a second as if the effort of talking was too much for him. 'My ex-mother-in-law lives alone, crippled with arthritis, and I have done what I could over the years. Her next move is into an institution, but with my contribution she was able to keep her independence. Now . . .' He spread his hands wide. 'And don't go putting me down in your book as a benevolent man, because I'm not. I am of the opinion that we are like animals when it comes down to basics. I helped my ma-in-law because I like her, I like her a lot, and if things had been different she would probably have been living with us.' He got up and walked over to the window. 'Do you know, they hadn't even the decency to call me into the office! Just sent a note by the office boy. Out! Finished!'

Then suddenly he turned and smiled, and at once his face looked young and boyish. 'You've given me the opportunity to let fly, and now I've done. It had to come out, and now it's said and over with. Thank you for coming. Even if it *was* on your way.'

When he opened the door he was grinning, and as she walked past him, carrying her hat, he reached out a finger, and

75

gently flicked the dark wing of hair away from her cheek.

'Goodbye, lass,' he said, and closed the door gently behind her, leaving Libby to stumble down the dark stairs, knowing she had been well and truly dismissed.

She was alone with Harry Brandwood in the lounge that evening. Carrie had gone up to her room, saying she had a headache, Oliver was in the billard room with his papers and the whisky bottle, and Ettie was upstairs with Sarah.

'Come here, Libby.' Harry caught her hand as she walked past his chair and pulled her forcibly onto his knee. 'For a courting couple we don't get many chances to be alone like this. Let's make the most of it, eh?'

His kiss was sensual and lingering, and Libby slid her arm round his neck and responded dutifully. Then as his hand moved to her breast she jerked away.

'Don't! Someone might come in. I don't think Carrie has gone to bed, and Father . . .' She sat bolt upright and put up a hand to tidy her hair.

Immediately Harry pulled her close again, covering her face with kisses. 'And what if they do, sweetheart? We're engaged to be married. Remember?' His face was hot, and his light brown eyes hazy with love. 'Love me?'

Libby sighed and turned her cheek into the comfort of his tweedy shoulder. Oh, yes, she did love this man. She had loved him for a long time now, all through the slow months of his wooing, accepting his devotion gladly. Whenever she needed him, he was there; he always would be there, steady as a rock. Once she had teased him and said he should have been christened Peter, not Harry. Peter, the rock.

And the other one, that thin tall man with despair in his eyes and a smile on his lips, alone in that room he called home with his pride, his tenacity. He would survive. Tom Silver would never submit to the indignity of unemployment which turned decent hard-working men into grey shadows as they trudged from one place to another, begging for work. His pride would sustain him, it had to. There was nothing she could do.

And the next time Harry kissed her, her fierce response was all he desired, more than he had hoped for, and whatever had been troubling her was gone. He knew his Libby. All sunshine one minute and shadows the next. Passion rising in him like a lick of flame, Harry wrapped his arms tightly round his bride-to-be as their kiss deepened.

Five

In July Sarah Batt's father died suddenly in the kitchen of the little cottage five miles from Westerley. Bending over to tie the laces of his boots, he ended his life as quietly as he had led it, his eyes wide open as if he too had been shocked by the suddenness of it all.

'Mrs Peel says I must stay for as long as you need me, Mam.' Sarah, eyes sunk into the hollows of her plump cheeks, stared down at her father's peaceful face with the broad hands crossed over the white shroud. 'The schools have broken up for the holidays, and Miss Libby and Miss Carrie will be able to see to her.' She leaned farther forward towards the plain wooden coffin. 'Who laid him out, Mam?'

Nellie Batt crossed herself devoutly before covering the waxen face. Physically an older version of her stout and capable daughter, with the same red hair and pale freckled skin, she was still in a state of shock. Only a small part of her accepted that her husband was dead, and she still expected him to come in from the fields, wiping the mud from his boots on the scraper at the door before going over to the slopstone to wash his hands.

'Why, Mrs Warburton, who else? She allus does the laying out, you know that, our Sarah.'

'Then she's missed his fingernails.' Sarah pointed. 'See, Mam, they're mucky. She might have cleaned them out with the tip of a knife or something. It looks bad.'

'That's soil, not muck.' Mrs Batt's flat voice rose in indignation. 'Your dad allus had black nails, especially the thumbs, with pressing his cuttings down into his pots, and with filling his pipe.' She glanced over to the rack of pipes on the wall. 'I don't know what I'll do with them now; there's two hardly

78

used, but I've got rid of his walking stick and his best jacket and trousers. A tramp came knocking not an hour before you got here, and I gave them to him. I think he thowt it were Christmas Day when I handed them over.' She turned away. 'You'd best go up and say goodnight to Patrick. He said he would stop awake till you came, an' knowing him he'll be lying there waiting for you. He's going to miss his grandpa, that child is,' she added, making no reference to her own feelings, which Sarah guessed were as cold and numb as her husband's still body.

Wiping her eyes, Sarah climbed the narrow twisting staircase leading up from the living room, then turning right at the top she went into the back bedroom and saw her son sitting bolt upright in bed staring at the door.

Patrick Batt, the living proof of Sarah's disgrace, was eight years old, and looked two years older. Tall for his age, he was a beautiful boy with hair as yellow as buttercups, the exact colour of Ettie Peel's as a child. His blue eyes slanted upwards at the corners and were set over a high-bridged nose. The Peel nose, Sarah thought now, struck forcibly with the uncanny resemblance of her son to his father, Willie Peel. Willie Peel, who had crept up the back stairs at Westerley and seduced her, lying in her arms and sobbing away his terror at the thought of having to go back to the hellhole that was France in that last year of the war.

Now it was his son's turn to shed tears of anguish in Sarah's arms. Over his bowed head she cursed the fate that had moulded him into such an exact copy, and even in her own sorrow she vowed that never, never would the Peel family find out the truth.

'Grandpa is with Jesus and Mary,' she soothed. 'Walking in a lovely garden where the sun always shines, and roses are in bloom in winter. His bad leg will never hurt him again. *Nothing* will hurt him. Jesus will see to that.'

'An' I will see to Grandma.' Patrick raised a small stricken face, the drama of the situation thickening his young voice with resolution. 'I made her a pot of cocoa and cut a slice of bread an' put jam on it, an' I can chop wood . . . and things,' he finished. 'Will Grandpa really have gone to heaven without making his confession?'

'Your grandpa had nothing to confess, love,' Sarah said firmly. 'He never said a wrong word, not in the whole of his life. He was the kindest, best man that ever breathed. Jesus will be glad to have him up there, I can promise you that.'

Then, as her tears rolled down her cheeks into the thatch of thick golden hair, she closed her eyes and sent up a private prayer of gratitude for the father who had pulled her close into his arms on the day she had arrived home, bringing trouble to their doorstep, and had promised her that her coming baby would be brought up to hold his head high.

When Patrick was six years old, astounding the teacher at the village school by his ability to read and write, she was back at Westerley, lavishing care and devotion on Ettie Peel.

'If they were to find out, they would claim him,' her father had said quietly one day, the pipe in his hand smoked out, his eyes suddenly bleak. 'Illegitimate or not, they would want him, not having a son of their own. Would be only natural.'

'Over my dead body!' his wife declared, rocking her chair so violently that it was in danger of tipping over. 'Why don't you come home, Sarah, and break with the Peels for good? Tongues would soon stop wagging here, and our backs are broad enough to stand it, anyroad. You could get a job in one of the big houses and the Peels would be out of our lives for good.'

Sarah shook her head. 'They will never be out of my life, Mam, even if I never saw them again. Patrick is his father born again, and being born on the very day his father was killed, he *is* Willie Peel born again, can't you see?'

In their religious superstition her parents did see at once, but what they could never understand was their daughter's obstinacy in wanting to remain at Westerley. It was no use trying to make them realize that Sarah's devotion to her mistress was the selfless love of a daughter-in-law, the protective caring for a woman whose grandson she now held in her arms, trying to comfort his childish grief.

'Lie down and try to get to sleep.' She tucked the covers up to his chin. 'We have to be very brave for Grandma's sake, an' I know you will look to her, love. I'm going downstairs now to talk to her, and tell her all the things she likes to hear about Miss Libby and Miss Carrie, to take her mind off. That's what

80

she needs, her mind taking off.' She kissed the flushed cheek, and felt herself jerked forward as two thin arms came from beneath the flannelette sheet and gripped her tightly.

'Are they really like two peas in a pod?' Patrick was stalling for time, willing her to stay. Sarah sat down on the bed and nodded, telling the tale he never tired of hearing.

'It's like one person, except that there's two. If they have their backs turned there's no difference, and even when they're both looking at you it's hard to tell. Same noses, mouths, eyes and hair, and most of the time they dress alike because they like nothing better than foxing folks, especially Miss Libby.' Sarah put out a hand and gently closed her son's eyes, seeing as she did so Mrs Warburton from the end house doing the same for her father when she was called to do the laying out. She bit her lip and fought back the threat of tears. 'Miss Libby is noisier than Miss Carrie. Always wanting her own way, and acting like a baby sometimes instead of a grown lady. An' worrying her mother with always arguing with her father; not a bit like Miss Carrie, who's all for a quiet life.'

'Miss Carrie's your favourite.' Patrick voice slurred on the edge of sleep.

Sarah stood up carefully, then began to back away. 'Yes, she is that. An' you know why? Because Miss Libby's always ferreting her nose into things that don't concern her, that's why.'

'An' Mr Peel?' The voice was whisper-soft now.

'Like a bull. A big, black, roaring bull. Put him in a field an' you wouldn't tell the difference.'

Sarah closed the door, letting the latch drop quietly into place. Then, with every stair creaking under her ample weight, she went downstairs to her mother, who was waiting for her, staring into the fire.

'Without a hand stretched out to me when life is too unbearable for me to carry on, I will die. Without *you* I will die.'

Mungo McDermot had done the unforgivable and telephoned Carrie at Westerley, throwing her into a blind panic, telling her that he would wait at the summer house all day for her to come to him. 'And every day until you do,' he had

81

finished, his voice hoarse with anguish.

'I can only stay for ten minutes,' Carrie told him, wrinkling her nose at the damp earthy smell in the little shuttered meeting place, bewildered at her claustrophobic reaction and the unresponsive stiffening of her body as Mungo held her close.

'Beatrice is always like this in the school holidays. She cannot abide me about the house.' He looked thinner than ever, all eyes, with a nervous tic throbbing at the side of his cheek. 'I interrupt her routine, she says.'

When his hand strayed to the loop-button fastening of Carrie's thin summer dress, she jerked away, then gripped his hand tightly to prevent it from straying further. At what moment, she asked herself, had she stopped loving him and seen him as he really was? A weak man who would have taken her virginity, maybe got her with child, with no intention of ever leaving his wife – just to gratify his own desires. The puritanical phrases milled round in her brain, as years of submission to a domineering father, combined with religious beliefs and a girlish naïvety towards the facts of life, rose to the surface and killed her infatuation stone dead.

'I don't believe you can't get out to meet me,' Mungo was muttering, his head bent, the thin spot on the crown of his head filling Carrie not with tenderness as before but with distaste.

She was very dignified that July morning, filled with pity as she wondered how she could tell him that she no longer loved him, that somehow love had died, forcing her to see him as he really was.

'You don't understand,' she said softly, trying to spare him. 'We are a close family. We don't, my sister and I, just leave the house without saying where we are going. If I said I was going for a walk or a bicycle ride it would be more than likely that Libby would say she would come with me, and besides, Sarah, who looks after Mother, has gone home for a while because her father has died.'

Sarah, this new, clear-headed Carrie now thought, who once gave in to a man like you and even now, eight years later, is too filled with shame to want to talk about her illegitimate son.

'You must not! You must never touch me like that again!'

Carrie forgot to be kind as Mungo's open-mouthed kiss descended, covering what seemed to be the whole bottom half of her face and filling her with nausea. Jerking away, she stood up, pulling her dress down and fastening the top buttons with shaking fingers. 'It's wrong! I'm not like that. I thought I was, but I'm not. You wouldn't do that if you had any respect for me.'

'You don't love me.' Mungo stared up at her, his mouth working convulsively. 'You led me on, and now you think you can cast me aside . . .' He waved a limp wrist to encompass the gloomy interior of the summer house. 'You have been the one bright star in my apology for a life, and now you tell me I mustn't touch you. Oh, God . . .' He dropped his face into his hands. Shaking with hard sobs he rocked himself backwards and forwards, moaning, whimpering, saying her name over and over again. 'Carrie, Carrie, oh, Carrie, my own sweet love.'

She had never seen a man cry before. She had seen her father incoherent with rage, heard his voice bellow as his face contorted with anger, and she had shrunk from the sight. But nothing, nothing had prepared her for this. Mungo's lack of control shocked her so that all she could do was stand there and watch him disintegrate from a man into a pitiable object devoid of dignity and self-respect.

And she had done this to him.

'If you leave me,' he was saying now, the words ragged and torn with anguish, 'if you leave me, then I will kill myself. I will do away with myself, I swear.'

Carrie felt the sweat break out all over her body, felt it run down her sides and stand in cold beads on her forehead. With one part of her she was kneeling down by his side, comforting, wiping his tears away, soothing, promising, but with the other part – the part that was in control – she was watching him with the aloofness of a bystander.

'You will *not* kill yourself, Mungo.' Her calm voice was the one she used to tick off a naughty child at school. 'People who threaten to do that never do. You have your boy to think about. He needs you more than any normal boy, and your wife . . .' she made herself go on, 'she needs you too, for support . . .' Her voice tailed away. How hypocritical can you be, Carrie Peel?

Never once, in all the time of your loving, did you give a thought to his wife and her needs. She backed towards the door. 'I'm going now, Mungo. I'm sorry . . .' Pull yourself together, she wanted to say, but that would have been too cruel. 'When you think about it calmly you will know there was never any future for us. Mungo . . . no!'

With a sudden movement he pulled her to him. Through the thin material of her dress she felt his body, every hard inch of it, pressing against her, devouring her with its closeness. One hand squeezed her breast, whilst the other held the back of her head, his teeth sharp against her tightly clenched mouth, his tongue probing, darting with insistence.

With all his strength he was straining and writhing, forcing her body to meet his demands and Carrie realized that to fight back would only inflame him the more. She went limp in his arms – not stiff, just totally unresponsive, some inborn instinct telling her this was the only way.

When he pushed her from him she fell painfully onto the rotting floorboards, hurting her knee, embarrassed almost to the point of faintness. Staggering to her feet, she opened the door and escaped into the warm sunshine. She was shaking as if with a violent fever, but she forced her trembling legs to obey and tottered towards the hole in the hedge and out onto the main road.

'Carrie! Come back! Don't leave me! Carrie . . . Carrie . . . Carrie . . .' Mungo's voice called out to her.

With head bent and taking small slow steps, Carrie set off for home, her knee throbbing and her heart pounding. If she could get into the house without anyone seeing her; if she could lock herself into the big bathroom and sink into a tub of hot water, then maybe she could wash away the memory of the morning. She shuddered as she thought of what might have happened. But now that it was all over she could tell Libby how foolish she had been, and some day they would laugh about it together, with their arms round each other, stifling their giggles as they done for as long as she could remember. Libby, the sensible one, who would never have got herself into a mess like this. Libby the strong one. 'Oh, Libby . . .' Carrie muttered, trudging on, near to home now, to her other self who would listen and understand. . . .

'It will be clogs to clogs in three generations. You mark my words.' Oliver Peel left the house in high dudgeon one August morning, bemoaning the fact that the postman was later than usual. 'The cotton trade is finished in this town; there's three mill chimneys with no smoke coming from them, and the way things are going Bridge Mill will be next.'

Used to the morning ritual, Libby and Carrie hovered in the hall, one twin handing her father his walking stick and the other his newspaper and bowler hat. Carrie, pale but composed, had stopped skimming hastily through the paper, holding her breath as she ran her finger down the obituary column in dread of seeing Mungo's death reported.

The fact that Libby, once she had given the tearful tale her full attention, had called Mungo's threat moral blackmail and had laughed his threat of suicide to scorn, helped to assuage the biting fear in Carrie's mind. It was no use saying that she felt responsible, that remorse was eating at her soul, waking her in the night sweating and shaking. Remorse was a wasted emotion. Libby had always maintained that; what people did of their own accord was their own responsibility. 'Not that circumstances don't sometimes push them over the edge,' she had conceded rather loftily, 'but in the main we work out our own salvations.'

Oh, to be like Libby, sure of herself, restless, with quick-silver reactions, taking over in a crisis and doing what had to be done without weighing the consequences. Like now.

'I'll take the post down to the mill,' Libby volunteered when it finally dropped through the letter box. 'Father obviously thought there was something here he wanted to see.' She held up a long buff envelope. 'This one looks a bit sinister. Maybe it's a summons. If he treats his workers with the contempt he holds for them I wouldn't be surprised.'

Ettie Peel appeared round the bend in the stairs, a loose wrapper over her nightgown. 'But there is going to be a storm, dear. The air is heavy with it.' She came down the remaining stairs slowly, feeling for each tread with a slippered foot. 'I think I have one of my heads coming on and, oh, I wish Sarah would come back. I know it's selfish of me, but I miss her so much, and she always knows what to do. Thunder terrifies me. It reminds me of the sound of guns, and then I get to thinking about Willie . . .'

Immediately Carrie went to her mother, leading her gently into the lounge.

'I'm here, Mother. I won't leave you.' She lowered her voice. 'And Libby needs to do something. The long school break leaves her with so little to do, especially this year when Father decided there was too much going wrong at the mill for us to take our usual holiday at Lytham St Annes.'

'But what will she do if the storm breaks?' Ettie, to whom worrying came as naturally as breathing, allowed herself to be led to the chesterfield.

'Tell her to ring for a taxi cab. Father can charge it to the mill.'

Ellie raised a small piteous face. 'Why does your father insist on walking everywhere? He may have this notion of showing the world something or other by not having his own car and chauffeur, but he doesn't stop to think that it makes me a prisoner in my own home. It's all very well for him to say I have Miss Gray to dressmake whenever I need a new outfit, and that all we need is delivered to the door, but, oh, how I would long just to walk round the shops one day. You know. I could manage to walk through the Arcade if I took it easy.'

She frowned and put up a hand to the hair that was once a bright buttercup yellow and now was faded and streaked with grey. 'And another thing. Why isn't Libby showing more interest in her trousseau? The wedding is in four months' time, and she hasn't even looked through the catalogue sent from Manchester. All that sewing and fitting to be done, and once she goes back to school there'll be so little time. And why does she insist on working next term? She should have left in July and spent the time in preparations. She told me one day she wouldn't care if she got married in her best blue jacket and skirt, and you know how your father has set his mind on a proper wedding with all the trimmings. Dr and Mrs Brandwood would be so upset if we made it seem like a hole and corner affair. Harry is their only son. It would be dreadful if we let them down.'

Carrie went over to the drinks cupboard and poured her

mother a glass of her favourite tonic wine. 'Drink this, Mother. I know it's early, but who cares? And try to stop worrying about Libby. She knows what she's doing. She'll probably get the tram and take her umbrella, and she won't melt even if it does rain. Libby would burst if she didn't get out of the house at least once a day, you know that.'

'I wish Sarah would come back,' Ettie said, sipping the wine and refusing to be cheered. 'What if her mother decides she needs Sarah at home now Mr Batt has died? She has a heart condition, Sarah once told me, and that boy . . . he must be a handful now, and surely the village won't hold it against Sarah any more. It's nineteen twenty-six, not nineteen hundred. People are more liberal-minded these days, even about illegitimacy. But Sarah never speaks about her son, and I respect her silence. She's such a *good* girl, Carrie, and she isn't always wanting to go to Mass like most Catholics.' Ettie took another pensive sip. 'Now that would set the cat among the pigeons. Your father would never hold with that. I can never understand him having Sarah back, not with his high principles. I would have thought a fallen girl would be the last person he would want in his household, so it proves he isn't as strict as he appears.'

Carrie turned away. Oh. Mother, poor trusting helpless Mother, she was thinking, if only Ettie knew the reason for her husband's supposedly liberal-mindedness. It would be the pot calling the kettle black for him to condemn Sarah, when all the time he was creeping up the back stairs to gratify his frustrated desires. She sighed and glanced through the tall window to where the trees stood motionless against a lowering sky. 'I think I will take a glass of wine with you, Mother,' she said, remembering having read somewhere that more suicides took place in stormy weather than at any other time.

'Oh Mungo. Please God you didn't mean it and that Libby was right,' she said silently as she watched the dark red liquid fill the glass.

If it rains, then it rains, Libby told herself, boarding the tram and settling herself in the seat nearest the exit. She would get off at the stop before Meadow Street and approach the mill that way. It would save going over the canal bridge, she decided, refusing to admit that her real reason for going into town was that she might possibly see Tom Silver.

And if he saw her, she had a genuine excuse for being in that street on a Tuesday morning, wearing her most becoming dress and loose jacket with its false ermine collar. He might say something sarcastic, but she would brandish the letters and explain she was merely being a dutiful daughter and delivering them to the mill.

The tram was clattering its way past the Corporation Park gates now. Along the wide pavement groups of unemployed men walked slowly, hands in pockets, heads bent, shoulders drooping. She saw one stoop and pick up a discarded cigarette from the gutter, examine it closely, then toss it aside in disgust.

Meadow Street was completely deserted when she turned into it. No landladies gossiping on doorsteps, no children throwing balls up against the walls chanting 'onesy, twosey, threesey, foursey'. Nothing but closed doors and a menacing boil of thunder clouds over the rooftops. Out at Westerley, where the view was not blocked by rows of terraced houses, the sky was yellow with sheet lightning, and even here the very air seemed charged with electricity.

Libby began to run. She forgot about looking for a chance encounter with Tom Silver; all she wanted now was shelter and the safety of her father's office at the top of the sloping mill yard. Suddenly there came a blinding flash, followed by a crash of thunder, and as she turned into the short street fronting the mill she heard a scream. She looked up at the tall chimney, surprised to see it still standing. Then, as she tore through the mill gates, she saw a young girl lying face down on the cobbles, arms spread wide.

By the time Libby reached her a crowd of women weavers, clogs ringing on the stones, had poured out from the weaving shed. One woman, her hair brushed up into an old-fashioned cottage bun, knelt down and lifted the unconscious girl into her arms. 'She's been struck!' she cried aloud. 'Me daughter's been struck! Oh, Mary, Mary, love! I'm here! Your mam's here. Oh, God, look at her eyes. What's happened to her eyes?'

'She's been blinded by the flash. See, she's staring straight at us, but she can't see nowt.' Another weaver, helping to support the girl in a sitting position, waved a hand in front of the strangely staring eyes, getting no response.

'Can you see *anything*?' Libby, heedless of her best outfit and of the rain now pelting down, took the limp hand in her own as she stared into the panic-stricken face.

The girl, no more than fourteen years old, a thin waif of a child with a black fent apron over her short-sleeved blouse and skirt, opened her mouth wide and screamed. Her loud, piercing shrieks brought more weavers running from the shed to stand in a circle round the little kneeling group.

'I can't see! Oh, Mam, I can't see!' The hand snatched itself away from Libby's grasp and began to claw the air. 'There were this big flash and I fell down and now I can't see. Oh. Mam! Help me! Help me, somebody! Help me!'

'We must get her inside.' Libby recognized Jimmy Earnshaw, her father's tackler, a small wiry man with a moustache too big for the rest of his face. She turned to him eagerly. 'It's probably only a temporary thing, but we can't do anything out here. Bring her into the office out of the rain.'

Gently the hysterical girl was helped to her feet, hands stretched out at either side.

'Tha'll be awreet, lass. Take it steady.' Jimmy Earnshaw, a former weaver with the expertise of a qualified engineer necessary to his role of tackler, a man who could tune a machine just by listening to the sound of it running, glanced at Libby. 'I never thowt to see you here, miss. You come to see the maister?'

Before Libby could answer, she looked up and saw Oliver Peel coming down the yard from the office block. Bare-headed in the pouring rain, his black hair already sleeked to his skull, he advanced towards them, head lowered like a bull charging a fence.

'What's going on here? Why have you left your looms?' Ignoring Libby, he spoke directly to his tackler. 'Get this lot back, Jimmy. What do you think I'm made of? Bloody money? The hooter hasn't gone, has it? Go on, the lot of you, before I send you all home.'

'This child's been hurt, Mr Peel.' Libby cringed as the man seemed to shrink in size. She almost expected him to doff his cap as he answered his employer apologetically. 'We was bringing her into the office before sending for the doctor. She's lost her sight.'

At that the girl began to scream again, and now her mother put both arms round her and rocked her backwards and forwards. 'If you won't send for the doctor, Mr Peel, then I'll take her home,' she said, facing Oliver with the rain running down her face mingling with her tears. 'An' we'll neither of us come in no more.'

'You can't afford to stay at home,' Oliver stated calmly. He pointed back down the yard. 'Anybody not back at their looms in one minute goes home.' He turned to the tackler. 'Jimmy, take their names and bring the list to me. They'll get their pay docked for the length of time they've been out here, every man jack of 'em.'

And with that he turned on his heel and walked back to his office.

'The callous bugger!' A woman with the wizened face of a monkey muttered in a low voice as she turned to walk back into the weaving shed. 'He knows we dursn't risk our jobs, the bloody sod.'

'One of these days I'll swing for 'im and gladly.'

The faces, pale from lack of sunshine and weary from standing at the looms in the humid atmosphere of the weaving shed, reflected a hatred so powerful, so intense that it was almost tangible. Libby, unable to credit what she had just witnessed, stood irresolute for a moment. Then the young girl pressed the palms of her hands over her eyes, held them there for a moment, and, raising her small pinched face to the rain coming down like stair rods, sobbed her relief.

'Mam! I can see! It's come back. The black has gone. I can see again!'

'The Lord be praised . . . oh, my little lamb, the Lord be praised.' The mother's arms were once again round her daughter. 'It were the shock, little love, just the shock.'

'Take her home, Maggie.' Jimmy Earnshaw touched the woman on her arm. 'I'll square it with the maister. Just thee get her home and coddle her for a bit. I'll make it reet.'

'Nay, tha won't!' Libby recoiled from the venom in the strident voice. 'We're going back to our looms like what he said. I'll see to her. It won't be the first time I've done the work of two.' She lifted a clenched fist and shook it in the direction of the mill office block. 'But I'll not forget, and one of these days I'll get even, if it's the last thing I do. If her sight had gone for good he'd have done nowt but bother about his bloody profit-making. I spit on him!' She rooted round in her mouth and ejected a stream of spittle onto the cobblestones. 'I spit on his immortal soul! May he rot in 'ell, the unfeeling sod!'

'I still think tha should tek her home, Maggie.' The tackler took off his cap, revealing a bald head at variance with the flourishing moustache. 'See how she's shaking. She's as white as a piece of bleached fent. She'll not find the strength to stand at her loom.'

'I'm all right now, Mam.' The little girl, smaller than Libby had been at eleven years old, leaned on her mother for support and walked unsteadily down the yard. But her mother hadn't finished, not quite.

'He knows I've got four more at home like 'er, an' me husband laid off since the strike. He was right when he said we can't afford. He holds the trump card, an' him an' his sort allus will. If I go home now he'll lock me out tomorrow, an' if tha doesn't keep tha' mouth shut, Jimmy Earnshaw, tha'll be locked out an' all.' Then, without a single glance in Libby's direction, she led the trembling child back down the yard and into the weaving shed.

'I'll have to go after her, miss.' The tackler wrung out his dripping cap and replaced it on his head. 'If them looms 'as been left there'll be 'ell to pay.'

Libby nodded once, then walked away in the opposite direction. First she passed through the outer office, with the trio of clerical workers on their high stools and the large safe in the corner containing the account books. Looking neither to right nor left she walked determinedly through the tiny room where the manager sat at his desk, and into the inner sanctum, her father's private preserve. This room was carpeted, with a desk, a telephone, and a smaller safe on the wall. She opened the door without knocking and walked straight in.

'Did you *see* me out there?' she demanded. 'Or did you take me for one of the herd? Father! I'm asking you a question!'

Oliver Peel had taken off his jacket and draped it over one of the chairs set in a semicircle by the window. There was a glass by the files on his desk and it was obvious that he had been drinking.

He jerked his head towards the closed door. 'Keep your voice down, for God's sake. I've enough on my plate trying to keep that lot in order without it coming out that I can't control my own daughter.' He opened a drawer at the side of his desk and slid the empty glass into it with a furtive movement not lost on Libby. 'What are you doing here, anyway? What are you doing traipsing down the town on a morning like this? Have you seen yourself? You look like something the cat's brought in. Why aren't you at home seeing to your mother?'

Opening her purse, Libby took out the letters and threw them down on the desk. 'You missed the post this morning, so I brought these. Doing you a favour, I brought the post down to you. That's all.'

She was still identifying with his weavers, staring at their maister with hate-filled eyes.

'You saw what happened to that child.' Libby gripped the front of the desk and leaned forward, her face almost level with her father's. 'She might have been killed, and if she had been you would have had her covered with a length of your flaming cotton and left her there till the twelve o'clock hooter blew.'

Oliver stood up, his six-foot frame towering over her. Outside, the sliding rain hissed across the yard.

'But she wasn't killed, was she, now? She wasn't even blinded like she was making out to be. She was out in the toilets where she had no right to be, and when the flash came she had the hysterics.' He picked up a fat ledger, balanced it in his hand, then dropped it with a thud onto the desk. 'So don't you think you can come down here, madam, and tell me how to behave. And as for bringing her in here . . .' He waved a hand round the room. 'I don't have weavers in my office. I never have and I never will.'

'Even when they are hurt and frightened half to death, Father?' Libby's voice was dangerously quiet.

'Even when they *think* they are hurt, and want to make out they are frightened.' Oliver said the words slowly, and as he spoke Libby saw the way the veins bulged on his forehead and his already high colour deepened to a purple hue with two bright spots on his cheekbones.

And all at once the compassion which was more inherent in her twin's make-up than her own rose to the surface. As they glared at each other she saw suddenly the way it was for Oliver Peel. A man who had to do everything for himself, never for a moment believing that anyone else could take the responsibility weighing so heavily on him. The threat of closure of the mill, the crippling competition from overseas markets. And then coming home every evening to a house peopled with women, and wife who had retreated both physically and mentally into a dim, complaining world of her own. Libby glanced over to the corner where once at a small desk her brother had bent his yellow head over his ledgers, and she thought how on that dark gloomy morning Willie's brightness of expression and his sweet temperament would have lightened the atmosphere with a touch of gold.

'Father . . .' she began. 'There are four more weeks left before I go back to school. I'm good at figures, you know that. Isn't there something I could do to help? I'm bored at home, I *need* to do something. I know I'm not a man, but I'm quick and practical. I could hold the fort on the days you go to the Cotton Exchange at Manchester. I learn fast and maybe even after I'm married I could come in in the mornings. Answering the telephone for Harry won't be enough for me. Already I dread being alone in that big house with nothing to do but arrange the flowers and entertain Harry's friends. I'm *wasted*, Father! I want to help!'

For a moment she thought he was actually going to explode. His deep-set dark eyes narrowed into slits in the puffiness of his face, and when he reached for a paperweight she thought for one wild moment that he was going to hurl it through the window.

'What bloody nonsense! What typical rubbish!' He sat down heavily. 'Oh, yes. I can just see me having a woman working alongside of me, ferreting about, getting in my way. And I can see Harry letting you.' He jerked his head towards the door. 'You've wasted enough time for me already this morning, and now you try to tell me it's time I packed it in. You think that because I'm reaching retirement age, I'm

93

finished. You're like your mother, always telling me it's time I sold out and went to live with her in a bungalow at Southport.' He snorted. 'I know better than most that this industry is in a steady decline, and it will get worse before it gets better. But let me tell you something, madam. Cotton is in the blood, it's in my blood like it was in my father's, and his father before him, and like it would have been in Willie's. If he had lived.' He seemed to slump deep into his leather desk chair. 'But with my son gone I have to carry on, and I *will* carry on. I'll keep that chimney smoking and that machinery going if I have to die in the doing of it, and without any help from anybody, least of all from you.' He jerked his thumb towards the door. 'And you can take yourself off, and get back to the house where you belong, and heaven help that man of yours when he finds he's married to an interfering woman who thinks she has the mind of a man.'

With tears stinging behind her eyelids Libby groped her way blindly towards the door. She had known and accepted for as long as she could remember that her father had a cruel streak in him, but his cruelty was – or had been – not so much in what he said but in the way he said it. He could wither her mother with a glance from beneath his bushy eyebrows, and he could reduce Carrie to tears with his sarcasm. But now, since the strike of three months ago, he had taken what he termed his weavers' 'disloyalty' personally, blaming the slow trickle of orders directly on them, incurring their hatred to the point where it threatened to explode into violence.

As she stumbled through the outer office not a head was raised from the fat ledgers. The three clerks, legs wound round the spindles of their high stools, carried on writing, struggling to see in the far from adequate light, even their backs showing fear and apprehension as to what might be coming next. Not one of them turned as Libby opened the door and stepped outside into the deluge, remembering too late that she had left her umbrella in Oliver's inner sanctum.

'And I'm not going back for it,' she muttered aloud. 'He's my father, and he's sent me out in this rain wearing a summer dress and a short jacket, and he *doesn't care*. He cares for nothing but his profits and his blasted mill.'

The gutters in Meadow Street overflowed as the drains

failed to take the onslaught of water. The sky hung low and grey over the chimney tops of the terraced houses. The curtain of rain hit the flagstones and bounced back again as she hurried along, unaware of the spectacle she presented of a girl obviously out of her environment, with muddied knees from where she had knelt on the cobbles, her ruined upturned straw hat tipped crazily to one side.

'Well, well!' She stopped suddenly, whipping round as the voice called from an open doorway. 'Miss Peel! What on earth. . . ?'

Tom Silver stepped from the doorway and planted himself in front of her. 'You'd better come in.' He took her elbow and guided her towards the door of number 14. 'You're soaked to the skin, lass. Come on, come on. I don't know where you think you're going, but you can't go anywhere like this.'

At the kindness in his voice Libby felt the tears, held in check, brim over and run down her face to mingle with the rain. She shrugged away from his solicitous grasp even as she allowed herself to be led over the doorstep into the dingy lobby, and up the stairs to the room at the top of the house.

'I can make you a pot of hot tea, and the first thing we must do is get those shoes and stockings off and get them dry. Come on. Off with that jacket, then give me your hat.' He produced a towel and handed it over. 'Look, you stop where you are and I'll go down and cadge a bucket of coal from Mrs Barton.' He nodded towards the tiny empty grate wearing its summer embellishment of a pleated paper fan. 'I stopped my coal recently, but she's a good sort. I won't be more than a minute.'

Libby heard him clattering his way down uncarpeted stairs, and for the first time felt the cold seep through her. The little room was as damp and cheerless as the grave, with the rain slanting down against the window and the faded oilcloth slippery to her feet.

When he came back he knelt down, screwed up a newspaper, placed a firelighter on top, arranged a heap of coal and applied a match, then covered the front of the grate with another paper spread wide. He nodded as the flames roared up the chimney, and from a coal scuttle by the side of the fireplace he took a bundle of wood and added it to the already leaping flames. Then he placed a small tin kettle on the gas ring and applied a match, nodding again and stepping back as it spluttered into life.

'And now those stockings.'

Embarrassed and confused, Libby lifted her head and shook it from side to side. 'I can't take my stockings off. Not here!'

'Then I'll have to take them off for you.' He grinned. 'Come on, lass. I'll hang them over this tidy here and they'll be dry in a minute.' He draped her jacket over the back of a chair and set it to one side of the blaze. 'You're shaking like a leaf. Don't look so worried, there's nothing going to happen. I'm not going to go mad at the sight of a bare leg. See, I'll turn my back and promise not to turn round till you give the word. Right?'

'They'll dry on my legs.' Libby tried to stop her teeth chattering. 'And I'm not shivering because I'm cold. I've just come from my father and I'm upset. He's upset me, that's all.'

She put a hand to her mouth. Now why had she said that? She hardly knew this man watching her so gravely, and yet at that moment she wanted nothing more than to put her head down and wail, and feel his hand on her hair and hear the soothing tone of his voice.

'Get those stockings off!'

Tom turned away to reach two mugs down from a shelf, then from a cupboard beneath he took out a small brown teapot and a packet of tea. 'And if you want to cry, then get on with it. Tears held in do nobody any good, and you've got a towel there to wipe them away.'

There was no mockery in the words, just a gentle understated consideration for her feelings. So, sniffing audibly, Libby unfastened her suspenders through the folds of her wet skirt, and peeled off the dirty, wet stockings.

'And your frock,' Tom said firmly. Still with his back to her he reached out and took a dressing gown from the rail at the foot of his single bed. 'There's not many folks round here sport dressing gowns, but this one was bought special a few years back when I went to a conference in Cambridge.' He threw it over. 'There were a few women delegates there, and I didn't want to shock them going along the landing in the nude. I don't wear pyjamas,' he added, and she suspected there was a hint of teasing laughter in his voice now. 'And there's something not quite right about a man going to the bathroom in his raincoat with a towel over his arm, wouldn't you say? Now give me the word to turn round when you're ready. I never have liked this view of Mrs Barton's back yard, with your father's mill shutting out what light there is. On a day like this it's enough to make even an optimist like me feel he's reached the very depths of his existence.'

Stepping out of her dress and pulling the rough blanket wool of the dressing gown round her, Libby told herself dramatically that the depths of her own existence had been reached the moment her father had let her walk out into the torrential rain. Oliver Peel had no love for her – the hatred and contempt he felt for her had shown in his narrowed eyes – and he had no love for Carrie either, mentally regarding them as one since the day they were born. Her mother he tolerated, that was all, his servants and workforce he treated with contempt, and some day he would get his just deserts. She was sure of it.

'Do you believe the devil can get into people, Mr Silver?' She held out her hand for the proffered pot of tea. 'I mean, so that they're angry all the time and you can hardly ever remember them speaking normally?'

Tom pulled up the little hard chair from the table by the window, turned it with its back to the fire and arranged her dress over it. 'Don't you think it's time you called me Tom, and let me call you Libby? You can't come out with a question like that to a stranger.' He sat down on the edge of the bed, holding his own mug of tea with both hands curled round it. 'Are you trying to tell me that you think your father is going mental? Because if you are, it's that doctor fella of yours you should be discussing it with, not me.'

Libby gave a visible start, then glanced down at the ring on her finger. She had forgotten all about Harry. In the whirl of her disordered thinking he had never come into the picture.

'When Harry's there my father seems almost normal,' she said slowly. 'He doesn't talk much to Harry, but on the other hand he doesn't ignore him altogether. Once when I told Harry my father had hit me, he seemed to think I had asked for it.'

'And had you?'

'No! All I want is to be treated as if I had a *mind*, a will of my own. I want to be treated as if I'm capable of being more than just a silly girl with nothing else to think about but getting married and setting up home. I *care* about people, Tom.' She said his name quite naturally. 'I sometimes feel that when I marry in December, I'll just be moving from one safe cocoon to another, and it stifles me. I should be happy, and I'm not.' She raised her head and stared into the fire. 'What's wrong with me? I mean to say, what am I doing here, sitting on this chair in your dressing gown, talking to you as if we had been friends all our lives?' She blinked back the threat of tears. 'And I'm selfish, too. My life is mapped out for me, safe and predictable, but what about yours? I haven't even asked you if you've had any luck in finding another job yet.'

Tom grinned, the couldn't-care-less grin that had infuriated her the last time they met. But now she realized it was merely a ploy to cover his despair. He shrugged his shoulders. 'When you go to see the clerk at the labour exchange you tell him you haven't been able to find work, and after a while you have to give three places each day where you've looked and failed, or they knock you off the list. Otherwise you are classed as not being genuinely in search of work.'

'Then what?'

'Well, there is always Poor Law Relief, and if they send the relieving officer round and he finds you have any coal, or furniture that will sell, or too much food on the shelves, then you have to sell it all before you can get relief.' He shook his head. 'But I'm not making out a case for myself. No, it's the married men with families who have to feed their kids on bread and jam if they're lucky and they've managed to pay the rent.' His face set hard. 'Talk about a land fit for heroes! I've seen men standing in line down at the labour exchange, men who were in the thick of it in France, and they have to listen to some clerk who sat out the war on his bottom laying the law down to them. It makes me despair . . .'

Libby watched him, her cheeks glowing with a colour that owed nothing to the fire now leaping in the tiny grate. When he went out of the room later while she pulled on her dry stockings and the creased dress, she prayed that he would hint that he wanted to see her again. But when she thanked him for his kindness he merely bowed his head and stood aside to let her pass.

When she stepped out into the street the wetness on her cheeks could not have been mistaken for the rain, for by now the storm had rolled away in a tumble of grey clouds over the chimney tops.

Six

Carrie suspected that Libby wasn't paying much attention to what she was saying, but then Carrie was used to talking to blank faces and glazed eyes at school. She had accepted a long time ago that whilst she was an adequate teacher she had none of her sister's flair for making a lesson come alive. Still, she had to talk to her and at the moment, as they sat at the table in the window of the first floor café overlooking the town's main shopping street, Libby was a captive audience.

'Mungo just won't take no for an answer,' she said, splitting a scone and spreading it with butter. 'He keeps trying to get me alone, and he stares at me, even when there are other teachers in the staff room. Great smouldering stares they are, and now, instead of making me feel sorry for him, they just make me feel sick. It's as though I can see him now for what he is, whereas before . . . I must have been out of my mind.'

Libby had insisted on waiting until the window table was vacant, and now she leaned over to peer down into the busy Saturday afternoon street thronged with shoppers.

'Looks can't kill,' she said, proving to a suspicious Carrie that she *had* been listening after all.

'He's so obviously unhappy.' Carrie, feeling better now she had her twin's attention, spread red plum jam over the butter on her scone. 'And I really am sorry for him, but what can I do?' She removed a crumb from the corner of her mouth. 'When I look back to the summer, I can't believe it was *me* behaving like that. All that rushing about, terrified in case anyone saw us together, and do you know, you won't believe this, but I had an awful pain low down in my stomach most of the time.' She shook her head. 'It's true, Libby. It was just like colic. I used to lie in bed thinking about him, then when I woke up in the morning he was there immediately in the front of my mind. And you know, I never once allowed myself to realize just how . . . how *weak* he was. He looks *weak*, all pathetic and cow-eyed. And I thought I *loved* him! Oh, I must have been *obsessed*! I can't believe it was me behaving like that.' She giggled. 'You know those pointed shoes we bought and regretted? Well, on the days I was seeing Mungo I sometimes wore them, and they were as comfortable as bedroom slippers, yet now I can't bear them on my feet. And when I think . . .' she shuddered, 'when I think how nearly I gave in to him . . .' She poured milk into the two cups by her side before lifting the heavy silver-plated teapot. 'I could have ruined my whole life, and he would never have married me, never left Beatrice.'

'Beatrice?' Libby swivelled her glance away from the window for long enough to accept the cup and saucer from her sister's outstretched hand.

'His wife.' Carrie took another scone from the plate lined with a fluted paper doily. 'They still fight. He came to school yesterday with a bruise the size of a half-crown underneath his eye, and he was all white and shaky. He looked dreadful.'

'I never liked the name Beatrice,' Libby said, moving the curtain with one hand to see better.

Carrie, exasperated now to the point of uncharacteristic irritation, put out a foot underneath the table and stepped none too gently on her sister's shoe. 'Libby Peel! You're miles away! Listen! I am asking your *advice*. Mungo managed to get me alone for a minute yesterday, and he said if I don't see him just once more to talk things over, he'll do it.'

'Do what?'

'Kill himself. Commit suicide.' Carrie looked round the crowded café and lowered her voice to a whisper. 'He's desperate, Libby. He's rung me up twice at home, and if Father ever answers the telephone he'll demand to know who it is, and if it comes out, well, anything could happen.' She bit her lip. 'And I know this sounds selfish and dreadful, but supposing Mungo does, well, you know, and leaves a note saying he's done it on *my* account, and then it gets into the paper? He's capable of it. He told me I would regret it if I didn't meet him.'

101

She stared open-mouthed as her sister suddenly pushed back her chair, grabbed her handbag and rushed towards the wide staircase leading down out of the café and into the street.

'Libby! Where are you going? What on earth . . .?'

Conscious of the inquisitive stares from the other tables and the sudden lull in the teacup chatter, Carrie gathered up her own bag. Covered with embarrassment, she walked as casually as she could to the check out till at the far end of the mahogany counter, where she handed over the bill and a ten shilling note to the middle-aged woman in a pink overall.

For weeks, Libby had seen Tom Silver's dark head everywhere – in the tram, walking down the street. Now he was really there – across the road by the bank, standing on the wide corner pavement talking to someone. He was hatless, his long black hair flopping over his high forehead, probably the only man she knew who went everywhere without a hat. Coatless too, in spite of the cold wind that had apparently blown the September Indian summer straight into winter.

Dodging the traffic, her own coat flying open, dropping a kid glove as she went, Libby ran straight up to him, her legs as wobbly as if she was just getting over the flu. Her feelings were in such a turmoil that she was incapable of caring about anything but the fact that he was there. After the weeks of longing he had finally materialized, just when she had thought she would never see him again.

'Tom!' Ignoring the man in a trilby hat talking earnestly to him, she actually clutched at Tom Silver's arm, feeling the bone hard through the thin serge of his shabby navy blue suit. 'How are you? I was over there . . .' she pointed back at the café, 'and I saw you. How *are* you? Have you found a job yet? You've been ill, haven't you? Oh, I can tell you've been ill . . .'

The man in the trilby hat, small ferret eyes missing nothing, mumbled that he would walk up to the Town Hall and wait there. Tom dismissed him with a nod, while Libby took no notice of his going at all.

'Libby Peel.' Tom looked down at her, at the flushed cheeks, at the rise and fall of her breasts beneath the soft blue wool of her high-necked dress. 'Come on, we'll walk a bit. It's too cold to stand here.' Taking her by the elbow, he turned her round and guided her firmly up the side street, round the corner and into the shelter of a wide shop doorway.

And Carrie, emerging from the café, flustered and disbelieving, stood on the wide pavement looking up and down, searching for her sister and seeing nothing. Eventually she went back up the stairs to the café and asked the pink overall behind the till that if her sister came looking for her, would she please say that she had gone home?

'I'll do that, love,' the woman said, then moved to the end of the mahogany counter nearest the stairs, the better to see Carrie stumbling down, small and bewildered, out into the street again.

Tom Silver was no fool. Since his wife had died he had known two women, and both times he had been the one to break off the relationship, knowing that there was something in him that stopped him committing himself completely. And now here was this lovely, intelligent young woman, all pride forgotten, staring up at him with her feelings shining from her brown eyes and trembling to his touch.

'What is it, Libby?' he said gently, then immediately regretted the question as her face crumpled and the dark eyes swam with tears.

'I don't know.' She twisted away from him. 'I just wanted to know how you were.' She shivered, and made no move to stop him as he began to button up her coat. 'I've been thinking about you being out of work . . . and everything, and I couldn't bear not knowing.' She seemed unable to take her eyes from his mouth. 'I wanted to come and see you, but it . . . I couldn't.'

As he lifted her hand with the diamond ring on the third finger, she realized for the first time that she had lost a glove. Not that it mattered; not that anything mattered now that he was here and she was standing close to him, with the keen wind blowing discarded cigarette packets and scraps of paper round their ankles.

He smiled the smile that had haunted her for weeks. 'Not married yet?'

She shook her head, seeing the way his collar was frayed at the edges and seemed too big for his thin neck. 'The wedding's in December, the day after the school breaks up for Christmas.' Her voice faltered, and it was as though the next words said themselves. 'But I can't get married, Tom. It wouldn't be right.' She took a deep breath, then put out a hand as if to steady herself. 'Can I see you again? Please?'

She was so small, so vulnerable, so obviously distressed. He stretched out a hand and lightly touched her cheek, then felt a sense of shock as immediately she held his hand in place against her cheek and turned her mouth into its palm.

'Look, lass, we can't talk here.' He glanced over her shoulder, away down the street. 'That man I was with – he has a small jobbing printer's business out Hoghton way, and there might be just a chance he could be taking me on.' He smiled. 'It won't be the same as my last job, nothing like, just wedding invitations and business cards, that kind of thing, but I can't afford to miss the opportunity.' He gripped both her arms so that he was holding her away from him. 'But I see that it's important that we talk, so when can I meet you?' He took a step forward so that Libby was forced to take a step backwards. 'See, there's a meeting of the Labour Council, an open meeting on Monday, at seven o'clock. I know Margaret Bottomley will be there as a representative of the women's section. Why don't you come along with her, then when it's over I'll take you home and we can talk?'

He looked round as if searching for a better solution. 'It's the best I can think of right now. Will you do that?' His voice was urgent even as he consoled. 'And don't do anything rash till then. Promise?'

He was embarrassed; Libby could sense his embarrassment, even as he tried to be kind. The enormity of what she had just said and done struck her like a sudden blow to the head. With her nerves jangling, she nodded wordlessly and held out her hand.

Solemnly, as if they had met unexpectedly and discussed nothing more important than the blustery weather for the time of year, they shook hands. 'Promise?' he said again. 'We'll have that talk first. Right?'

As they walked away in opposite directions, she turned her head and saw that he was running, loping along at the edge of the pavement, to rejoin the man who might offer him a job.

She waited until he reached the corner by the Co-op emporium, hoping he would turn and wave, but he ran on, leaving her to make her way back to the café, then on to the tram stop and Westerley.

When Libby walked through the front door she saw Sarah Batt sitting on the high throne-like chair in the hall, being comforted by Carrie and her mother.

'She just broke down.' Ettie, still in her housecoat, with her faded hair hanging down her back, looked relieved to see Libby. 'She's been like this all week, not herself, and going in her room to cry, and I can't get a word out of her.'

Carrie gave her sister a look which said that any explanations about what had happened down town could wait. 'Down at the mill, fortunately,' she said, interpreting Libby's glance towards the door of the billiard room.

At once Libby knelt down on the dark red and blue patterned carpet, so that her eyes were on a level with Sarah's pinkly puffed eyelids.

'Right! Now you have to tell us what's wrong, Sarah, because if you don't then there's nothing we can do to help, is there?'

Sarah's plump face set into lines of obstinacy as she made to get up, only to feel Libby's hands on her arms forcing her back. She sighed and gulped back a fresh flow of tears. It was no good. She knew Miss Libby of old, and Miss Libby wasn't one for taking no for an answer.

'It's my boy.' The words were dragged up from deep inside her. 'When I went home last weekend he was coughing fit to burst.' She picked up the corner of her afternoon apron and twisted it into a point. 'He's been off colour for weeks now, an' nothing me mother gives him seems to help. She's been scooping the top of a turnip, filling it with honey, and putting brown paper under his vest, and even letting him sleep downstairs with the steam kettle going, but nothing helps.' Her voice thickened with anxiety. 'I'm that frightened. I should have had three brothers, but every one of them were took off with the cough . . . with the consumption,' she added, saying the dread word aloud. 'An' it runs in families. It *does*, an'

105

nobody can tell me no different, an' me mother knows it as well. I could see the fear on her face.'

'Nonsense!' Libby spoke with firmness. 'You must be talking about – what – thirty years ago? Doctors know more about it now. Besides, your boy lives out in the country with all that fresh air and milk and eggs and cream. It's an environmental disease, Sarah. What your son's got is more like a touch of bronchitis. Some of the kids in my class have that, but they're sleeping four to a bed mostly, and not getting enough nourishment. It's different in your son's case.'

'*Why* is it different?' Sarah's indignation dried her tears. 'What do you think me mam has to live on? There are no soup kitchens in the country like what there were down in the town when the strike was on. And with the fire going day and night, who's to fetch and chop the wood now me father's gone to his rest?' Worry was making Sarah forget her place, and once started there was no stopping her. 'I was warming a pat of butter at the fire on Sunday morning, and it slipped off the dish onto the coals, and you know what me mother did? She sat down on a chair and put her apron over her head and cried. She cried for ten minutes without stopping, an' *you* talk about milk and eggs and cream! Oh, aye, and fresh air. Well, I grant you that's cheap enough, but it's the only thing what is.'

'Oh dear.' Ettie put a hand to her head and swayed, overcome as usual by any unpleasantness. 'We never thought . . . we had no idea.'

'No. Your sort never have, do you?' Sarah was burning her boats with a vengeance, all the pent-up anxiety releasing itself in a flood. 'How do you think I feel when I see good meat on the table every day of the week an' knowing there's nothing I can do about it? Many's the time I've wished I could just send even the gravy to them. Just the gravy, never mind a nice thick slice off the joint. I'd think God had stepped down from his heaven if I saw my lad sink his teeth into a meat butty. Do you know that?'

'Take Mother upstairs.' Libby spoke almost to herself, but at once Carrie obeyed.

'Do this,' her twin had said when they were children. 'Do that,' and at once Carrie had obeyed. 'Do this,' her father had said. 'Do that,' and again she had done what was asked of her.

For wasn't Libby the one looking into the mirror whilst she was merely the reflection? Even her first attempt at writing had come out back to front, only decipherable by holding it up to a looking glass. And now Libby was again taking charge. So, gently persuasive, Carrie led the distressed little woman up the wide stairs, leaving her sister to deal with a Sarah they knew little about, a Sarah with a life of her own far from the confines of Westerley.

'Poor Sarah.' Ettie raised a piteous face to her daughter. 'We forget they have feelings, don't we?'

'Now what we are going to do,' Libby was saying downstairs in the hall, 'is this. I will get Doctor Harry to drive out and see your boy this evening.' She stood up. 'The doctor is very good with children. He will examine your son, and whatever is necessary will be done. You must go too,' she added, 'then if there is nothing to worry about Harry will drive you back here. If you are needed, then you must stay there. Mother will have to do without you for a while. It might even do her good. She relies on you far too much. I would come as well, but Carrie is going to an organ recital in King George's Hall with a friend, so I will have to stay at home with Mother.' She waved a hand impatiently. 'It's ridiculous that Mother won't stay in the house alone, but there it is. I can't think what she's going to do when I get married and Carrie tries to lead a life of her own. Why some women allow themselves to become so helpless I don't know.'

All the time Libby had been talking, arranging, organizing, Sarah's mind had been whirling round and round like a moth caught in a gas lamp. The thought of seeing Patrick again without waiting for her next weekend off was an opportunity she could not bring herself to refuse. Then to have him examined by a clever doctor like Doctor Harry – and he must be clever when it cost folks a mint of money just to see him for a few minutes – oh, dear Mother of God, how could she refuse? She twisted her apron into a harder knot. Libby's doctor would know what to do. Sarah bit her lip so hard that a blood blister formed. And it would be all right because Doctor Harry had never seen Willie . . . he hadn't been coming to the house when Willie was alive, so he would never put two and two together. Men weren't like that, anyroad. But if Patrick died because she was too frightened to accept help – oh, dear sweet Jesus! She couldn't lie awake, not one more night, imagining the worst. She was nigh out of her mind with worry; it was eating her away, and she could take no more.

'Can you do that?' Libby was saying into the telephone. 'I know it's a lot to ask, Harry, but you must see . . . We were staying in tonight anyway. You can be there and back in two hours.'

Like a butterfly Libby had flown straight from one crisis to another, persuasive, sure of her fiancé's cooperation. It was as though she had never met Tom Silver down the town, never trembled at his nearness and asked him to meet her again. First things had always come first with Libby. Besides, Harry was the rock she had clung to for a long time now, and it was unthinkable that he would let her down.

She raised her voice impatiently as he made objections. 'This is something I'm asking you to do for *me*, Harry. For all of us.'

'He's coming.' Libby replaced the receiver and turned to march into the kitchen with Sarah following like a devoted dog at her heels. 'I'll get a basket of things together whilst you go up and get your coat and hat. We're lucky that it's a Saturday and the doctor doesn't have an evening surgery. So things are working out already, aren't they?'

Then, infuriating Mrs Edwards in the kitchen by taking things off the pantry shelf without so much as a by your leave – the boiled ham that was for the Sunday tea and the eggs for the deep custard to go with the stewed damsons – Libby filled a basket to the brim. It was as if the episode of less than an hour ago had happened to another person altogether, a wild woman who had completely taken leave of her senses.

It was cold in the pantry with its stone floor and deep shelves. It smelled of apples, pickled onions and spices. Mrs Edwards watched in grim silence, arms folded across her one-piece bosom.

'Sarah's mother is ill,' Libby told her. The lie came easily. Sarah's secret was Sarah's secret, and her silence about her son had been respected since long before Mrs Edwards' time. Libby walked briskly out of the kitchen, watched balefully by the disgruntled cook. Now she had to start again with tomorrow's menus, and if they thought she was going to put herself out then they had another think coming. Oliver Peel was stingy enough with his money as it was. If he had to make do with cheese and onion pie for his Sunday tea instead of a nice thick slice of boiled ham, then he could like it or lump it. Mrs Edwards thumped the mixing bowl down on the table so that the spoons jumped into the air to fall back with a tinkling clatter.

'A straightforward case of bronchitis,' Harry said, coming back to Westerley exactly two hours later, ruddy-faced and cheerful. He jerked his head towards the door of the lounge. 'Sarah has gone straight up to your mother. I think she feels a bit guilty now about all the fuss, but worry's a funny thing. It grows like a fungus once you let it catch hold.' He sat down on the chesterfield and patted the cushion by his side. 'Come here, love, and let me look at you. Let me hold you, and touch skin that isn't sweaty, and look into eyes that aren't bloodshot . . . Oh, God, it's been one hell of a week. Half my patients have flu, or think they're going to have it, and my father is slowly passing some of his patients over to me. Not that it does my ego any good.' He laughed his uninhibited laugh. 'They take one look at me and ask straight off where my father is. You have to be at least fifty before some of them class you as a real doctor.'

Libby stayed exactly where she was. 'What was he like, Sarah's son? I've often wondered. She won't talk about him, ever. She must have been genuinely worried to agree to you going out to see him. Is he like Sarah, all red hair and big teeth and a bit, well, you know, a bit slow?'

Harry shook his head, reached into his pocket for his pipe, held it out for permission, then started to fill it.

'I was surprised. Really surprised. He's a little corker, that lad.' He puffed for a while and threw the spent match into the fire. 'Bright as a button, with an intelligence far beyond his years. He more or less confided in me that both his grandma and his mother worry their guts out about him. He'd got hold of a *Pears Cyclopaedia* from somewhere and he was reading it when we got there, sitting up in bed and going through it alphabetically, reading it as if it were a book of fiction, and understanding most of it if I'm any judge.'

'And his chest?'

'Rattly, granted, but nothing a week in bed and warmth won't cure.' The pipe was going nicely now and Harry leaned back, a man at peace with the world. 'Whippet breed definitely, not like Sarah and her mother with arms and thighs on them like a couple of lady blacksmiths.'

'Then you went for nothing really?'

He shook his head. 'I went for *you*, love. For your sake, and that's enough for me. Now come here, and let's forget young Patrick Batt. Let's talk about the wedding and decide where we're going for our honeymoon, and what changes you're going to make in the house, and important things like the kind of flowers you are going to have in your wedding bouquet.'

Libby moved reluctantly to sit by him and he put his arms round her. When she stiffened in his grasp he rubbed his cheek against hers as if to force a sign of responsiveness from her. When he kissed her she clamped her mouth so tightly shut that he pushed her away to stare at her in bewilderment.

'What's the matter, love? Look, Libby, I'm too tired and old to play games. I've told you, it's been one hell of a week.'

She twisted round to stare into the fire. 'Harry – I'm so very, very sorry, but I can't marry you. I know it's a terrible thing to say now at this moment, but better now than later. I'm sorry.'

'*What* did you say?' Roughly he pulled her round, holding her so that her arms were pinioned. Then he kissed her roughly. 'Do you know what you just said? Do you?' As he felt her lack of response he drew back. 'Stop play-acting, Libby! Stop it!' The colour in his cheeks slowly drained away as he stared at her in wide-eyed amazement. 'You *mean* it, don't you? What brought this on?' He made a move towards her, then as she shrank away his temper flared.

'What is it *now*? Is it because you still want me to move my practice down into town and work a clinic for the under-privileged? Because we've been over that, Libby, over and over.' His face darkened. 'You can keep your Bolshie ideas after we're married. You can go to your meetings, and you can wave a red flag as often as you like, but I won't be intimidated. If I want to treat patients who pay me in a lump sum instead of

110

sixpence a week to the doctor's man, then that's my affair. My father worked all his life to build that practice up, and I intend to carry on where he leaves off. You've got it all wrong, Libby. A new-born baby with a dislocated hip is just as pathetic as a baby bowed with rickets, and a child can die of diptheria without being half-starved into the bargain. Wake up, Libby! Stop setting yourself up as some sort of saviour, because it doesn't suit you. Beneath all that idealistic talk you're still *you*, knowing which side your bread's buttered and accepting it. So come here, and never let me hear you say you won't marry me ever again. If you leave me I'll be just as bereft as if I was an out-of-work labourer in a flat cap standing on street corners. I bleed, too, Libby. Never forget that!'

They were both very tired. Libby had held the afternoon's emotions in check from the moment she walked through the door. Then for more than two hours she had sat with her mother, listening to Ettie wondering plaintively how it would be at Westerley without Sarah.

'I feel in my bones that Sarah needs to be with her mother and the boy. She says her mother hasn't picked up since her father dropped dead. One of these days she won't come back from her weekend off. I feel it in my bones,' she had said again. 'And there's Carrie. She's bound to meet the man she wants to marry before long, and that will leave *me* here alone in this big house with your father.' Ettie had shivered and stared with watery blue eyes into a future that looked as bleak as the Lancashire moors.

Harry had been called out to a patient at five o'clock that morning, and had left his dinner to drive out with Sarah – and now he was faced with Libby's rejection. But he felt his anger evaporating as he saw the way she held herself still, as if she wanted to say much more and was determined not to do so.

'Let's not quarrel, love, I know things aren't easy for you here. Maybe it's not such a good idea my popping round every day. Weddings are nerve-racking things.'

'There isn't going to be a wedding.' Libby's expression hardened. 'I'm sorry, Harry, but I can't help it. To marry you would be a terrible mistake, feeling the way I do.' She started to pull the ring from her finger, only to have her hand taken in a firm clasp.

'I won't listen!' Harry pushed the ring back, then squeezed her left hand hard. 'I have to drive my parents over to see their new house tomorrow; on Monday I have an evening surgery and two consultations, so we'll have to leave it till Tuesday.' He gave her a quick sideways smile. 'On Tuesday I'll pick you up from school at four o'clock, and we'll drive out somewhere for a meal. Then if you still feel the same you can tell me.' He released his tight hold on her hand and gave it a little shake. 'And now I'm going, but remember this.' Gently he cupped her face in his big hands and as he smiled at her she saw the hurt bewilderment in his brown eyes. 'I love you more than life itself. I'll never let you go, not if I have to chloroform you to get you down the aisle.' He glanced round the big room with its overstuffed furniture and preponderance of potted plants. 'I want to get you away from this mausoleum, with your father drinking himself to death across the hall and your mother thinking herself into invalidism upstairs. You were meant to be happy, Libby, and happy is what you're going to be.'

Without attempting to kiss her he walked to the door, a thick-set brown man in his tweedy speckled jacket, a well-fed, confident man with his comfortable life mapped out for him. So different from the tall, gaunt man with his hair blowing untidily in the wind, running along the pavement for the chance of a job he would hate even if he were lucky enough to get it. They were such worlds apart that Libby felt she could not bear to dwell on the comparison.

When Tuesday came it would all be settled. One way or the other her life would never be the same again. She bowed her head as the silent tears ran slowly down her cheeks.

The hall was already full when Libby took her seat with Margaret Bottomley at the back. The women were in the minority, but the rows of men sat united, their faces serious and intent, some of them leaning forward the better to hear the speakers on the platform.

'This town is in a bad way.' The speaker, a miner, spoke with a fiery delivery that belied his puny appearance. 'And what do our bosses care? He raised a fist and shook it. 'I'm no

Marxist, and neither are most of the men who think like me, but we have one thing in common in this fight of ours. We are all asking for a fair wage for a fair day's work. They – the bosses – can go on living in their big houses for all we care. We don't covet what they've already got. No! All we want is a fair slice of what's going. We just want what's ours by right, and that's a decent standard of living. Is it wrong wanting that?'

Libby could see Tom Silver's dark head four rows in front. He looked down now and again and she guessed he was making notes. He was so naïve, she thought tenderly, believing better conditions would come through the Labour Party. It was men like her father who made the conditions, the rich and the educated. Why couldn't Tom Silver see that? She looked round, startled, as a heckler seated directly behind her, jumped to his feet, shouting and waving his arms about.

'Nay, nay. Of course it's wrong wanting just that! You lot would be satisfied with half a loaf, but I say we deserve a *whole*! Labourism? You lot are nowt but Tories in a different hat. You want to be definite one way or another!'

'He's a Communist,' Margaret whispered. 'He even went so far as to stick one of their posters on the board outside the police station last week. Cheeky blighter. The police will have him if he doesn't watch out.'

Libby turned and saw the eager, screwed-up look of dedication on Margaret's face. She looked harder and saw an unhappy woman, and in a revealing instant realized that political argument could never be the centre of her own existence. It was exciting, it was fascinating, but it wasn't enough. She shivered, holding her arms close round her as if to ward off a sudden freezing wind. What *was* there to satisfy this restless feeling always bubbling up inside her. Would even Tom Silver be able to give her what she wanted, when she wasn't sure herself?

She wrinkled her nose at the smell of closely packed bodies and cheap tobacco, then drew herself slightly away from the woman sitting on her other side. Shifting her position on the hard bench, Libby closed her eyes and willed the meeting to end.

*

When Tom sat beside her on the slatted seat on the top deck of the tram and paid her fare, she knew the pennies he was counting out in his hand represented more to him than mere coinage. She could see her reflection in the window, all eyes beneath the tiny cloche hat, the fur collar of her wrapover coat snuggled up to her chin.

The shiny material of Tom's jacket looked as if it would disintegrate at the slightest tug, and his bony knees had poked blisters in his trousers. He was a man who did not care very much how he looked, she guessed, but surely, in the time he had been in full employment, he could have provided himself with a coat? His shabbiness caught at her throat, irritating her and at the same time making her feel ashamed of her own warm clothing.

He was talking about the meeting, laughing at the affectation of a Councillor Tomlinson, a big-stomached man who persisted in wearing a cloth cap.

'He never wanted to be a councillor; it's just that he truly believes that his ideas, if they could be put into practice, would improve the lot of working people. I think he must have read every book, every pamphlet, every paper on what the Party stands for. You'll never catch old John out, not on any point of order. He has a case for housing, wages, anything you can think of, and there's no putting him down.'

'He stood up well to the heckling,' Libby said confusedly. They were nearing the terminus now, and they might have been two casual acquaintances returning from the meeting, making conversation about what had taken place. She followed him between the rows of seats to the platform, held onto the rail until the tram pulled up, then with a nod of thanks accepted the arm he held out to help her down.

'Now,' he said, as they walked down the wide road towards the lane leading to Westerley, 'what's all this about, Libby?'

He made no move to touch her, not even when her heel caught in a patch of uneven ground. He's proud, she thought, feeling her heartbeats quicken. He's going to leave me to make all the running, and oh, dear God, what do I say? I can't tell him that all I want is to be near him. She tried to see his expression, but now they had left the well-lit road and were turning into the lane where deep shadows filled the long spaces between the lamps. His face was no more than a pale blur.

They walked on in silence for a while, then she stopped suddenly. 'This is where I live,' she told him. Through the gap in the hedge down the long, winding drive was Westerley, with lights gleaming from the downstairs windows and from the upstairs front bedroom where Ettie would be reading, trying to get to sleep.

Tom stuck both hands in his pockets and whistled softly. 'And there's just you and your mother and father live in that mansion of a house?'

'And my sister.' Libby felt her face burn at the implied sarcasm. 'And the maids,' she added defiantly. 'Mrs Edwards, and the maid of all work, and Sarah who looks after my mother.'

'I never knew you had a sister.'

'I used to have a brother, too, but he was killed in the war.' She brought up her eyes to meet his and saw that he was watching her carefully.

'What do you want of me?' he asked abruptly.

She was trembling now, rather frightened, but when he suddenly pulled her to him and held her so close that there was no point at which their bodies did not touch, and then put his mouth over hers, she responded to him with an almost animal-like ferocity.

'There!' His voice had a challenging all-male aggressive ring to it. 'There, Libby Peel. Is *that* what you want? Did you want to find out if my kiss was less clinical than your doctor lover's? Were you for finding out the difference, then?'

When she hit him, an open-handed slap on his right cheek, he threw back his head and laughed out loud. Pulling her to him again he ran his hand down her back, down her spine, lingering on her buttocks, so that she felt it as intimately as if she had been unclothed.

'Would you marry me, Libby? Would you come with me and be my love in that room you saw? Would you stop in there all day long and cook my tea on the gas ring, and manage on less than you spend on frocks and shoes, and silly hats like the one you've got on now? Because I tell you straight – not a penny would I take from that father of yours.'

She could feel every inch of him. It was as though she was

115

being made love to, there in the dark of the wild night with the wind tossing his words away and the lights of Westerley shining out behind his head like some incongruous backdrop to a Victorian drama.

'I . . . I . . . You're frightening me!' She struggled to break free, but it was as though she were being held in a vice.

'Right!' Suddenly he let her go. 'If you really want me, then go inside. Go into the house this minute and pack a bag, and come out to me.' He thrust both hands in his pockets. 'I'll wait ten minutes, and if you don't come then I'll know you've changed your mind. Go on now! Make it snappy! I'll be waiting.'

Without further words he turned and walked a few yards down the lane to stand in the shelter of the high hedge, a dark waiting blur, with head held high and the collar of his jacket upturned against the seeking wind.

While he waited he strained his eyes against the darkness, dimly assessing the rolling meadows and the dark blue haze of hills in the distance. Dear God, he thought, this is one gamble that has to come off. Then, because even in the worst of times his northern sense of humour never quite deserted him, he admitted to himself wryly that he had always been a gambling man. Even in France on the Somme, coming unexpectedly face to face with a real bloody German, he had accepted that the best form of defence was attack. He could smell the acrid musty smell of the mud and dead bodies as he remembered the German, a lad of no more than seventeen years, lowering his bayonet in that one weak moment of indecision. Then his jaw tightened as he remembered too the look of bewilderment on the young face as the German realized that his indecision had cost him his life.

But the war had been over now for eight years come next month and Tom Silver was still fighting. Now the war was against misery and poverty. The grit of the unmade road crunched under his shoes as he walked back to the place where he could see the big house, a cocoon of warmth and light, a haven for those who could afford to be sheltered inside its walls.

What he had just done was cruel, but then he had always accepted that there was a cruel streak in him. He narrowed his eyes and held his breath for a moment as he saw a curtain move at an upper window. That lass, Libby Peel, with her half-formed ideals and the longing in her eyes for something to give a touch of drama to what she considered to be the boring pattern of her days . . . that lovely, lovely lass was no more for him than he was for her.

Tom turned away, back down the lane with his slogging soldier's walk, to the main road and the terminus where a tram stood ready for its rhythmic clanging journey back into town. But tram rides cost money, and anyway he needed to walk. He needed to despise himself a little for the way he had behaved and, besides, walking took longer and kept him out in the air, away from the room at the top of the house that smelled of the misery he swore to eradicate some day.

And the Libby Peels of this world had no place in that scheme of things, no place at all.

Seven

By the middle of November, with the wedding of Libby Peel to Doctor Harry, son of Dr Henry and Mrs Brandwood, only five weeks away, Carrie found herself trapped in the school's basement cloakroom by the man she had been avoiding for weeks.

'You have at least to *talk* to me, Carrie! You owe me that!'

Mungo's face was violin-shaped with self-pity, and a faint bruise showed up in a yellowish tinge at the side of his jaw. 'I need a friend so much, Carrie, someone to *understand*. And who else is there but you?'

He stood before her in the narrow passageway between the rows of hanging coats, felt hats and shoe bags, holding out an arm so that she was trapped between him and the wall. He was so close she could feel his breath on her face; so close that she could see the despair in his eyes, and so close that even his hoarse whispering came to her like a shout.

'Mungo!' She tried to duck beneath his arm, but his hand came down and clamped itself on her shoulder. 'Someone might come down! Mungo! Don't be so stupid. The bell will go any minute, and if they find you down here with me . . . oh, God, Mungo, let me go!'

His mouth was against her ear. 'You're driving me mad,. Carrie. It's hell coming here day after day when you won't even look at me properly. I'm not made of stone. Carrie! Two people can't have meant what we did to each other, and then act like strangers!' He made a sound halfway between a groan and a sigh. 'Is there someone else? Tell me. Have you met someone else?'

'No!' Carrie jerked her head away only to have her chin grasped and twisted round again. 'No Mungo! There isn't

anyone else. I've told you over and over, you're *married* and I
. . . I no longer love you.' Her brown eyes were pleading.
'There was no future for us, you know that, and now you must
get on with your life and leave me to get on with mine.' Tears of
frustration sprang to her eyes. 'You have to be a man, Mungo,
and accept that it's all over.'

'Never!' To her horror, he brought his head down and
fastened his mouth over hers. His hand slid down her back to
hold her close. The more she struggled, the more his thwarted
passion flared, and when he felt her lack of response he began
to kiss her closed eyelids, her nose, her cheeks, whispering
incoherent broken words of love.

'Carrie . . . Carrie . . . oh, my little love. I *need* you. I must
have your love. Oh, dear God, please be kind to me, please!'

When the voice of the headmaster sounded behind them,
Mungo released his hold of her so abruptly that Carrie felt her
knees give way. Grasping at a school gaberdine raincoat to
save herself, she slid down to sit on the narrow bench in front of
the row of pegs, knocking a shoe bag to the floor. Shaking so
violently she could actually see her legs trembling, she looked
up and met the furious, incredulous stare of the small man
respected and feared by both teachers and pupils alike. Mr
Eccles's eyes glittered behind the rimless spectacles worn
habitually halfway down his hawklike nose.

And at that very moment the clattering of outdoor shoes on
the flight of stone steps leading down to the basement heralded
the onrush of Form Four hurtling in from their PT lesson,
followed by Miss Clayton, with a scarlet band round her short
hair, her cheeks polished red by the cold wind.

'Come with me! Both of you!' Mr Eccles nodded first to
Mungo, then to Carrie, before leading the way with his small
head poked forward and the back view of his trousers hanging
loose over what seemed to be a non-existent behind.

'What's up?' Miss Clayton caught at Carrie's arm, then
stepped back as Carrie brushed her impatiently aside.

'Now then. No talking!' Miss Clayton bellowed the command automatically, her eyes fixed on the trio disappearing
up the basement steps.

'Snogging behind the coat racks, I bet.'

The gym mistress whipped round just too late to catch the

girl responsible for the whispered words.

Upstairs in his study overlooking the rhododendron-fringed drive Mr Eccles MA faced the two cringing members of his staff.

'Never,' he said, in his reed-thin, trembling voice, 'never in the whole of my career have I been faced with a situation so degrading, so shameful, so repugnant.' He lifted his small pointed chin. 'I am not going to ask you what was going on because I could see only too well.' Taking out a white handkerchief he mopped his forehead. 'Teachers have a very special responsibility to their pupils, a grave and serious responsibility to show an example, to be themselves beyond reproach. And yet I find you . . .' here words failed him for a moment, 'doing what you were doing in *my* school, in class time . . .' Picking up a lined ruler from his desk, he threw it down again. 'What were you doing out of your classroom, Miss Peel? Just for the record, of course.'

Carrie seemed to be finding difficulty in forming her mouth round the words. 'One of my girls had come upstairs without changing into her indoor shoes, and as they were in the middle of copying something from the blackboard I went to fetch them for her.'

It was the truth. It was a typical Carrie gesture, the self-effacing Carrie who was used to fetching and carrying.

But Mr Eccles waved her explanation aside with a downward motion of his long thin hand. 'And you, Mr McDermot? What is your excuse?'

Mungo gave an eloquent, all-revealing sideways glance at the trembling girl who looked as if she might faint at any minute. The truth was that he had seen Carrie through the glass panels of his classroom door, hurrying on some errand, and decided it was too good an opportunity to miss. Telling his class to read over the poem they had been analyzing, he had simply followed her. Now his mind was too numb with the implications of what was happening to attempt any alternative explanation. So he remained silent . . . a silence that grew and lengthened as Carrie lifted her head to stare at him in bewildered terror. Surely Mungo would admit that he was to blame? Even though it almost certainly would not help, surely as a gentleman he would at least try to absolve her from *some* of the blame?

Mr Eccles's mind was made up. As well as his genuine disgust at the scene he had just witnessed, there were wider issues to consider. For instance, an almost forgotten meeting of the town's Rotarians when Oliver Peel, with a few snide remarks, had made him look like a fool. The fact that at the last meeting of the board of governors he had been advised to cut his staff or raise the school fees to an unacceptable level. His instinctive dislike of Mungo McDermot, who had refused to fight in the war whilst the headmaster's eldest son had been wounded. And lastly, the seconds he had stood there down in the basement cloakroom, a Peeping Tom, enjoying a vicarious thrill at the sight of the man and woman locked together, writhing together in what appeared to be an embrace of such unbridled passion that his own loins had tightened with an almost physical pain. For that alone they stood before him damned.

'You can get your things and go,' he said quietly. 'You will be hearing from the authorities in due course, but I will not have either one of you in my school again. In another minute the children would have seen the disgusting spectacle, and I will not have their minds sullied by your depravity. The rumours will be bad enough as it is, but for the time being I will take your form, Mr McDermot, and Miss Clayton will see to *your* pupils, Miss Peel.' He jerked his chin towards the door. 'Now go! Do what you have to do in a field or behind a hedge somewhere, but leave my school. Now, this minute!'

As Carrie turned to obey, Mungo came suddenly to life. As she looked back for a brief moment she saw him leaning across the wide desk, mouthing incoherent words lost to her. Then she ran across the wide landing into the mercifully deserted staff room. She collected her coat and hat from the cupboard, then ran back down the stairs and out into the damp cold of the November morning.

She was not, she told herself, a totally innocent party. What had happened was only the culmination of what had been going on during the long summer afternoons when she had lain with Mungo in the summer house, responding to his caresses. If this was to be her punishment, then she would face it as bravely as she could. No, let Mungo plead to be forgiven, let him grovel before Mr Eccles and beg to be reinstated. She, Carrie Peel, would leave with dignity.

Then, as the tram clattered its way towards her and she moved into the middle of the road to board it, the terror she had held in check suddenly exploded inside her. Groping her way between the rows of seats like a blind woman, she sat down to find she was shaking so much that she could hardly get her fingers round the coins in her purse.

Somehow she would have to find the courage to tell her father. That same night she would have to face him and say, 'Father, today I was sent home from school because the headmaster, Mr Eccles, found me down in the basement cloakroom in the arms of one of the teachers, a married man.'

She made small sideways movements with her head as if to shake the inevitable from her as the tram clattered and rocked away from the town, dropping off its passengers, leaving her at the end to sit there alone, head bowed, too terrified even to cry.

'You must tell Father the truth.' Libby put an arm round her sister's shaking shoulders. 'You must tell him how this man has been making your life a misery for a long time. How he has been following you round at school and forcing his attentions on you, and how he overpowered you this morning so that the headmaster jumped to the wrong conclusions. You must get all that out before Father has a chance to shout you down.'

Carrie's voice filled with bitter scorn. 'But it wouldn't be *true*, Libby! Oh, yes, it was exactly like I said this morning, but Mungo wouldn't have pounced on me if I hadn't been going with him all the summer. He's not a maniac.' She started to cry again. 'He's gentle, really, and, oh God, it'll be even worse for him. He has a wife and child to support. How will he get another teaching post now? He's finished, Libby – this will finish him. I know.'

'I thought you said you'd stopped loving him?'

'I *have*!' Carrie wailed. 'I don't know how I even *thought* I loved him! But that doesn't mean I can't be sorry for him.' She shivered. 'Oh, that awful Mr Eccles! When I heard his voice, all the blood inside me froze. I'll never forget that moment for as long as I live!'

When she saw Libby turn away, her shoulders shaking, she thought at first her twin was crying in sympathy. Then to her amazement she saw that Libby was laughing.

'Oh, Carrie . . .' Libby turned round, tears of laughter brightening her brown eyes. 'Don't lose your sense of humour, love. It isn't the end of the world. You'll get another teaching post in a better school, one like mine, where you can give the kids a peep at a world they never knew existed. Not teaching kids who are only passing time till they marry the son of one of their father's friends, or go straight into father's firm.' She came and knelt down by the side of the bed, putting her hands on Carrie's knees. 'Oh, I can just see that dried-up little man standing there with his little prissy mouth wide open and his eyes standing out like chapel hat-pegs. He hasn't got a bottom has he? When I saw him on your last Sports Day I couldn't believe it, but I swear that underneath his pants and his combs – he's sure to wear combs – there's nothing, just a flat, empty nothing.'

Carrie drew a shaky breath. 'I've often wondered myself what he sits on,' she said. Then as they rocked together, Libby added, 'and if Father goes too far – if he goes on about morals, then I'll remind him of what I saw that night. "And just which pot is calling the kettle black?" I'll say. I will! I'll be away from this house soon anyway, so what does it matter?'

When Oliver Peel, without knocking, banged back the bedroom door with a slam that almost jerked it off its hinges, he saw two faces turn to him. Two identical faces, with the laughter he had heard as he stood outside wiped from them as if their old nanny had taken a damp flannel and washed the merriment clean away. Straddled in the doorway like a huge black bull, nostrils dilated, face flushed to an apoplectic purple, he bellowed, 'Where does he live? That's what I want to know!' He took a step forward as the two faces registered first dismay, then a cringing terror. 'That was Eccles on the telephone, feeling it was his duty, the sod, to break the news to me first before we get what he called the official letter. But he thought it unethical to give me the name and address of the man responsible for this filthy humiliation.'

With one movement he shot out an arm and flung Libby to one side. 'And you can keep out of this, madam! This is one time when you don't speak for your sister. One time when she stands on her own two feet, instead of acting like your bloody shadow.' Taking Libby by the arm he frogmarched her towards the door. 'But she's not your bloody shadow, is she? Tarred with the same brush she might be, but she's capable of getting up to her own nastiness, isn't she?'

Furiously Libby tried to break free from the iron grip, only to hear Carrie's voice ring out loud, clear and commanding. 'Go, please, Libby. I want you to. Please . . . please.'

Oliver's whisky-laden breath fanned hot on her face as Libby immediately stopped struggling, but before the door was slammed in her face she called out, 'Don't tell him, Carrie! Whatever you do, don't tell him!'

Then she was outside on the landing, breathing hard, clenching her fists and muttering to herself. 'If he lays a finger on Carrie I'll kill him myself. I swear it. He isn't fit to live! He's cruel, vicious, and I hate him so much I wish he was dead! If he dropped dead right this minute I would jump on his dead face, then go down and enjoy my dinner! I would! I swear it!'

'Your sister isn't coming down for her meal.' Oliver took his place as usual at the head of the table. Libby pushed her chair back and half rose to her feet, but he motioned her back with a wave of the hand holding the carving knife.

'Oh, dear . . .' Ettie Peel took a long, deep breath, then held a hand to her heart. 'What has Carrie been doing?' She gave a piteous glance in her husband's direction. 'I heard shouting, but I thought it was Libby. It's not like Carrie . . .' Her voice wavered.

'Tell her.' Oliver ran the carving knife up and down the sharpening steel. 'Tell her if you wish. The matter is out of my hands now until I choose to do something about it. Go on! Make your mother ill. It's up to you.'

Libby held her anger tight inside till she felt her blood must surely be at boiling point. She saw the way her mother's lower lip trembled and the faint bluish tinge to her lips, and pity, overcoming the anger, forced her back to her chair again.

'It's nothing, Mother.' To her own surprise, her voice came out quite calm. 'Carrie had a bit of an argument with the headmaster at school today, so she's thinking of changing to another teaching job. It was time, anyway. She's far too good for that tinpot private school where parents too well off to know better send their kids.'

'Oh, dear.' Ettie Peel helped herself to one small boiled potato. 'But it *will* be nice to have Carrie at home till the wedding. There's so much to do. Oh, I wish she could meet someone like Harry.' She dribbled a spoonful of mashed carrots onto her plate. 'The man who is going to be your best man, Libby – he's not married, is he? Wasn't he at university with Harry years ago?'

'He's married to his mother,' Libby said clearly, venting her anger by being deliberately provocative.

'Oh, dear,' her mother said, refusing the gravy. 'I see,' she said wistfully, not seeing at all.

'I don't know what Father said to her, but she didn't tell him Mungo's name or where he lived.' Libby ran out to the car as Harry drove up to the front of the house. 'But we're going there now. We have to warn him that Father is on the war-path. Otherwise there'll be murder done.' She climbed into the passenger seat. 'Come on then. I'm not exactly looking forward to it, but it has to be done. Father will get his address somehow, and the sooner Mungo McDermot knows what to expect the better.'

Harry raised his eyebrows. 'But what about his wife? He's a married man, isn't he? You can't just barge in and confront him, Libby. His wife won't know anything about his . . . dalliance with Carrie. Surely you see we can't interfere? It's none of our business, love.'

'What happens to Carrie *is* my business. What happens to Carrie happens to me.' Libby's small chin jutted forward. 'Carrie told me that Mungo's boy is kept at home because he's deaf and dumb, so if we can't get Mungo alone I'm going to say I've come about the possibility of the boy attending school.' She nodded twice. 'But we *have* to get Mungo alone. It will all blow over in time, but for the moment he has to lie low.'

'You can sit outside in the car if you would rather,' she added as they drove down the long tram route to the town, turning left eventually at Libby's direction. 'It's off here, I think. Number twenty-two. I used to come down here for piano lessons when I was a little girl.'

'I didn't know you played the piano.' Harry said this with the air of a man who had long ago accepted the fact that he did not know much about anything at all.

'I don't. It was a complete waste of time,' said Libby, peering through the car window at the numbers on the doors of the terraced houses set back behind tiny front gardens.

'Heaven preserve me from bossy women,' Harry whispered fondly as they stood on the short paved path waiting for an answer to their knock.

'Why? Do you know any?' Libby answered sweetly, as the door opened almost at once.

Ten minutes later Harry started the car and drove back down the street. 'So where did that get us?' he asked. 'That woman had been drinking, did you know that? Brandy, I would guess, and by the colour of her I would also guess that her liver is part rotted. She's going to be in trouble if she doesn't watch out.'

Libby wrinkled her nose fastidiously. 'She *was* awful, wasn't she? Grotesque. I thought hard drinkers stopped eating? But there wasn't much evidence of that – she must weigh at least fourteen stones.'

'Glands.' Harry was more relaxed now the mission was completed. 'But the boy was pathetic, wasn't he?' He signalled to turn right. 'You know, you could be right about that child needing help. He isn't mentally retarded, not at all. He was taking it all in. He was lip-reading, that lad, *and* making sense of it too. And don't ask me how. A child born deaf like that is only dumb if he is never taught to speak, and if that boy has never learned to speak then how could he lip-read?' He stopped to allow a man and a woman to walk out into the road to board the tram. 'But his mother soon put *you* in your place when you tried to suggest schooling, didn't she?'

Libby wrinkled her nose again. 'She smelled, Harry. Her clothes and the house weren't dirty, but *she* smelled . . . ugh! No wonder her husband looks elsewhere.' She turned sideways. 'Where do you think Mungo is? She doesn't know anything yet, does she? When she said he hadn't been home

126

from school, I didn't know what to say. Heaven help him when he does decide to return. Carrie says she hits him, and I can well believe it. I wouldn't like to meet her in a dark passage at night. I bet she packs a hefty punch.'

Harry, driving with his usual caution, was well content. This was the Libby he had fallen in love with and would love till the day he died. Bossy, outrageous, funny, taking up causes with enthusiasm, then dropping them as suddenly. Helping, caring Libby – naïve at times and immature, childlike even, though she would flare into instant indignation if he said so. But that didn't come from inherited characteristics, but because of that man, her father. Harry sighed. If ever a man was in need of psychiatric treatment, then that man was Oliver Peel. He alone, with his Victorian ideas of how to bring up daughters, was responsible for the mess Carrie seemed to be in. Treat a woman like a child and she would behave like one. Deprive her of parental affection, and she would seek that affection elsewhere. And Libby . . . Harry gripped the wheel hard. He would never know what had caused her to try to break off the engagement a month or so back. All he knew was that, though quieter of late and less prone to dramatic out- bursts, she was now anticipating their wedding day with a quiet serenity that made him love her more than ever – if that were possible. Taking one hand from the wheel he placed it on her knee, and was rewarded when she covered it with her own hand, answering his pressure with a loving response that made his blood rise until his farmer's face was suffused with a ruddy glow.

'Nearly home,' he said.

Less than ten minutes later Harry was again at the wheel of the car with Libby beside him and Carrie seated in the back.

'I'm sure I know where to find Mungo,' Carrie was saying. 'It's not far. Turn left here, Harry. Now right. Here! This is the place.'

Stopping the car, he saw that they were beside a high hedge, and all at once he was remembering the old manor house, drooping into decay even when he was a boy. Now he sup- posed it was no more than a derelict ruin, cloaked in trailing ivy, with no future for it but the trundling rumble of bulldozers when the town council decided the time was ripe for development. Hardly the place for . . . He raised a resigned eyebrow as Carrie, getting out of the car, asked them to stay where they were, promising she would be as quick as possible.

'Let her go,' he told an indignant Libby. 'She knows what she's doing, and as far as I can remember there's a little summer house just inside that hedge. She won't be going all the way to the house, not on a night as dark as this.'

'So that's where they met.' Libby sounded smug. 'I often wondered where Carrie met him when she was late home from school. Talk about a dark horse! Fancy that,' she added.

'Let's forget Carrie for a little while.' Harry put his arm across the back of the seat and drew Libby to him. 'Oh, love. I'm just counting the days now, aren't you?'

'I hope she knows what she's doing.' Libby returned his kiss absent-mindedly. 'If she's not back in ten minutes I'm going in there after her. I am!'

Mungo was there, inside the summer house, in the dark, sitting on the edge of the chaise longue and smoking, flicking the ash on to the pile of spent cigarettes at his feet.

'It's all right, it's only me.' Carrie closed the door behind her and, guided by the red glow from what must have been his umpteenth cigarette, went to sit beside him, keeping her distance and speaking slowly and firmly.

'You have to go home, Mungo. You have to go home now, and face her . . . face Beatrice. I've had to face my father, and you must face her. This is something you can't run away from, Mungo, but . . .'Her voice faltered. 'You have to keep away from my father, for the time being. He will find out who you are, and where you live. Not from me. Never from me. But he *will* find out, and when he does he'll come for you.'

She started to put out a hand towards the silent cringing figure sitting beside her on the rickety sofa, then drew it back. 'What we did – what we were doing last summer was wrong, and this is our punishment. But running away won't help. It's not like running away from the war, Mungo, because the war was far away, but this is here. You have to be a man.' She sighed. 'Mungo! Are you even listening to me? Are you?'

When he began to cry she felt the pity drain out of her,

leaving her mind crystal clear. Her sympathy wilted away, so that she had a sudden desire to get up and go, leaving him to wallow in his grief. She asked herself how she had ever imagined she loved this man. How *could* she have loved him, and dreamed of him every waking moment? Ached for his touch, and felt a day wasted when they had not been together? Run out to meet him, climbing through the hedge all those warm summer days to lie with him in this musty place. Lied to Libby . . .

'Libby and Harry are waiting for me outside on the road in the car.' She stood up. 'They went to your house tonight and saw – saw your wife.' She fought down a desire to slap him as he moaned like a wounded animal. 'Oh, you needn't worry, they didn't say anything. They were only trying to warn you.' She opened the door slightly, letting in the damp night air. 'It's going to be foggy, Mungo. If you come now I'll ask Harry to run you home. We can drop you at the end of your street.'

'I'm not going.' The first words he spoke sounded thick in his smoke-rasped throat. 'I'm never going back there, ever!'

Carrie was achingly tired. It had been, she was sure, the worst day of her whole life, and now she could take no more. 'If you don't get up and come with me, I'll go and fetch Harry. He's big and strong, and his evening has been ruined already through my fault and yours. He's also a very patient man, but he's a doctor and I know he will never leave you sitting there, rotting like the leaves.' She kicked out with her foot. 'You'll catch pneumonia if you stay here all night; you must be frozen stiff now, so are you coming of your own free will or shall I go and fetch Harry?'

Carrie waited as he stumbled past her out into the darkness, through the gap in the hedge and over to the waiting car.

'Will you take him home, Harry?' Carrie made the request humbly, only to step back in surprise as Harry leaned over the back of his seat to open the rear door.

'Is he ill?' It was the doctor in him speaking now. 'Unable to walk?'

Carrie turned to where Mungo cowered against the hedge, lighting yet another cigarette, the flame from the match trembling in his shaking hand.

'No he's not ill. Just very frightened,' she said slowly.

'Then get in.' Harry turned back again. 'He can walk. I'm damned if I'll take him home. He's not a naughty schoolboy. Anyway, I've had enough. I need a drink.'

'Harry is right.' Libby's voice rang with pride at the unexpected limits to her fiancé's benevolence. 'Enough is enough.'

As they drove away, Carrie, rubbing at the window and peering out into the darkness, saw Mungo take his first stumbling steps in the direction of the town. A faint lingering pity welling up inside her died, leaving in its place a healing sense of relief, and the comforting knowledge that from now on the man called Mungo McDermot would in time be no more than an unpleasant memory.

From now on, the forgetting could begin.

Eight

'One thousand four hundred looms stopped mainly as a result of the strike; valuable orders lost while our continental rivals collected the orders. *We* taught them to weave, and now the foreign buggers are taking *our* trade!'

Bleary-eyed, Oliver Peel looked up from his desk and waved the tackler Jimmy Earnshaw away with a dismissive gesture.

But the little man stood his ground. 'That faulty loom's still banging up, maister. The weft's not leaving the shuttle right. I can stop on and feckle it if you want me to.'

Oliver knew the worth of Jimmy Earnshaw. The small man with the bushy moustache and deeply lined face had a hundred and fifty looms in his charge. He was better than a qualified engineer at improvising with a weight or a wedge when the tension of a machine needed keeping up. He also knew that Jimmy had the sensitive feel necessary to maintain the correct delivery of the cloth, and without him the weavers would be all at sea. But at that moment a banging loom seemed of little importance.

'Get on home, Jimmy,' he said, keeping his right hand on the whisky bottle in the half-open drawer of his desk. 'It'll keep till morning.'

The little man chewed hard on the plug of tobacco wedged in the side of his mouth, and turned reluctantly to go. He didn't hold much cop for the man slumped behind the big desk, but there were times, and this was one, when he felt heart sorry for him. Oliver Peel looked dreadful, all red-necked and bloated, with his eyes sunk deep into pads of swollen flesh. Aye, he were a sick man if ever there were one; it would be a hard man what couldn't feel pity.

'Goodnight then, maister.' The tackler opened the door, then turned, adjusting his soiled mercerized cotton scarf. 'It's a terrible night out yon.'

'Goodnight, Jimmy.' Oliver took the bottle out of the drawer and tipped it into the glass hidden behind the files on his desk. It had taken him three days to find out the address of the man who had brought shame and humiliation to his house, and now he was ready for revenge.

The whisky bottle was empty when he pushed himself unsteadily to his feet. He took his bowler hat and thick melton overcoat from the stand in the corner, and putting the hat on first struggled awkwardly into the heavy overcoat. Normally his drinking did not begin in earnest until he had eaten his evening meal and retired to the billiard room with his accounts. Now the drink was inflaming his empty stomach and firing his muddled brain. He turned out the light and walked unsteadily to the door, remembering to lock it behind him before dropping the keys into his pocket.

Mr Crankshaw, the mill manager, had left at the same time as the weavers streaming out into the mill yard when the hooter blew. Curling his lip at the man's uncluttered desk, Oliver walked through the outer office and into the yard. For a moment it was as though he was blinded. He swayed, stretched out a hand and touched a cold damp wall. Then, as he shook his massive head from side to side like a wounded animal trying to clear its vision, he saw dimly in front of him the outline of the mill gates.

Some warning told him that tonight was not the night; that to take the short cut along the canal bank to the street where Mungo McDermot lived was foolhardy in the extreme. But the whisky urged him on. Lurching in a reeling walk, he turned down the short street and made his perilous way down the stone steps leading to the murky waters of the canal.

It was a stretch of rough bank often used by colliers as a training ground for their whippets, where boys dangled twine in a vain attempt at fishing, carrying their pathetic catches home in glass jamjars tied round with string. Certainly not the place to be on a dark night, with fog swirling up from the dirty water, concealing the dusty grass verge and merging it with the uneven path. Two hundred yards, that was all, before

Oliver came to the steps leading to the house whose number was burned into his brain.

He had no clear idea in his mind as to what he was actually going to do to the apology of a man who had, so his informant had told him, sat out the war on his backside. Oliver groaned aloud. Willie had given *his* life for his country – that bright shining young life holding such promise. But of one thing Oliver was sure; Mungo McDermot wasn't going to get away with it. He, Oliver Peel, would see to it that he never worked again, even if he personally had to confront every bloody board of bloody governors to blacken a character that already stank to high heaven.

Carrie – well, she was a woman, and could always find plenty to do around the house. He had never held with his daughters working, anyway. Women should stop at home where they belonged – where God intended them to be. Besides, with Libby gone, her sister would be a comfort to her mother.

Mumbling to himself, Oliver caught his foot on a loose stone, lost his balance and staggered to the right, one arm flailing to save himself. The stunted grass bordering the canal was slippery, and as he fought to regain his balance his feet slid from under him. The splash his heavy body made as he fell into the water seemed to be swallowed up by the fog which closed round him, and as he sank the evil-smelling water rushed into his open mouth, choking him.

The silk-lined heavy overcoat soaked up the water like a sponge, dragging him down again as he surfaced. He opened his mouth to shout for help, flung out an arm to grasp the stunted grass at the side of the bank, then sank back into the water.

His bowler hat, its sleekness polished by Carrie that morning, floated away like the hump of a wet black seal. The water was in his ears, his mouth, filling his lungs as his frantic struggling took him farther away from the bank into the middle of the fog-shrouded canal. Kicking out he tried to get rid of his shoes, but sodden with water they only helped to drag him down again.

The realization that he was dying penetrated his drink-fuddled brain, and as he choked and struggled the name screaming through his head was that of his son.

'Willie! Willie!'

Then the dark waters closed over him for the last time.

When the fog lifted early the next morning, wafted away by a
cold wind, they found him, every tissue in his massive body
sodden with water. When Harry identified him in the mor-
tuary he turned his head away and ordered that the coffin be
immediately sealed. When Libby and Carrie, stunned and
disbelieving, stood in the newly opened Chapel of Rest they
saw no more than a plain oak coffin surrounded by high-
banked chrysanthemums behind an alcove lined with purple
velvet curtains.

Carrie was weeping silently, but Libby, dry-eyed, stared at
the box which held the remains of the man she had tried in
vain to love and had finally hated.

'It's all my fault.' Carrie repeated the words she had been
saying ever since the police had called to report the finding of
the body. 'He was going to find Mungo,' she had wailed.
'That's the only reason he was where he was, and now I have
to live with that for the rest of my life.'

'He was drunk,' Libby said. 'He could have stepped out in
the road under the wheels of a car. It was the drink killed him,
so stop it! Carrie! I won't hear you torturing yourself with
remorse. Our father was sick in his mind, and if he *had* been on
his way to find Mungo, who knows what might have happened?' She turned to Harry for reassurance. 'If he hadn't
been drinking he could have got out of the canal, and if he *had*
found Mungo he might have killed him.' She lifted her chin.
'Better to have drowned than have committed a murder.'

With his arms round both girls, Harry led them out of the
darkened alcove, past the curtained partitions and down the
steps, nodding to the undertaker who watched them go with
clasped hands and a suitably doleful expression.

'We should have had him brought back to the house. It
seems dreadful leaving him there all alone.' Carrie got into the
back of the car and buried her face in her hands.

Libby, with two high spots of colour burning on her cheekbones, turned round from the passenger seat.

'And have Mother upset more than she is already? With him lying there in the billiard room with a lily in his hand, and Mother lying upstairs in bed having a heart attack at the thought of it? Father is *dead*, Carrie. There is nothing you can say or do that will bring him back again. He's dead, and Mother is alive. She's the one we have to be thinking about. I am right, aren't I, Harry?'

'You never loved him.' Carrie's voice from the back seat was no more than a whisper, but on hearing it Libby whipped round again.

'Did *you* love him, Carrie?' Her voice rose. 'Did any one of us love him, if the truth were told?' She beat with a clenched hand on the back of the seat. 'Father was impossible to love, and dying hasn't suddenly changed him into a plaster saint. So stop being a hypocrite, Carrie, because that's what you are!'

Harry, driving with his usual caution, raised both eyebrows as he decided to let them get on with it. It was an uncanny experience listening to the sisters quarrelling. It was as though Libby was talking to her own conscience and it was answering back through Carrie.

'You're so hard!' Carrie was moaning through her sobs. 'You'll be telling me next you're glad he's dead!'

'I am not glad he's dead.' Libby, the voice of reason, spoke again. 'But I can't *feel* anything. I can't at this moment think of one kind thing he ever did or one kind word he said. I wish I could, but I can't.'

'He was our father . . .'

'Oh yes, he was our father. He got Mother pregnant, then when there were two of us and girls at that he turned away from Mother and from us, to Willie.' Libby's head drooped. 'It was Willie, always Willie . . .'

'Do you think he'll be with Willie now?' Carrie's voice was calmer and through the driving mirror Harry could see her dabbing at her eyes with a screwed-up handkerchief. Silently he willed Libby to say what her sister wanted to hear, then gave a resigned sigh when the answer came.

'I doubt it. Unless Willie went straight down to hell. Because that's where Father will be, make no mistake about that.'

So why, Harry asked himself as he stopped the car outside

135

the big house with every one of its windows curtained out of respect, why in the name of all that made sense was it Libby who with her sister's arm round her, was crying her eyes out as they went up the steps together?

'The wedding must go on. Exactly as planned.'

Ettie Peel, dressed in the morning for once, was sitting in the high-winged chair by the fire, the day before the funeral. Harry stared at her as if he doubted the evidence of his own eyes. It couldn't be, and yet the small, timid woman seemed to have grown physically since hearing the news of her husband's death. Gone was the hang-dog expression and the nervous habit she had of rolling finger and thumb together. It was as though with the dominance of Oliver's presence removed from the house she had come into her own, found that she could make decisions, and with the discovery grown in stature. For hours she had been closeted in the billiard room with Mr Crankshaw, the mill manager, listening, accepting advice, and agreeing that for the time being the mill would carry on as before.

'We owe it to the weavers,' she had said. 'You must engage an under-manager, Mr Crankshaw. That will be possible, I suppose?'

Then, assured that with the recent closure of two mills in the town there was likely to be a queue for the position, Ettie had nodded, satisfied, and thanked the bewildered little man for his cooperation.

Harry, entering the house as Oliver's mill manager was leaving, had thought that he too had grown in stature, running down the steps and heading in the direction of town like a man who had just had a purpose in life handed to him on a plate.

'You can trust me, Mrs Peel,' Mr Crankshaw had said. 'I will try and see you don't have to worry. I promise you that.'

But Ettie looked far from worried as she talked about the wedding, now only four weeks away.

'People will talk,' she said, 'but let them. Your parents had planned to move to their retirement bungalow before Christmas, and your new assistant starts the first week in January, Harry, so if we postpone the wedding there are going to be a lot

136

of people with their plans upset. And besides, the concept of a whole year of mourning is going out of fashion. We saw enough of that with the old Queen.' She nodded at her two daughters sitting side by side on the chesterfield. '*I* will wear black, of course, perhaps with a touch of white at the throat, but you must wear the outfits you had planned to wear.' A suspicion of a smile lifted the corners of her mouth. 'You are carrying lilies, Libby, and your dress is mauve georgette, Carrie, so the niceties are being adhered to, in a way.'

'That is very noble of you, Mrs Peel.' Harry was ashamed of his overwhelming relief. Not even to himself had he admitted his despair at the thought of the postponement of the wedding. He glanced over to where Libby sat, staring into the fire as if they were discussing a matter which had nothing to do with her. A far from imaginative man, he had wakened in the night a lot lately from a dream where he waited at the altar in vain for his bride to walk towards him. Once he had gone through the whole of the wedding ceremony only to lift the veil from his wife's face and see that it was Carrie smiling up at him. Then turning round in horror he had seen Libby in a bridesmaid's dress laughing at him, tossing her head back and laughing, with all the astonished guests in their pews gazing at them in open-mouthed dismay.

'I don't know what we would do without you, Harry.' Ettie groped for a handkerchief and dabbed at her dry eyes. 'We're a pretty helpless lot without a man. You think everything is in order for tomorrow? I hope we haven't left anybody out, but poor Oliver, he hadn't many friends . . .' She sighed. 'Even the collection at the mill for a wreath was pitifully small. I suspect Mr Crankshaw put most of it in himself. I would have liked to have thought that the weavers were saddened by Oliver's passing. It would have been nice to have seen some of them walking behind the hearse . . . As it is, there will only be three cars.'

Libby opened her mouth to say something, only to be gently kicked into silence by a sideways movement of Carrie's foot.

'It will soon be over, Mother.' Carrie's eyes filled with tears. 'We are the only ones who matter really. Father never gave a damn about what other people thought about him, and if he knows, I don't suppose he's caring now.'

'I just wish he could have died in his own bed.' Ettie's next sentence caused an amused exchange of glances between Libby and her fiancé. 'It would have made the whole thing more decent somehow.'

Oliver Peel was buried in the windswept cemetery on the very day the coal owners' terms were agreed in Lancashire.

'How Father would have gloried in the miners' defeat.' Libby, ready before Carrie, walked without knocking into her sister's bedroom. 'But I'm not so sure it *is* defeat. The trade unions will go from strength to strength now, and a lot of the pits will go bankrupt. Nothing will ever be the same.'

Carrie, pulling on a pair of black kid gloves, widened her eyes in protest. 'How can you talk politics at a time like this? Sometimes I think you have no feelings.'

Libby gave a twitch to the back pleat in her twin's coat. 'It's because I have feelings that I worry, can't you see? All that suffering and all that hunger, all for nothing. I'm not sure what we should be mourning today, Carrie. Our father, who if he were still alive would be storming up the stairs waving the newspaper and shouting that the coal owners will have the whip hand from now on, or for the whole futile army of tired and defeated men going back for less than they were getting before. I'm sorry, but it's all mixed up in my head, and I can't decide who or what to cry for. Does that make sense?'

'It's time to go now.' Carrie walked over and opened the door. If Libby could keep from crying, then she would too. But thinking about the miners did seem out of place that day. It wasn't right, somehow. Then, as they went down into the hall and she saw Harry Brandwood, subdued in a dark suit with a black tie, come forward with his hands outstretched to her sister, Carrie felt the tears spring to her eyes.

Libby had Harry, while she had no one. Then as she blinked the tears back she realized that she too was crying for entirely the wrong reasons on that sad and doleful day.

Poor father, she thought, as with Sarah Batt beside her Ettie came down the stairs to ride into town for the first time in years, her head tilted as if it were a celebratory outing she was going to and not her husband's funeral.

138

Poor, poor Father ... Carrie walked out to the sleekly polished black funeral car, her throat tight with the tears she swore she would not shed.

Although by northern standards it was a very quiet funeral, Westerley opened its doors that day to more people than Carrie could remember. There was the vicar and his wife, Harry's parents, Mr Crankshaw from the mill, the family solicitor, two of Ettie's cousins from Manchester visiting the big house for the first time, and even little Jimmy Earnshaw, the tackler from the mill. Ettie had seen him standing on his own, well back from the funeral party at the graveside, and had gone over to him to whisper a few words as he stood there, twisting his flat cap into an unrecognizable shape. And now there he was in the lounge, holding a glass of sherry carefully by the stem, an embarrassed captive audience as Libby chattered non-stop beside him on the chesterfield.

Mrs Edwards had done them proud, and the dining table, with two extra leaves slotted into position, groaned with a spread that was more like a banquet than a funeral tea. There was a side of ham, a pressed tongue, bowls of salad, a huge fruit cake, plates of scones, fairy cakes and a fresh fruit salad flanked by a jug of thick yellow egg custard.

It was just like a party, Carrie decided, a party that would never have taken place if the master of the house had been present. She watched carefully as Martha Cardwell jerked nervously from sideboard to table, handing round cups of tea from the Rockingham tea service. To Carrie's knowledge the cups and saucers had only been taken out of the display cabinet before to be washed and replaced.

There was no sign of grief on Martha's flat expressionless face, and yet surely she was feeling *something*? Carrie shuddered, then turned her head swiftly as a burst of laughter came from the window seat where two of her father's old Rotarian friends shared a joke together. Why had they come? What was the point in paying respect to the dead, when during his life Oliver Peel had earned far more dislike than respect?

And look at her mother – talking animatedly to the vicar's wife about the Christmas Bazaar and promising to help with the handicrafts stall. It was years since Ettie had been to church. Only the week before she had explained to Libby that it would be impossible for her to go and hear the banns for the wedding read out.

'I can't kneel, and I would only have to go out halfway through the service. You know what being shut in with a crowd of people does to me.'

And yet here she was, excited at having her two cousins to visit, plying them with food, and being the perfect hostess.

It was as though, with Oliver's death, the whole house had suddenly come to life.

Leaving unnoticed, Carrie walked across the hall, curled her fingers round the brass doorknob of the billiard room, opened the door and slipped quietly inside.

Although the blinds had been lifted and the long plush curtains drawn back in the other rooms of the house, this room, her father's special bolt hole, had been left shrouded in funereal gloom. Carrie walked over to the window and slid the heavy dark green curtains back, hearing the brass rings clink together as the room was flooded by the grey diffused light of a winter's afternoon.

Bolt hole. Yes, that was the word for it. This was where Oliver had escaped night after night to sit at his desk, the whisky decanter to hand, working on his papers, a lonely man unable to delegate even the smallest part of his worries to his workforce. His own fault, oh, certainly his own fault. Carrie sat down in the chair with its hand-carved, curved back and arms, and ran her fingers round the leather-bound blotter. And as she sat there she became for one moment her father, sitting alone, hearing the sounds of footsteps on the stairs, the telephone ringing in the hall and Libby's voice or her own answering. Seeing Martha coming in to make up the fire, and swivelling round in his chair as she bent over the coal scuttle, her small rump outlined in the too-short skirt. Simple, unlessoned Martha, to whose arms he had crept for comfort.

Carrie shivered, crossing her arms and trying to rub away the chill seeping into her bones. Now she was seeing him grope his way in the fog down onto the canal bank, bent on revenge. Why else had they found the slip of paper in his pocket with Mungo's name and address written on it in his decisive hand?

And no matter how many times Carrie had told herself there was no love behind Oliver's intentions, she still felt it was her fault.

Pushing the chair back and jumping up so quickly that it spun round of its own accord, Carrie almost ran from the room, wrenching open the door and stepping into the hall to meet a burst of chatter, the clatter of crockery and the sight of Mrs Edwards, flushed with the excitement of it all, bustling into the dining room with yet another loaded tray of food.

'I'm going out for a walk.' Running down the stairs with her black coat flying open and a scarf tied round her hair, Carrie bumped into an astonished Libby who was busily chivvying Jimmy Earnshaw into the lounge for a final cup of tea.

'You can't go out! Not now!' Libby gripped her arm. 'What will people think?' She stepped back as Carrie pushed her none too gently aside. 'And anyway it'll be dark soon.' She followed her sister to the door and into the vestibule. 'Are you all right? You look terrible. What's wrong, Carrie?'

As Carrie opened the big front door the late afternoon dampness wrapped her round like a soggy blanket.

'What *could* be wrong? It's only Father's funeral, isn't it? Why don't you go back in there and put a record on the gramophone? Then maybe you can all have a bit of a dance.'

She was running away from the house, dodging round the parked cars, down the drive, out into the lane, taking in great gulps of cold air as if it were the first proper drink she had had that day.

The tears were there, a solid wedge of grief, an overwhelming pity for the father she could not love. Turning left at the end of the lane she walked away from the direction of the town, past the detached houses set high up from the road and fronted by flights of stone steps. As the smart black coat had no pockets she wrapped her cold hands in the ends of the woollen scarf, and walked on with head bent, letting the tears flow, feeling them running down her cheeks.

She saw the man's shoes first, black lace-up boots like her father's weavers wore, but different in that they were polished until the toecaps gleamed. He was walking quickly, and when she expected him to pass he stopped and spoke, so that she raised her tear-drenched face in startled surprise.

141

'Libby Peel! Why are you crying? What are you doing out all alone in the dark like this?'

The voice was unrefined, but not unpleasant. Even in her distress Carrie noticed that. He was staring at her in amazement, his dark eyes puzzled, stretching out a hand to her, then letting it drop back to his side.

'But you're not Libby, are you?' He shook his head from side to side, taking in the face he thought he knew – same nose, same mouth, same high cheekbones, but with one startling difference. The eyes. These eyes, brown and long-lashed, wet with tears, were gentle and kind, not bold and challenging. He frowned. He had kept that face in his memory not for any sentimental reasons, but because Libby Peel's face was one not easily forgotten. And yet . . .

Carrie took a hand from the enveloping scarf and dashed the tears from her cheeks. 'I'm Libby's twin sister,' she said softly. 'Did she not tell you about me?'

The man shook his head again. He seemed unable to take his gaze from the tear-drenched face staring up at him, and again he felt the overwhelming urge to take this girl into his arms and comfort her. Not as once he had trailed a finger down her sister's face in teasing fashion – nothing like that.

'She said she had a sister, but not a twin.' He smiled. 'But now I see you are not really alike, not really, not at all . . .' His voice tailed away, but he made no move, just stood there, looking hard at her in disbelief.

'My name is Tom Silver,' he said at last, and held out his hand.

Putting her own into it, Carrie felt in the strong, firm clasp the first sensation of peace that had come to her that day.

Nine

'And he thought you were me?' Libby threw down the almost finished pair of pink crêpe-de-Chine camiknickers into which she was stitching a lace insert. Her face was suddenly as rosy as the material. 'Well, go on. Tell me what else he said.'

Carrie stared with surprise at her sister's flushed face. For a reason she couldn't quite fathom she had put off telling Libby about her meeting with Tom Silver until the week after the funeral, and now her twin was demanding to know why.

'Why didn't you tell me about this before?' Libby lowered her head. 'Did he ask you about the wedding?'

Carrie was sweetly reasonable. 'Love, it was the day of Father's funeral. If you must know, we talked about funerals, not weddings.' She smiled gently, remembering. 'He agreed with me that there is something pagan about burying a person with a ham and tongue spread, and relatives you haven't seen for years appearing as mourners. I was surprised how understanding he was.'

Libby picked up the sewing and stabbed her needle into the lace. Her voice was sharp. 'Well, I hope he didn't say he was sorry to hear that Father had died. Our father was one of the bloated capitalists Tom Silver despises. He has real Bolshie ideas, that man. He was sacked from his job on the *Weekly Times* because of them, and he was going to work at a jobbing printer's out Hoghton way. Did he tell you how he was getting on there?'

'He only stayed three weeks.' Carrie bent her head over her own sewing, a pale blue trousseau nightgown for Libby, with fine feather stitching down the bodice. 'He starts work on the evening paper in the New Year. He said the other place was soul-destroying.'

Libby sniffed. 'Not enough scope in a small business for bother-making, I expect. I'm surprised the evening paper is taking him on. I would have thought that after being victimized he would automatically have been blacklisted. The two weeks the paper was out of print during the strike must still rankle with the management. Maybe Mr Silver is learning to keep his mouth shut.'

'It's obvious you don't like him very much.' Carrie winced as she noticed the size of the stitches in Libby's sewing. 'You've never talked about him. I would have thought you would have to know someone pretty well to dislike them so much.'

'I know his *sort*!' Libby pricked her finger, sucked at it furiously, then hurled the half-finished camiknickers to the far corner of the chesterfield. 'Oh God, how I hate sewing!' She ran her hand through her fringe until the calf-lick at the hairline pushed the hair up on end. 'So he thinks there's something pagan about funeral teas, does he? Well, *I* think there's something even more pagan about a bride tarting herself up in pink camiknickers just because she's getting married. Are you *sure* he never mentioned the bloody wedding?'

Calmly Carrie went on with her sewing. When Libby swore it was a sure sign something had upset her badly, something far more important than the sewing she detested so much.

'He never said a word about the wedding,' she said gently. 'Why? Should he have?

'No!' Libby shouted the denial. 'Are you seeing him again?'

This time it was Carrie's turn to put down her sewing and push it to one side. 'Seeing him again? Good heavens, no. I met him accidentally, we talked for a while and that was that. What are you so agitated about?'

'I am not agitated.' Libby spoke through clenched teeth. 'It's just that Mr Silver is not a man I would like to see you getting friendly with. He's only one step up from one of Father's weavers, even if he does fancy himself as an equal.'

'Libby Peel!' Carrie's voice was teasing. 'Listen to who's talking! I thought you were the one who always said all men were equal in the sight of God.' She wagged a finger. 'That used to be one of your favourite sayings, and anyway Tom Silver doesn't wear clogs and a greasy muffler. He even sounds his aitches, and blows his nose into a handkerchief instead of through his fingers.'

'That's not funny!' Jumping to her feet, Libby made for the door. 'That was *crude*, not funny. And don't you go thinking that just because you talked to him for a few minutes means you know him better than I do. Because you don't! Tom Silver is a jumped-up, arrogant man. It amuses him to pretend to be friendly with people out of his class. He mocks all the time, yes, he does, *and* envies those who live in better houses and don't go on strike just to get their own way. He's got a chip on his shoulder as big as a whole forest of trees. He should have been working in Moscow, not Hoghton! He probably prays to Lenin instead of God!' She turned, her face contorted with an anger bordering on terrible despair. 'So don't go mentioning his name to me ever again. Not ever! Do you hear?'

When the door slammed to, Carrie sat with a hand to her mouth for a moment, staring out through the big bay window at the scudding clouds. So her mother had been right last night when she had said that Libby was suffering prewedding nerves. 'Just let's keep our fingers crossed that she doesn't change her mind in the next few weeks,' she had said. 'Libby will never meet another man more right for her than Harry. He has the patience of a saint with her, and he's going to need all that patience in the years to come. But Harry is strong underneath all that apparently easy-going nature. He can handle our Libby, and my guess is he's waiting until he gets married to show a bit of stick.'

'Mother!' Carrie had laughed her surprise.

'And not before it's needed,' Ettie had added, softening her words with the smile that came more often to her lips lately.

Carrie picked up her sister's sewing from where it had been thrown in a heap, shook it out and, with her tongue protruding slightly from between her lips, began unpicking Libby's tortured stitches.

On some occasion, most likely at one of the Labour meetings Libby used to attend, Tom Silver had annoyed her . . . Carrie frowned as she threaded her needle, holding it up and squinting at the light. But the man she had met and talked to that dark afternoon had no unkindness in him, she could swear to that. Why, she could never remember seeing such warm eyes in a man's face. There had been an almost feminine understanding in them as she had choked back her sobs and told him how the funeral party had upset her. She had felt no sense of shame in talking to a stranger like that. Then look how he had insisted on walking her home, shaking his head when she had said with truth that the dark lane leading to Westerley held no terrors for her.

'May God go with you, Miss Peel,' he had said before walking away, and somehow, going back into the house with all the lights glowing and overhearing one of Ettie's cousins thanking her hostess for a 'nice' time, she had been able to see the funny side. The whole thing had got into perspective somehow.

Martha Cardwell had been sent packing by Ettie the day after the funeral. 'So Mother knew,' Carrie had said. 'She must have known all the time. So why didn't she assert herself when Father was alive?'

'Because she would never have won, that's why. Because Mother wasn't born a fighter. She's only coming into her own now because there is no one actively opposing her,' Libby had declared.

'The oracle has spoken!' Carrie had teased, and their eyes had met in shared laughter.

'These things will never be ready in time for the wedding,' Carrie now muttered to herself as she put the camiknickers down and started on a row of French knots round the neck of the nightgown. 'Not that Libby will care. She's only tried her wedding dress on once since it was finished, and if georgette doesn't hang properly it looks awful. At least her veil is long enough to cover the back, and oh, please God, let it be fine on the day. It's quite a long walk from the car to the church door, and what could look worse than white stockings and satin shoes all splashed with mud?'

Still muttering to herself Carrie bent her head and got on with what had to be done, as nervous and worried as if she herself were the bride-to-be.

And upstairs Libby lay on her bed staring at the wall, seeing nothing.

'Tom Silver *is* rude and arrogant! No matter what Carrie says. I know him, and she doesn't. He isn't worth even the nail

146

on Harry's little finger. He isn't!'

Turning her head into the pillow, Libby bit her lips hard.

'Oh, why did he have to come into my life again just when I thought he had gone away? Why did he have to come back?'

There was a most terrible moment when, coming down the aisle on Harry's arm with the ivory georgette dress hanging beautifully and the embroidered net veil caught up in a cap with pearls and orange blossom flowing out behind her, Libby thought she saw Tom Silver disappearing out of the church door.

There was the same tilt to the dark head, the same set to the thin shoulders, but when the man turned round and she saw how mistaken she had been, the colour drained from Libby's cheeks and her hand on Harry's arm trembled.

This was the man she loved, she told herself, and later that night, at Southport, when he took her gently in the big bedroom at the hotel overlooking tree-lined Lord Street, Libby clung to Harry fiercely with a passion that delighted and touched him.

'Oh, Harry . . . Harry . . . I do love you so much, so very much.'

Over and over again she whispered the words, lying in his arms, with the pale blue nightdress lying in a heap at the foot of the bed, and the pink crêpe-de-Chine camiknickers lying across a chair where Harry had dropped them as he undressed her, his brown eyes shining with adoration.

Then, when he was sleeping deeply with his head against her shoulders, Libby stared up into the darkness, vowing that she would be a good wife to this man.

'I was a good teacher, and now I'm going to be a good doctor's wife,' she told him when they came back to the red-brick house at the other side of the park to Westerley. 'You'll wonder how you ever managed without me.'

Harry, bursting with pride and love, took her face in his hands and gazed deep into her eyes as he left on his rounds that first morning after the honeymoon. 'I'll make short shrift of this morning's patients,' he promised. 'All the time I'll be longing to be back here with you. Around one o'clock, darling.

147

Will that be all right?'

Waving him off from the porch, Libby told herself how lucky she was to be married to such a man. To walk straight into a house like this, furnished with the antiques his parents had left behind, saying they were too big and too dark for their new bungalow at the seaside. To be mistress of her own house, to arrange things exactly as she wanted them arranged, to go into the kitchen and tell the cook-general – another legacy from Harry's parents – what they would like for lunch, and to leave the daily help, a pleasant little woman, to her brushes, dusters and mops.

And to have nothing to do . . .

Slowly she walked back into the house, into the lounge where a coal fire glowed, with the brass fire irons and the brass fender giving off sparks of reflected light. Glancing at the Westminster-chime clock on the mantelpiece she saw the time. Eleven o'clock. At school the children would be in from their mid-morning break, sitting at their desks, hands on heads, waiting for permission to open their desks and get out their English grammar exercise books. She wrinkled her nose at the remembered smell of urine emanating from boys and girls who slept three, four and sometimes five to a bed. Sleeping in rooms where the sickly stench of bugs came from the walls, and where fathers lolled unshaven in front of empty grates. A side of the coin that even Harry, for all his goodness, refused to recognize.

She had loved those children. In spite of their nit-infested heads and the dirt ingrained underneath their fingernails, she had loved them. And now here she was, an idle woman with nothing to do.

When the telephone rang she ran to answer it. Perhaps it was Carrie? Oh, yes, please, let it be Carrie! She would invite her over that afternoon, and together they would go through the house and decide what changes were to be made. The curtains in this room, for instance. Libby thought they were hideous, absolutely revolting.

'Yes?' She frowned as a high-pitched voice crackled in her ear.

'Is the doctor there? I would like to speak to the doctor. It is urgent, very urgent.'

Libby sat down, holding the receiver against her ear, picking up the pencil lying at the side of the notepad on the polished mahogany table.

'If you will give me a message I will let the doctor know as soon as he comes in. He is out on his rounds at the moment, I'm afraid.'

The voice at the other end of the wires was high with indignation. 'But surely you are able to get in touch with him? I have to see him right away. *Now!* I am in such pain . . . such pain.'

'Who is that speaking, please?' For someone in agony the voice was very strong and peevish, Libby thought. She licked the point of the pencil and waited.

'This is Mrs Morgan. Mrs Morgan from Bramwell House. Who is that? You don't sound like Dr Brandwood's girl. What has happened to Phyllis?'

'Phyllis went when Dr Brandwood retired. I am Doctor Harry's wife.' Unconsciously Libby was adopting her school-marmish voice. 'If you will tell me your symptoms I will see that my husband gets your message when he comes in at one o'clock.'

'My *symptoms?*' The loud voice rose an octave. 'Since when was it necessary to describe one's symptoms over the telephone? Dr Brandwood knew all about my migraines, and he always came round straight away. To give me an *injection*. I can't possibly wait until one o'clock. Surely your husband left you a list of the people he was visiting? All you have to do is ring round until you find him. That's what Phyllis always did.'

'I am not Phyllis.' Libby gripped the telephone hard, raising her eyes ceilingwards. 'And I suggest you go and lie down and wait until the doctor returns. If you are a sufferer from migraine, then surely you know that is the best thing to do anyway.'

'How dare you!' The voice crackled with such ferocity that Libby held the receiver away from her ear. 'I have been a patient of Dr Brandwood's for over ten years and never, never have I been spoken to like this! You can tell your husband when he comes in not to bother coming to see me. I will find a doctor who knows how to get his priorities right. Someone with a little more sympathy. Goodbye!'

When the line went dead, Libby sat quite still for a moment before hooking the telephone back onto its stand. It was silly, she told herself, but the exchange of words had left her quite shattered.

When Harry came in at half past one for a lunch already drying in the oven Libby told him about the call. 'Mrs Morgan from Bramwell House?' Harry frowned. 'I'll have to go round there straight away.' He shrugged his shoulders when Libby reminded him that he hadn't eaten since half past seven that morning. 'Look, love, Mrs Morgan and her husband are two of my best patients. They pay promptly, and migraine isn't exactly what you would class as an imaginative illness. It can be completely demoralizing when it strikes.'

'Well, it hadn't struck this morning!' Libby followed him to the door, still protesting. 'You should have heard the way she shouted at me. A person with migraine can hardly lift a head from the pillow. She was rude, Harry, rude and arrogant!'

He turned and drew her to him for a moment. 'Well, real or imaginary, love, Mrs Morgan is my patient and besides, she exerts quite an influence in this town. Insult Mrs Morgan and you insult half the county. I must go and at least try to pour oil on troubled waters. I can't afford to lose that account. It's a bad start, Libby, a bad start.'

'And I'm to blame?' Libby drew away from him to glare into his anxious face. 'Oh, Harry. Women like that aren't worth bothering about. You'll most likely find she is finishing a good lunch when you get there.'

She went back into the house, closing the door none too gently behind her. But within the hour Harry was back, obviously fighting hard to keep his normally controlled temper.

'Mrs Morgan had left orders not to let me into the house.' He threw down his bag. 'And there was a car I thought I recognized outside in the drive. So that's one account closed.' He shot her a guarded glance. 'School-marm tactics don't work when you are talking to patients, Libby. I must ask you to be more tolerant in future, even if you feel in your mind that the caller could be malingering.'

'I know children,' Libby said, with a calmness belied by the anger sparkling from her brown eyes, 'children who come to school with a fever or worse because their mothers realize they can be kept warmer at school than in an unheated house. Mothers who turn mangles with their insides dropping out. I've *seen* them, Harry, and yet you expect me to have patience with a pampered woman who imagines she has a headache? A spoilt woman who only needs to crook her little finger for you to go running? Is that smarmy bedside manner of yours what you trained seven years for?' She waved a hand at the telephone. 'And am I expected to kowtow and jump to attention when a woman like Mrs Morgan calls the tune? Well, I can't do it! It's degrading.'

She looked very beautiful in her anger, but this time Harry was not impressed. This time he ignored her.

'I see you have a lot to learn, Libby. If you will have a sandwich sent through into the surgery, I'll eat there. I have some paperwork to do before I go out again.

'He was as bad as Mrs. Morgan.'

Libby sat opposite Carrie in the lounge at Westerley the same afternoon. 'Oh, Carrie, we've quarrelled already, and I thought when we got married the bickering between us would stop. I thought we disagreed so much because the wedding and everything was getting on my nerves, but I was wrong. I looked at him this morning, Carrie, and I didn't *like* him, let alone love him. What am I going to do?'

Carrie hid a smile as she listened. Her twin was talking quickly, waving a hand to emphasize a point, eyes flashing, cheeks flushed. And, oh, it was good to have Libby in the house again, even for a short time. With Libby around the whole world seemed different. Even her more outrageous statements had a touch of comic drama about them. Privately she was glad Harry had stood up to his wife. He was learning already, and the time would come when Libby would settle down in her role as doctor's wife, playing it with as much dedicated intensity as she played every other part. At least it made a change from politics. Carrie sighed. Only yesterday Mr Crankshaw had been up from the mill, explaining to her mother that the cotton trade was so seriously hampered by heavy rates and taxations that the coming year was going to be a testing time.

'It's all on account of the tremendous cost to the state of the coal strike,' he had said. 'Did you read in the paper that the miners' secretary on a visit to Moscow has prophesied a revolution in England? Inevitable, he says. He believes that the government and the mine owners between them beat the working man down in his demand for a living wage. But he says their victory will be the dearest victory that British capitalism ever won.'

Oh yes, it was a good job Libby wasn't on *that* hobbyhorse. At least her marriage to Harry seemed to have damped her ardour for the Labour movement. Now it only remained to be seen which soapbox she was about to leap on.

Carrie had not long to wait.

A month later, when the February snow lay dirty and trodden in the streets of the town, Libby announced that she was giving a small dinner party for the express purpose of introducing Carrie to a Burnley friend of Harry's, a divorced man by the name of Roger Fish, son of a mine owner. Since his wife's desertion he had been fending for himself, leaving his small girl in the charge of a series of unsuitable housekeepers.

'He's looking for a wife.' Libby, making no attempt to be circumspect, filled Carrie in with the details. 'There's a house, neglected of course, but you could soon set that to rights. Not good-looking, but then, what do looks matter? I don't mean repulsive,' she added, 'just a bit bald, and with a laugh that grates, but once you get past that he's nice. You'll take to each other at once. I'm sure of it.'

'What shall I wear?' Carrie asked the question with pretended innocence, and wasn't in the least surprised when Libby took her quite seriously.

'Your rose-coloured overblouse with the black velvet tie, and your velvet skirt. I'll wear my black velvet. You should stand out nicely against that.'

'Libby!' Carrie's eyes brimmed with ready laughter, but her sister failed to see anything remotely amusing. So Carrie sat back, in the way she had always sat back when Libby started on her 'steam-roller tactics', and allowed herself to be taken over. Conditioned by closeness, Carrie nodded and agreed.

To tell the truth she was glad of the opportunity to get out of the big house for a while. Ettie, actively fearing Sarah Batt's imminent departure now that her mother was becoming too frail to look after her grandson, had already lost some of the euphoria which had sustained her since Oliver's death. She was in danger of sinking into semi-invalidism again, and when she did so Carrie knew her role would be that of the unmarried daughter, a slave to the house and her mother's whims.

This Roger Fish – well, he didn't come into it. She wasn't a slab of meat to be sold to the highest bidder and besides, a bald head and a laugh that grated . . . oh Lordy! The corners of Carrie's mouth twitched with laughter again, but with great effort she managed to keep her face straight as Libby went on planning the dinner party.

'A week next Friday, then?' Having arranged everything to her satisfaction Libby rose to her feet and started upstairs to say goodbye to her mother.

'I'll be there,' Carrie promised. 'Bois-de-rose, overblouse and all.'

'Harry will fetch you,' said Libby, over a disappearing shoulder. 'At seven o'clock sharp. And if he's called out to a patient, then I won't be responsible. I just won't!'

'How can a man be so stupid as to keep mixing us up when we're dressed in completely different frocks?'

Libby beckoned Carrie out of the room as the two men settled down with their afterdinner cigars and the decanter of port.

'Roger Fish isn't even *trying* to get us right, in my opinion. Something tells me he thinks we're funny. A couple of freaks in a circus tent. The next time he calls me Carrie, then apologizes, I shall say something very rude.'

Carrie followed her down the hall and into the drawing room. 'So you don't think he fancies me as the next Mrs Fish, do you?'

'Or me,' Libby said promptly, and as their laughter exploded they clapped hands to their mouths and sank down together on the overstuffed sofa, leaning on each other, rocking together in shared merriment.

'He's not all that bald.' Carrie sat up, wiping her eyes. 'And

153

his laugh isn't that bad, either. A bit squeaky, but you could get used to it if you were hard pressed enough.'

Libby, with one of her abrupt and bewildering changes of mood, suddenly gripped her sister's hand. 'You're not still pining for that awful Mungo man?'

'No, I'm not.' Carrie tucked her handkerchief back up her sleeve. 'I never think about him. Mr Eccles took him back, apparently, and I'm glad. Mungo was the breadwinner. He needed his job more than I did. I wouldn't be surprised if he hadn't convinced the headmaster that *I* was the one who did the grabbing that day down in the cloakroom.' She shuddered. 'Not that it matters now. It's all water under the bridge.'

Then at the mention of water they both stared at each other, their dark eyes wide.

'And yet *he* was the one directly responsible for Father drowning.' Carrie sighed. 'I wake in the night sometimes and wonder how I could ever have imagined that I was in love with him.' She shuddered. 'I must have been out of my mind.'

'Have you seen Tom Silver again since that day?' Libby turned her face away, trying to keep her voice light.

'No, never,' Carrie said, the sudden blush warming her cheeks surprising her. Then, as the two men came in from the dining room, they were confronted by two identical faces, wearing two identically guilty expressions.

Now what's been cooking, Harry thought, coming forward with a smile on his ruddy face, and taking care to leave the place next to Carrie free for Roger Fish.

'I will drive you home, if I may.' The bald head inclined itself towards Carrie solicitously. 'And I must thank *you*, Libby, for a most enjoyable evening.' The high-pitched laugh wobbled nervously. 'Perhaps before too long you will all come and have dinner with me? My present housekeeper is a splendid cook. She'll be glad of the opportunity to display her skills.'

'That would be lovely.' Libby's brown eyes were wide and innocent as she exchanged a glance with her twin. 'Wouldn't that be lovely, Carrie?'

'Delightful.' Carrie narrowed her eyes at her sister's treachery, but outside in the drive she allowed herself to be helped into the passenger seat of the car.

'You must show me the way.' The nervous laugh twittered again. Carrie explained that it was only a five minutes' drive to Westerley, her conscience pricking slightly. It had been un-forgivable of Libby to throw them together like this so obviously, but Roger Fish was, she felt, a lonely man, covering up his loneliness by a too-ready laugh, and the heavy-handed joke of not being able to tell them apart.

'It must be difficult bringing up a little girl without her mother.' Carrie's voice was gentle with sympathy, filled with a genuine remorse at her off-hand manner all the evening.

The man by her side shot her a quick glance from beneath surprisingly bushy eyebrows. She was very beautiful, this girl who was the image of her sister. More beautiful than the other one in an undefinable way. Following her instructions, he drove the car round the drive and up to the steps leading to Westerley. Then thoughtfully he turned off the engine. She was tender-hearted, too. The wine with the meal and Harry's generous pouring of the port afterwards blurred his vision as he looked at Carrie's oval face above the high collar of her velvet coat. She drooped her head and fiddled with the clasp of her silk purse.

'I hope I haven't offended you. Libby told me that your . . . that your wife . . .' The gentle voice faltered.

'My wife went off with someone else.' Roger Fish felt his own voice deepen dramatically. 'She never wanted the child, and when Claire was born it seemed to take Elaine farther away from me.' He sighed, his face so close that his breath made the marabou trimming flutter enticingly. 'I will never understand how a woman can leave her baby, but there it was, and now, well, I just do the best I can.'

'Oh, I'm so sorry.' Carrie put out a hand and touched his sleeve. 'Would you have her back, your wife, if she came?' The brown eyes were filled with compassion, causing him to draw in his breath sharply. 'It could be that she was depressed after the baby came. It happens sometimes, and maybe this – this other man – maybe she was just infatuated. There can't have been much about him to take a wife away from her husband and child, but women sometimes fall in love with the most unlikely men.'

It was an intimate moment there in the car with the doors and windows closed, and the scent she was wearing made his senses reel. This Carrie Peel, with her quiet ways, gentle voice and dark eyes, was a dark horse if he was any judge of women. And since his wife's desertion Roger Fish prided himself very much on being a judge of women.

'There are times,' he whispered unforgivably, 'when my life is as dark as the lives of the ponies down my father's mine.' He thought Carrie swayed towards him; he could have sworn it – women always fell for a bit of the old sob stuff. With a swift movement he pulled her close to him and then, as he felt the scented warmth of her, his mouth found her soft lips.

As the kiss deepened and his hand slid down Carrie's back to draw her even closer, he felt himself thrust away with a strength he would never have believed the small girl possessed. When he reached for her again, telling himself that all women played hard to get at first, the stinging slap to his right cheek made him reel back in astonishment. What he did not know, what he could never have been expected to know, was that to Carrie Peel he was not, in that moment, a maudlin man who had had too much to drink, but a man wild with angry frustration, holding her captive against the wall of a basement cloakroom.

In the next moment Carrie had reached for the door handle, wrenched the door open and almost fallen out of the car, frantic in her desire to get away from him. As he sat there, dazed, a hand to his burning cheek, he saw her run wildly up the steps to the big front door, then disappear inside without a backward glance.

'Well, bugger me!' Roger sat there, leaning on the wheel for a moment, then pulling the door closed started the car and drove away down the drive, muttering to himself at the vagaries of women, and in particular of the girl who had been thrown into a blind panic by one harmless kiss.

He was on the main road, heading for home, when the sight of the silk purse on the seat beside him made him curse aloud again. There was no way he was going to turn back and knock at the door of the big house set at the end of the winding lane. He sighed, and took the turning leading to the doctor's house. A quick explanation and a handing-in of the purse at the door, and he could be away. Back to Burnley and the housekeeper would would be waiting up for him, her housecoat tantalizingly open and her willing body ready for his caresses.

He drew up at the front of Harry Brandwood's house just in time to see Harry getting into his car and driving swiftly away, leaving Libby standing on the doorstep with her figure in its black dress etched against the light streaming from the hall.

'Are you coming in?' Libby took Carrie's purse from him. 'Harry has gone out on a case.' She held the door invitingly open. 'Another panic that could easily have waited until tomorrow; another case of the one who pays the piper calling the tune.'

There were two spots of bright colour high on her cheek-bones. She was gloriously, beautifully angry, and Roger did not hesitate. He might have summed one of the sisters up wrongly, but this one, well, she was a completely different kettle of fish. Snatching the trilby hat from his bald head he followed her into the lounge and accepted the drink she offered him, telling himself that as rum goes went, this beat the best of them.

When, twenty minutes later, he staggered out once again to his car, a hand to a burning cheek – the left one this time – he was laughing silently, accepting the fact that he was too drunk to drive, then reminding himself that he had driven in a far worse condition than this.

'God Almighty!' he muttered as he clung to the wheel, his head spinning. Two of them! Two identical faces, and two identical reactions. All in the space of half an hour. By the time he was well on the road to Burnley the two faces had merged and become one, and he was laughing uproariously, slapping the wheel with the flat of his hand, his high-pitched laugh filling the interior of the little car.

'Roger Fish is not the man for Carrie!' Libby was sitting up in bed when Harry came up the stairs, so tired that the normal ruddy colour of his face had faded to a patchy grey. 'I never want to see him again. How you could have possibly thought he was her type I don't know.'

Too tired to demand an explanation, Harry began to

undress. 'I thought the evening went off rather well,' he said mildly, then went out and across the landing to wash his hands and clean his teeth. When he climbed into bed, a solid, comfortable figure in his striped pyjamas, with his hair brushed flat against his head and a clean handkerchief in the pocket of his jacket, Libby settled herself in his arms, laying her head on his shoulder, her hair tickling his chin.

'I wasn't going to say anything yet, but I should have . . . is it too soon to think I might be going to have a baby?'

Harry's thoughts as he sank into a sleep from which the telephone bell was to propel him out of bed and into his trousers at five o'clock the next morning were a mixture of pride and satisfaction. Now his Libby would have something more to occupy her mind than a jealous monitoring of the restricted time he was able to spend with her.

It was as well he could not see the expression on his beloved's face as she stared up into the darkness, her palm still itching from the slap she had administered to Roger Fish's leering face, a heavy depression settling on her as she realized that now she would be more a prisoner to the house than ever, that her craving for excitement and freedom was to be thwarted for a long, long time to come.

Ten

'It will be a boy. I know it will be a boy. I *order* it to be a boy!'

It was the end of March before Libby told her mother about the coming baby, wanting to be, as she confided in Carrie, quite sure first.

Ettie's heart was playing her up again now that she was realizing that even without Oliver's brooding presence Westerley was still a house where the most frequent comings and goings were by the tradesmen to the back door.

Carrie seemed, to her mother's eyes, to be drifting more obviously into spinsterhood with every passing month. Without her twin she was only half a person, a shadow, and since the dinner party in January Libby seemed to have abandoned the idea of finding a husband for her sister.

But a baby . . . well, that was what they all needed. Ettie smiled at Sarah Batt busy in the corner with her sewing. 'We *order* a boy, don't we Sarah? And more than that – I have a feeling he will be just like Willie.' Her blue eyes grew dreamy. 'The Lord works in a mysterious way, and somehow I know He is going to give me back my Willie in my grandson. I have never felt that Willie was really dead. I always felt that one day the door would open and he would walk in with his fair hair shining and his blue eyes teasing, the way they always did. And now I know. Libby is going to give him back to me, aren't you, love?'

'Mother!' Libby exchanged a glance with Carrie. 'That's a fanciful notion. It could be a girl. There's a fifty-fifty chance of it being a girl. You know that.'

'No!' Ettie rose from her chair in her excitement. 'Sarah! Give me a length of cotton from the workbasket there. And

Libby, give me your wedding ring.'

'What on earth for?' Libby, pleased at seeing her mother's face crease into lines of animation, decided not to argue but to humour her. Holding up her left hand she slipped the heavy gold band from her third finger. 'Now what?'

'Lie down. Put your feet up on the chesterfield. Sarah, thread the cotton through the ring. Now, hold it in your fingers over Miss Libby's stomach. Like this, Sarah. No, don't put any pressure on it.' She clapped her hands together. 'If it swings round and round then it will be a girl, but if it swings backwards and forwards, then it's a boy.'

'I don't like to, Mrs Peel.' Sarah, her round face troubled, held out the ring and the length of cotton. 'I don't think we are meant to tamper with fate like this. The Lord will send Miss Libby whatever he thinks fit, and I'd rather not . . . It's wrong, that's what it is. Wrong!'

Ettie's face fell, but Libby, lying flat with her toes upturned, spoke sharply. 'Sarah! Don't be so silly! It's only a game! C'mon now, this is even better than reading *Old Moore's Almanac*. Let's see if it really is Willie's reincarnation I've got in here!'

'I won't do it!' Flushing bright scarlet, her round eyes starting from her head, Sarah threw the ring from her. 'You've no cause to speak like that, Miss Libby! You're upsetting your mother. Just look at her. If she has an attack it will be all your fault!'

'But it was Mother who began it.' Bewildered, Libby sat up, and as she bent to pick up the ring from the carpet she saw Sarah Batt's feet in their sensible lace-up shoes scurry away. Then, as she raised her head, she saw the door bang closed behind the hurrying figure.

'*Now* what have we said?' Libby stared at the door, then sighed as she saw the way her mother lowered herself back into her chair, steadying herself on the arms, then dropping suddenly as if she had an arthritic hip. 'What's got into Sarah lately? *I'm* supposed to be the one who makes scenes and goes off in huffs. Pregnant women have a free licence to do that!'

'She's a Catholic,' Ettie said sadly, as if that explained a lot, then looked hurt as her daughters burst out laughing. 'Perhaps it was a silly thing to do. It's just that I want it to be a boy so much . . . so very, very much.'

'I'll do my best, Mother.' Libby stood up and went over to the window. 'By the time those green leaves have turned to brown you'll know one way or the other.'

She turned round, snatching up her coat from the chair where she had thrown it when she came in, thrusting her arms into the sleeves in her old restless way. 'Oh God! I'll never have the patience to wait until then. I'm tired of being pregnant already. Harry's quite disgusted with me because I haven't even felt sick yet. Most of his patients go into a decline from the minute they conceive. Still, it's early days yet. I may start eating coal and fancying beetroot with custard any day now!'

But at the end of a disappointing August, when rain fell almost daily from bleak grey skies, Libby was still disgustingly healthy and so bored she felt there were days when she could throw herself on the carpet and scream aloud.

Reading the local papers from cover to cover she saw that Tom Silver had been made a councillor. There was a photograph of him staring into the camera with a dedicated expression in his dark eyes, and a report which said that for a new boy Mr Silver was already making his presence felt. On one occasion he had stood up and berated his fellow councillors for taking plants from the conservatory in the park for their own gardens. And on another occasion he had brought to the notice of the meeting the state of the market place when the stalls were taken down on Wednesdays and Saturdays.

'Hordes of ragged children scrambling about for cut oranges and bruised apples,' he had said. 'We know the high incidence of unemployment in this town, but must we revert to Dickensian times? Are our children so undernourished that they have to forage in overflowing dustbins?'

He had gone down personally, the report stated, and talked to the children, taking the names of some of them and visiting them in their homes. What he had seen had appalled him.

'Houses so poorly furnished that there weren't enough chairs to go round. Bugs in the walls, and bare flag floors. Mothers with nothing to give their children but great doorsteps

161

of bread sprinkled with margarine and sugar, and everywhere the smell of poverty . . .'

Libby put the newspaper down and stared into the coal fire burning high in the wide tiled fireplace. It was as though Tom Silver was there in the room with her, talking, pointing with a thin finger, black hair falling forward over his forehead, reminding her that there was one law for the rich and another for the poor, and always would be if something wasn't done. He was reminding her of the children, the bright pupils who, having missed their chances of a grammar school education, were now thrown out of work by the closing of the mills, and forced to queue at the labour exchange. For what? Three shillings a week at the most.

Libby shivered. She had been in danger of forgetting all that.

She was like a big fat cow, waddling around, feet splayed, back arched, stomach sticking out. With characteristic dramatic honesty Libby berated herself. Complacent wasn't the word. No, the word was unfeeling, uncaring. Her pregnancy had slipped by and in the long waiting months she had slipped quietly into the category of those who had, and to hell with those who had not.

She would write to Tom Silver. She would sink her pride, because after all she was a married woman now, and the humiliation of that September night when he had called her bluff was a thing of the past. She would write to him and congratulate him on speaking out, and more than that, she would pledge herself to join the fight after the birth of her baby.

Heavily she got up from the chair and went over to the writing table, but when she bent her head over the thick notepaper and wrote the date at the top in her flowing hand, the headache that had been threatening all day erupted into a thousand hammers beating at her skull. Her throat ached and suddenly the room took on the dimensions of an overheated prison cell. Pushing the paper away, she walked flat-footed into the hall.

For Libby to think was to act, and within a few minutes she was outside, a long cardigan hanging loose over her smocklike summer dress, her head bare as she breathed deeply of the humid air blanketing the street like a shroud.

She had meant to walk down to the park gates and wander up the Broad Walk towards the duck pond, her usual afternoon walk, but the main shopping centre of the town was only five minutes' walk away and beyond that was the market place. Libby walked on, ignoring the stares of passers-by. With characteristic defiance she had made little attempt to disguise her condition, refusing to stay in during daylight hours, as was deemed to be right and proper by her contemporaries. To be pregnant was normal. To be large and ungainly was normal also, and if people wanted to stare, let them stare.

She plodded on, past the Town Hall and over the road to the market, where at the end of that Wednesday market day the stallholders were packing their goods away into crates before beginning the task of taking down the stalls. By now her head was throbbing and her face burning as if she had been sitting in the sun too long. She had brought no basket, no purse, and if she had done so she would have handed out the money to the children she saw diving underneath the stalls, waiting with hands outstretched for the display oranges cut into two pieces to show their juiciness.

Horrified, Libby watched the children, some of them wearing clogs and some boots several sizes too big for them. Waiflike children, with white faces and straggly hair. Dirty-legged, cheeky mites, more ragged than any she remembered teaching in her church school before she had married and forgotten how poor the poor could be.

The cobblestones seemed to be pushing their way up through her thin summer shoes with their pointed toes and bar-straps. Now Libby left the fruit and vegetable stalls to cross to the secondhand clothes stalls, with their hanging rows of musty-smelling coats and frocks, and their rows of shabby shoes and tangled piles of stockings.

'Are you all right, love?'

Libby blinked as a woman dismantling a stall spoke kindly to her.

'You look all in.' She came round the front of the stall and touched Libby's arm. 'Don't you think you'd better be getting home, love? It's starting to rain, and from the look of that sky we're in for a real wetting. Would you like to sit down for a bit? There's a box behind here, and I think there might be a drop of tea left in the can.' The woman turned to call out to her neighbour on the next stall. 'This lass is all in, but I can't get her to say nowt. I think she's sickening for something. Her time's not up yet, though. She hasn't dropped. She's carrying too high to be going into labour just yet awhile.'

Libby walked away, hearing them talking about her as if they were referring to someone else. She could not understand it. She had come down here to find Tom Silver. She hadn't known it before, but it was quite clear now. What wasn't clear was the fact that now there were stalls where she had thought to see an empty market place, with Tom standing on a make-shift platform telling a mysteriously disappearing crowd that he was on their side.

'That's right, love. Get back home.' The woman's voice spiralled after her as, stolidly placing one foot in front of the other, Libby forced herself to walk on. She was muddled, with the heat pricking all over her body. She welcomed the rain, she really welcomed it. In fact, she would lift her face and feel the cool drops wetting her skin.

'It's a long way to Westerley.' She said that aloud, then smiled at the absurdity of it. 'It's a long way to Tipperary.' That was how it should go. Tipperary, not Westerley. She would laugh at such a silly mistake, if only her throat hadn't closed up in that painful way.

She was trudging past the park gates when she remembered suddenly that she no longer lived at Westerley. That was good. Where she lived wasn't so far as Westerley; where she lived was only a few turnings farther on. And when she got inside out of the rain Tom Silver would be there, setting a match to the fire and ordering her to take her stockings off. He would be bossy but kind, his thin face set into lines of mocking humour. He would give her a mug of tea, not a cup, because folks in the street where Tom Silver lived never drank from cups. Cups with fluted rims edged with gold were for the sort of woman she had become. The women whose babies were put into treasure-cots with organdie drapings, not into an empty drawer lined with newspapers and old blankets.

The red-brick house with the surgery built onto the side was there, just a few more steps, and it was here she lived, and she was glad, because she could go no farther. . . .

'You have looked after scarlet fever patients before, nurse?' Harry took the shabby Gladstone bag from the little woman and led the way upstairs. He failed to see the glint of indignation in Nurse Tomkin's grey eyes behind the whirlpool lenses of her round spectacles.

'Yes, doctor.' The answer was mild and deferential, but what Nurse Tomkin was saying underneath her breath was that she had nursed more scarlet fever patients than what he'd had hot dinners. With her sixtieth birthday farther behind her than she was prepared to admit, Nurse Tomkin had done her training in a Manchester teaching hospital and been filled with righteous indignation when the powers-that-be had refused to accept her application to go to France during the war. Properly trained she might be, but she still believed that a hot bread poultice slapped onto a wheezy chest worked wonders. Aye, and a good suck at a whole bag of acid drops, with the spit shot into a bowl, was the only method guaranteed to cure bleeding of the gums. Scarlet fever! She had her remedies for that, too. She'd soon have it sweated out of this young doctor's wife.

But even Nurse Tomkin, trained not to show her feelings, drew in a sharp breath of dismay when she saw her patient propped up on the pillows, eyes glazed, mouth dry and cracked, rasping from the tortured throat.

'How far gone is she?' The short-sighted eyes took in Libby's swollen stomach, rising like half a barrel beneath the sheets. 'Near her time?'

'First week in October.' Harry stood by the bed, an unprofessional anguish creasing his face into lines. 'I didn't want to have her moved to the isolation hospital. I want her nursed here, at home.' He laid his hand on his wife's burning forehead, then bent his head closer as Libby muttered feverishly in a high garbled voice, her eyes as filled with terror as if she were living out some unbearable nightmare. 'I couldn't bear to see her taken away.'

'Quite right, doctor.' Nurse Tomkin glanced round the

room with approval. 'It's understood that there's no one to come in here but me and you?'

Harry nodded. 'Anything you want – anything . . .' He backed towards the door. 'Just ask.' He tried to smile. 'Since this epidemic began they are sleeping them two to a bed in the hospital.'

'You go down to your surgery.' Nurse Tomkin rolled up her sleeves, baring arms as red and mottled as if she had sat in a hot bath for far too long. 'What I would like is a camp bed, or even a sofa over there by the wall.' She dismissed a mahogany tallboy with a wave of her hand. 'That can go out for a start. I would like to sleep in here. There's no call for a night nurse, though that was mentioned.' She bent down and rolled up a rug laid by the side of the bed. 'I'll put what I don't want out on the landing, then I'll want a tray with my own things. Own cup, own knife and fork. You have help in the kitchen?'

Well, that was a daft question, she muttered to herself as the doctor left the room at last. Of course they would have help in a house like this. She stared round the bedroom at the highly polished furniture, the silver hair brush on the dressing table, the dark green satin eiderdown and the pillows edged with hand-crotcheted lace. Still muttering, she stood with her neat head cocked to one side, mentally making a list of the things she needed. Those china ornaments off the mantelpiece could go, and all that clutter on the dressing table. This room would be as near to a hospital ward as she could get it, or her name wasn't Nellie Tomkin.

She was picking up a silver-framed photograph when surprise made her hold still for a moment. 'Now what?' she asked herself out loud. 'What was a photograph of old Mrs Batt's grandson doing here in this room?'

She stared down at the laughing face of a fair-haired boy, squinting into the camera as if the light was too much for him. Well, well . . . She glanced over to the girl in the bed. She had been told that her patient was one of the Peel twins, and yes, the Peel house was where Sarah Batt worked for a Mrs Peel whose husband had been drowned last year.

Nurse Tomkin's small mouth pursed itself up, as if anticipating a kiss. No wonder Sarah Batt was so devoted to the Peel family when the married daughter kept a photograph of Sarah's

166

illegitimate son Patrick on her dressing table. She sniffed. The Peels must be an unusually broad-minded family.

Carrying a side table out onto the landing, Nurse Tomkin followed it by the photographs, and a lot of what she called unnecessary clutter. There would be no harbouring of dust whilst she was in charge or she would know the reason why. Then, mentally armed with a list of what she considered *was* necessary, she went downstairs to worry the life out of the cook in the kitchen.

On the way back upstairs she stopped on the landing long enough to pick the photograph up again. Holding it close to her near-sighted eyes she stroked her chin thoughtfully, her mind ticking over as she worked out dates.

For two days Libby hovered between life and death. Sponged down with vinegar and water, fed from a feeding cup filled with boiled water and sugar, her every breath monitored by the stalwart little figure in the dark blue dress and white starched apron, Libby rambled, tossed, protested feverishly. Now and again she opened her eyes to see a pinched dedicated face leaning over her. At times she suffered the indignity of an ear pressed to her bare stomach, and when at last the fever broke and the sweat poured down her sides, she felt the soothing touch of a sponge washing her all over her hot sticky body. She felt strong arms lifting her against high-piled pillows, and when she protested feebly a voice cajoled her into submission. If she moaned at night, the wrinkled face was there, hands lifting her head to spoon the sweetened water into her mouth. If she wanted to pass water, the bedpan, warmed to comfort, was slipped underneath her bottom and left there for just long enough and not a minute longer.

Whilst Libby was sick Nurse Tomkin loved her with a fierceness that would have put the most devoted of mothers to shame. It was as simple as that. For a long time now all Nellie Tomkin's compassion had been lavished on the ailing, the dying, only to be withdrawn when they recovered. And recover they usually did under her round-the-clock ministrations. For the healthy, Nellie Tomkin had very little time. Her acid tongue and biting sarcasm, nurtured on a life embittered by disappointments, meant that in the village where she lived alone in a tiny cottage she was thought by some to be a witch.

167

So when at the end of September she saw Sarah Batt walking down the lane after attending Mass in the old priory, she planted herself in front of her with her broad feet in their usual ten-to-two position.

'This your weekend off?' She stared at Sarah's red hair, peeping untidily from the ugly cloche hat pulled low down over the narrow forehead. It was said that Sarah Batt had never looked at a man since her downfall of roughly nine years ago, but with her country-fresh complexion and her round blue eyes she was a comely enough lass. This alone was enough to sharpen Nellie's tongue. 'It's a small world, wouldn't you say, Sarah?'

'Aye.' The only way Sarah could have walked on was to have pushed the determined little figure aside, but her eyes narrowed nervously as she waited for what was to come next. Gossipy Nurse Tomkin never so much as passed the time of day with the folks of the village unless she had something unpleasant to impart. Sarah waited with a premonition of dread seeping through her.

'I've been nursing somebody you know very well.' The eyes glittered behind their thick lenses. 'One of the Peel twins. The married one, Miss Libby, married to Dr Brandwood.'

Sarah's expression was now the resigned stonelike passivity of someone waiting for the axe to fall. 'Oh, yes?'

'She's better now, but whether she'll survive her confinement is another question altogether. It's a good job she was far on in her pregnancy because they are coming round to thinking that scarlet fever contracted early on can damage the unborn child. They are sending for me again when she's due. Dr Brandwood was mighty pleased with me. I thought for a while I was going to have two patients to nurse. He's besotted with that wife of his.' The uneven teeth showed in the semblance of a smile. 'But she'll survive, that lass. Plenty of spunk there. I only had to turn my back during that last week and she was out of bed. Strong as an ox with spirit to match, that one.'

Sarah stared down at the ground, her eyes following the progress of a flurry of red-gold leaves from the trees bordering the lane. Why didn't the old witch come to what she was determined to say? 'I must go, Nurse Tomkin.' Sarah took a

168

step forward, then sighed as the plumply solid little figure stood her ground. 'My mother is far from well and I'd like to do a batch-bake before I get the train back this evening.'

'Your mother has a hard life looking after that lad of yours at her age.' The greying head nodded twice. 'How old is he now? Nine? Ten?'

'Patrick will be ten in November.' Sarah lowered the ugly felt hat, wishing she had the nerve to push the old woman out of the way. 'I have to go. Excuse me, Nurse Tomkin. Me mother will be wondering where I am. I stopped to make my confession, and I'm late already.'

Nellie Tomkin, a lapsed Methodist herself, sniffed her disapproval at such heathen ways. Then she dealt her stomach punch.

'A funny thing, Sarah. Well, at least it was a bit of an eye-opener to me not knowing the Peels like you do.' She paused, savouring the moment. 'I saw a photograph of your Patrick in my patient's bedroom.' The eyes, magnified to nightmare intensity by the thick lenses, picked holes in Sarah's suddenly quivering face.

'But you couldn't have. They – the Peels – they've never seen Patrick. Never set eyes on him.' The healthy colour drained from Sarah's round face, leaving the freckles standing out like brown measles. 'You must have made a mistake.'

'No mistake, lass, though when I asked Mrs Brandwood who the little lad was, she said it was her brother Willie who had been killed in the war. Naturally I kept my mouth shut, but it's a funny do all right. What do you make of it, Sarah?'

What Sarah made of it caused the ground to come up and hit her smack between her eyes. As the blood left her head, she crumpled at the knees, the grey sky with its scudding clouds dipping and wheeling around her.

And now the face bending over her, slapping her cheeks, loosening the top button of her coat, was filled with compassion, the evil glint in the eyes quite gone. With Sarah Batt's sudden and unexpected metamorphosis into a patient, Nurse Tomkin was all solicitude.

'It was only a little faint, lass. Come on now! Up's-a-daisy!'

Trembling and sick, Sarah felt the small woman pull her to a standing position, with arms as strong as steel ropes.

'Shock does that sometimes. Drains the blood from the brain. See, I'll walk home with you, lass.'

Nurse Tomkin was all sympathy now, but Sarah's refusal was immediate. 'Thank you. But I am all right.' She forced a wan smile. 'I don't know what came over me. It was likely going to Mass without a bite of breakfast.'

Pulling her hat down even farther over her face, she walked away without another word. She could not have thought of anything to say if she had tried.

When she got back to the cottage her mother was sitting in her chair by the fire, her head back and her eyes closed. Seeing her like that, defenceless, with the yellow tinge to her skin and so thin that her clothes hung loose, Sarah made up her mind. Now that Nurse Tomkin had guessed the secret so carefully guarded all these years, Westerley was as out of bounds as if it were a hundred miles away. Because when Miss Libby's baby came and Nurse Tomkin was in charge, the interfering busybody wouldn't be able to keep her mouth shut. Sarah knew it in her very bones, and she moaned despairingly. Because when Nurse Tomkin remarked on the uncanny likeness between Patrick and the dead Willie, then Miss Libby would know straight away. Miss Libby hadn't been in the back row when brains were dished out, and she would know . . . oh, dear sweet Mother of Jesus, she would know all right. She would remember Sarah's reluctance ever to speak about her son; she would remember the panic whenever she had tried to probe; she would ask that nice Doctor Harry to describe Patrick. And, worst of all, she would tell Mrs Peel.

When the dinner was over and Patrick had gone scrumping with his pals in the fields beyond the village, Sarah unburdened herself to her mother. 'I *know* Miss Libby, and when her suspicions get warmed up she'll ask the doctor to drive her out here to see for herself.' Sarah's broad face crumpled. 'Oh, Mam, when they see Patrick there won't be no turning back. Mrs Peel has never really cottoned on to the fact that her Willie is dead. She even prays that Libby will have a boy to take his place, never dreaming that her grandson is here, growing up so like his father that it *is* him born again.' Her mouth tightened. 'Oh, why couldn't Patrick have had red hair? Or black? Why couldn't he have looked like you or me dad? Why did he have to be the dead spittin' image?'

'They can't take him from us.' Mrs Batt winced and without thinking laid a hand over the pain in her back. 'There's no law. Is there?'

Sarah found she was having to look away from the suffering on her mother's face. It was time she came home to stay. Nurse Tomkin had been right. Bringing up a rough, highly strung boy was no task for an ailing, elderly woman. Sarah felt the tears spring to her eyes and blinked them quickly away. She knew what was wrong with her mother. Grandma Batt had gone the same way, wasting to the size of a little bird, with her skin that strange pale yellow colour. And her mother knew it too.

'Why don't you have the doctor, Mam?' Carefully she tried to keep her voice light. 'He could perhaps give you a rubbing bottle for your back . . . or something.'

'There's nowt wrong with me that a rubbing bottle can cure.' Mrs Batt straightened up in her chair, but the pain lay like a dark shadow on her face even as she tried to smile. 'You mustn't let nobody take that lad from you, Sarah. We've fetched him up and he's ours. And Miss Williams at the school says he will likely pass the scholarship to the grammar school.' The faded eyes shone with pride as she got up and pushed the kettle over the flames. 'I keep thinking how proud your dad would have been of him. He would have been so chuffed with a grandson at a grammar school.'

'Then it's all settled.' Sarah got two pots down from the dresser. 'I have to go back after tea, but I'm going to tell them that after next week I'm coming back. For good. I'll tell them a lie,' she said, keeping her back turned. 'I'll say that you aren't well enough to look after Patrick no more.'

'And no more I am.'

When Sarah turned and saw the resigned dulled expression on her mother's face she felt terror grip her tight, as if a hand had suddenly squeezed her heart. And when she left to catch the train back to Westerley in the late afternoon she knew she was making the journey for the very last time.

Eleven

'But it's ridiculous, Mother! Two of us living in a house this size. Eight bedrooms and only three of them slept in. Mrs Edwards has the whole of the top floor to herself, and now that Libby has gone, and Sarah . . .' Carrie's voice tailed away as she saw the ready tears spring to Ettie's eyes at the mention of Sarah's name.

'All these years,' Ettie mourned. 'After us taking her back when she had disgraced herself, then her leaving just when it suited her. Young girls don't know the meaning of the word loyalty these days.'

'But Sarah's first loyalty was to her own mother, and her son.' Carrie knew she was wasting her time, but went on just the same. 'And besides, Sarah wasn't exactly a young girl. She was twenty-seven, Mother. It was time she tried to make a life of her own.'

'But she doesn't seem to want even to *remember* us.' Ettie touched her eyes with her handkerchief. 'All these weeks and never a line.'

'Sarah never was much of a scholar,' Carrie reminded her. 'I doubt whether she could put a letter together. And she was proud. You know that. Anyway, what has Sarah leaving got to do with us staying on here?' Her normally serene expression was clouded with concern. 'If we lived in a smaller house I might be able to find another teaching position. At least I could *try*.'

She was still young, Carrie reminded herself. She could feel herself daily settling deeper into the role of unmarried daughter, fetching her mother's reading spectacles, going into town to change her mother's library books from Boots. Not bothering to wear her skirts at the fashionable length; playing the piano in the evenings, and getting on with her self-imposed task of covering the dining chairs with tapestry seats. Nothing ever seemed to happen, and yet, when she lay in bed, staring up into the darkness, it was as though she was holding herself still, expecting something to happen. Some exciting turn of events that would fill her days with more than the humdrum everyday running of a house. Not for the first time she wished she were more like Libby. What Libby wanted, Libby got. Not a vestige of martyrdom lingered in Libby's bones. Carrie frowned at the delicate stitching stretched over the frame on her lap. Was that what *she* was becoming? A martyr, sacrificing herself on the altar of her mother's possessiveness?

In a louder voice than she had intended she said, 'Well, I think we *should* look around for a smaller house. Perhaps one of the detached houses by the park. Nearer to town so that you could walk to the shops.'

Ettie held up a hand, a surprisingly strong hand as Carrie had so often realized when, helping her mother up to bed, the grip had tightened on her arm.

'The Peels have lived here for well over a hundred years. Westerley is part of your heritage, Carrie, and some day you will marry,' Ettie added vaguely, 'and your son will go on living here. When I'm gone,' she finished sadly.

'To have a son I need a man first.' Carrie ignored the wounded expression on her mother's face. 'I am nearly twenty-four, Mother. All my friends are married, with homes of their own. I'm the odd one out, Mother. My life is passing me by. I won't go on spending my days keeping this place going. It's too much.'

When Ettie's lower lip began its customary trembling, Carrie forced herself to look away, but she accepted the fact that for the time being anyway the question of the house must be shelved. There was something about the small quivering figure sitting opposite her that made her insides melt with love. Oliver Peel had made his wife what she was, and it was too late to change her now. Carrie turned her head as the telephone rang in the hall.

'That will be Libby,' she said. 'Are you coming to speak to her?' As she turned with a hand on the brass doorknob, she saw the way her mother was already levering herself up from her chair, an anticipatory expression in her dulled eyes. 'Oh, God help us,' Carrie whispered as she took the receiver from its hook, 'When a telephone call makes our day.'

'I waited until it was all over.' Harry's voice, ringing with triumph, came passionately alive over the wires. 'Libby went into labour last night, and it's a girl, a beautiful girl, weighing six pounds four ounces, with ten toes and ten fingers.' There was the break of emotion in his voice as he went on, 'A straightforward birth with no complications. Libby sends her love.'

'A girl,' Ettie said, coming into the hall and leaning against the wall as if for support. 'That is so strange. I was sure it would be a boy.'

'But aren't you *glad*?' Carrie, guiding her mother back to her chair by the fire, felt as deflated as a pricked balloon. 'Aren't you pleased you have a granddaughter, and that Libby's all right.' Going over to the sidetable she lifted the sherry decanter. 'We must celebrate, Mother! You are a grandmother, and I'm an aunt. Surely a little drink won't upset you? Oh, Mother, *please*! Please be glad. For Libby's sake let's be happy together. Please?'

'You know sherry always upsets my liver.' Ettie smoothed her skirt down over her knees. 'But *you* have one, dear.' She saw the expression in Carrie's eyes and added, 'Well, of course I'm glad that Libby has had her baby safely, especially after her being so ill with scarlet fever. But they can't very well call a girl Willie, can they?'

Carrie closed her eyes for a moment. 'I have to be more forceful. I have to be more firm. I have to get out of the house for at least part of the day.' She was muttering to herself as she poured a far larger sherry than the time of day warranted, tilting her head back and half draining the glass before she took it back to her chair. Her needlework waited for her, its soft colours as muted as the atmosphere in the large, chilly room.

Nurse Tomkin was in her element with a new-born baby to care for, especially one that resembled a skinned rabbit with twig-thin legs and a mauve tint to its mottled skin. Bustling

174

round the bedroom with her flat-footed walk, she felt a sensation of gloating power as she nurtured the secret beneath the white starched bib of her apron – the secret that could, at a word from her, throw the Peel family into a proper flummox.

The week after Sarah Batt had slid in a faint at her feet, Nurse Tomkin had answered a knock at the door of her cottage to find the red-haired young woman standing there, her face reflecting a terrible anxiety.

'It's about that photograph, Nurse Tomkin.' Sarah had blurted out the words, then followed her into the cottage, refusing to sit down, just standing there red and troubled, so troubled that even Nurse Tomkin's spiteful curiosity had taken second place to her genuine concern.

'You *knew* that photograph wasn't my Patrick. You knew that when you stopped me that day coming home from Mass.' Sarah's hands, chapped and swollen by a lifetime of service, twisted together as if she was working up an invisible lather. 'So what are you going to do about it, Nurse Tomkin? Are you going to tell them that I have a boy who is his father born again?' Sarah's voice rang with passionate pleading. 'Because if you do, then they'll come for him. And when they see him they'll try to make me realize how much they can do for him. They'll tell me they can send him to a good school. Then they'll give him their name.' The round eyes swam with tears. 'Mrs Peel has never believed that her son was dead. Never, not to this day. And when she realizes that Patrick was born on the very day that Willie died . . .' Sarah took a step forward and for a moment Nurse Tomkin thought she was going to go down on her knees.

It was the Irish Catholic in her, she decided. That red hair and her mother's maiden name of Mary O'Leary – no wonder this sturdy daughter of hers had let a man have his way with her, with all that superstitious passion smouldering behind those blue eyes.

'If you give me away then I will kill myself.' Sarah repeated this in a harsh whisper. 'If you tell the Peels what you have found out then I'll do away with meself. I swear by Our Lady. I will cut me throat with the bread knife. I will! I mean it!'

'Then who would bring your Patrick up?' Nurse Tomkin's voice was brisk. She didn't hold with histrionics. 'Don't get so worked up, Sarah. See here now. Come and sit down. I'll make us a pot of tea, then we can talk about this in a sensible fashion.'

'I don't want your tea, an' I don't feel like being sensible!' Sarah Batt had gone as white as on the day she fainted. 'I just want your promise that you won't say nothing. I want you to swear it on the Bible, Nurse Tomkin.' She lowered her voice a fraction. 'Me mother won't live all that much longer. I know what ails her as well as you do, and when she's gone then there will be just me and Patrick. For the first time just the two of us.' Sarah's blue eyes glared defiance. 'I'll work me fingers to the bone to keep him. I'll get up afore it's light and go and scrub out the shippens over at the farm, then work in the sculleries or the *fields*, if they will take me on.' Her body was shaking as violently as if she had St Vitus's Dance. 'I will catch the train into Preston and go on the streets if need be. But they will never have him, the Peels won't. Never! Never! Never!'

And now, as she faced Libby sitting up in bed, Nurse Tomkin felt the sensation of gloating power again. With a few words she could set ripples widening that would have repercussions far more exciting than any of the little hoohas she had managed to stir up in the whole of her long and industrious life.

Libby spoke fretfully. 'But you don't understand, Nurse! I don't *want* to feed my baby. My husband agrees with me that she will come on just as well on Cow and Gate. The very idea of breast-feeding disgusts me.'

Nurse Tomkin could scarcely believe it. Mentally she compared the lovely face with Sarah Batt's homely features suffused with anguish on the day she had come to the cottage. That had been real mother-love, a word this little madam didn't know the meaning of.

One who had, and one who had not.

In that moment of revelation, Nurse Tomkin made up her mind. Sarah Batt's secret would be safe with her. Not for anything was she going to hand the Peel family their grandson on a plate. They had enough. They didn't deserve that little lad with his corn yellow hair and his bright eyes that charmed one even when he was at his most impossible.

'Then if you won't give the baby her ten o'clock feed, you'd

176

be better off without your cup of coffee, Mrs Brandwood. Your liquid intake will have to be curtailed for the next few days at least.'

Nurse Tomkin nodded decisively, then with her starched apron crackling as if it had a life of its own she stalked out of the bedroom and down the stairs in search of her own morning cuppa and two or three Marie biscuits.

Carrie politely nibbled the sugar-coated biscuit held out for her approval by the dignified elderly assistant in the shop in the town's main shopping street.

'Yes, you can include a tin of those in our order,' she agreed, handing over the neatly written list. 'They are rather nice.'

Then, with a wicker basket over her arm containing nothing more than four library books, she walked down the street and turned the corner, making her way to the offices of the evening newspaper to hand in the announcement of the birth of Libby's and Harry's daughter.

It was a golden day, an autumn day with the trees in the cathedral grounds scattering brown and yellow leaves and the wind for once no more than a soft sigh. She was wearing a beige costume with a little Peter Pan fur collar and a small cloche hat to match pulled down over her forehead, hiding her fringe and leaving the side pieces of her dark hair framing her face.

The little outer office was crowded, and the young man behind the counter seemed to be taking a long time to pacify a flat-capped Irishman who was arguing loudly. Carrie heard the glass-fronted door open, then felt an embarassing blush stain her cheeks as a delighted voice hailed her.

'Miss Peel! Carrie! Yes, definitely Carrie! How are you? You remember me?'

It had been a long time but, oh yes, she remembered Tom Silver. She had followed his career in the papers, smiling at some of his more outrageous remarks in the reports of council meetings, and now that he was actually there, standing by her side, smiling, she realized that she had never forgotten him for a single moment.

There was a genuine note of pleasure in his voice as, after waiting for her to hand in the notice, he took her by the elbow and walked with her down the steps and into the sun-warmed street. Then, with the trams and the buses streaming out from the Boulevard, he told her that he could well be spared for half an hour at least and that she must come and have a drink with him in the big hotel on the corner.

When they were seated in an alcove with their drinks on the little round table in front of them, he turned towards her so that he could look full into her face. 'Now, Carrie Peel! Hello!'

She looked down at her hands, only shakily composed. There was something so intimately gentle in his look and his voice that for a wild uncontrolled moment she thought she was going to cry. She had been crying the last time they had met, the only time they had met, she remembered, and with an effort she pulled herself together.

'Libby has had a baby. I was putting the announcement in your paper.' She busied herself taking off her gloves and then stroked them into position on her lap. 'A girl. They are going to call her Isobel.'

'So that's Libby settled.' Tom smiled at her. 'And you? What are you doing with your life now, Carrie?'

There were shadows on her face, and he felt an illogical desire to stretch out a finger and smooth them away. When he had thought about Libby it had been with a sort of compassionate affection that filled him with remorse for treating her so cruelly that September evening in the lane outside the big house. Now *this* one – this one with Libby's face but with that difference in the eyes – had been put from his mind with conscious deliberation.

'There's nothing to tell about me,' she was saying softly. 'But you? *You* are a celebrity. I read about you in the paper. You're still fighting battles, aren't you, Mr Silver?'

'Tom,' he said, then nodded towards the group of men shaking hands as they met at the bar, pot-bellied men with florid complexions, drinking their beers before moving through into the dining room for expense-account lunches. 'I haven't joined *their* ranks, if that's what you mean, Carrie.'

'But the strike is over and forgotten,' she said guilelessly. 'The miners are back at work and my father's mill is flourishing, even in spite of foreign competition. What does a man like you *do* when the town is sliding back into prosperity?'

178

To her surprise he threw back his head and laughed out loud. 'Carrie! What have you been doing with yourself? Oh, aye, things might have been looking up for the likes of them.' He jerked his head towards the bar. 'Masons, Rotarians, pit and factory owners. They never need to worry where their next meal's coming from. Everything they do is put down to expenses, like those drinks they're enjoying now.' He shook his head at Carrie, then flicked the fur collar on her coat with an impatient finger. 'No, the hope for the future doesn't lie with the likes of them. The only hope for better working conditions is through the Labour movement, though I've been disappointed in the way some of the Labour councillors seem to lose contact with the very people they are put there to serve. We've a long way to go yet before we reach an ideal society. And if you do say too much in defence of the needy you're accused of having Bolshie leanings.'

'I do hope you don't lose your job again.' Carrie noticed how the green pullover underneath his dark jacket had been badly washed so that the wool had erupted into little bobbles. Hardly knowing what she was doing, she put out a hand and touched his sleeve. 'You've been victimized once. I know that because Libby told me. So isn't once enough? You can't fight the way things are, Tom.' She said his name shyly. 'There will always be those who have and those who have not.' She paused. 'Libby went through a stage of not wanting to accept that; she wanted everyone to have the same advantages she had, but she seems reconciled to the idea that a system like that could never be.'

'And you?'

'I have thought about it.' She was very serious as she tried hard to be honest. 'It's just that I can't see how it would *help* for me to become poor overnight. My father and grandfather worked hard, you know. So – I get on with what I have to do, and what I have to do at this moment is take care of Mother and Westerley. And I feel the same resentment as if we sat by an empty grate all day and I went out to the corner shop to get things on tick. Oh, I know I must be shocking you, because you'll be thinking one can't compare, but that's the way I am. I would never have chained myself to railings for the vote. I could never stand on a platform shouting the odds. I'm not

179

one of the intellectual elite. I wasn't even a very good teacher, nowhere as good as Libby.' She smiled. 'I go to church to evensong, and half the time I can't believe what I'm praying about. My ideas are half formed; they must be. All I want is to be happy, and to make the people I love happy too.' Her hand shook as she lifted the tall sherry glass and drained it. 'And now I must go, or Mother will work herself into a state wondering where I am.'

Tom stood with her on the pavement outside the newspaper office, and when she raised her face to the sun he thought her dark-fringed eyes had a bruised look about them, as though she had not been sleeping well. He realized he did not want to let her go.

He shuffled his feet. 'I'd like to see you again. Soon.' To his surprise his thinking was too confused to mention a definite date. 'May I telephone you?' Suddenly he took her hand in his. 'Oh, Carrie. I'm putting myself across badly, but there's so much I'd like to show you.' He was looking deep into her eyes as the tooting of a car horn made him turn quickly.

And afterwards Harry Brandwood was to tell Libby that Carrie had stared at him as if he were a complete and utter stranger.

'I took Carrie home,' he told Libby, eating his lunch with her in the overheated bedroom from a tray on his lap. 'It saved her catching the tram, but I don't think she was glad of the lift.' He chuckled. 'The way she was holding hands with that man – a man I don't recollect ever meeting, by the way – I got the feeling she would have preferred to ride on the tram just to be alone. She certainly hadn't much to say to me.'

'What was he like?' Libby put her knife and fork down, her face suddenly peaky above the pale blue bedjacket. 'Did she tell you his name?'

'No.' Harry went on eating, oblivious of the tension in the air. 'But he worked in the compositors' room of the evening paper. She told me that.' He chewed happily. 'A tall, thin chap with long hair. No hat. Not a man your father would have approved of, I can tell you that much.'

'Not a gentleman?' Libby's voice dripped ice.

'Well, hardly. Not at first glance.' Harry speared a piece of sliced carrot on his fork. 'I wasn't holding up the traffic, nothing like that, but Carrie didn't bring him over to introduce us. If you ask me, she was sorry I appeared like that.' Innocently he rubbed salt in the wound. 'She was looking very pretty. More animated that I've seen her for a long time. I've been worried about Carrie lately. She allows herself to be manipulated, and with all due respect, love, your mother can be a bit overpowering. In a helpless way, if you know what I mean.'

Libby, taking a tight hold on herself, controlled the urge to lean over and tip what was left of her husband's lunch onto his lap. The thought of Carrie holding hands with Tom Silver was making her feel sick. The binder round her swollen breasts was suddenly like a tourniquet, cutting off her life's blood, so that she found it hard to breathe. And there was nothing she could say. She was stuck there in bed for another ten days at least, with that bossy woman glaring at her through her thick spectacles, with the baby crying in that high plaintive wail. And now her sister was betraying her by meeting Tom Silver on the sly and being intimate enough with him to hold hands in the street.

The euphoria she had felt just after the birth had drained away, and now her immediate desire was to strike out at whoever was nearest – Harry, munching stolidly through his lunch, his face ruddy and contented.

'I've told Nurse Tomkin that you agree with me about stopping breast-feeding,' she said casually.

Harry, forgetting his natural good manners, spoke with his mouth full of food. 'You have *what*?'

'I sent her out for bottles and a tin of Cow and Gate. She's downstairs now mixing it up, or whatever you do with it.' She picked up her own fork and began to eat.

'But why?' Harry stared at her in amazement. 'Why did you tell her that? It isn't true, damn it. You have enough milk there to feed half a dozen babies.' Bewildered and angry he pointed to the corner where the baby whimpered in her frilly cot, making smacking noises with her tiny mouth. 'She needs your milk, Libby. Breast-feeding is your *duty*, it gives the baby an immunity to certain diseases, besides being easy and natural.' He touched the bolster case pinned round his wife's swollen breasts. 'Besides, your stomach will go flatter quicker if you breast-feed. It's your *duty*!' he said again. 'As a doctor I forbid you to send all that good milk back.'

'I'm not a cow, Harry.' Libby, assuaging the hurt he had inflicted on her by telling her about Carrie and Tom Silver, set her face into lines of determination. 'Besides, I refuse to be tied to feeding times. I refuse to be cajoled into the barbarity of it.'

'The barbarity of it?' Harry rose to his feet, holding the tray in front of him and looking round wildly for somewhere to put it. 'Good God, woman! What kind of talk is that? I look at you sometimes, Libby Brandwood, and I wonder what I see. There are women in this town who are having to feed their babies on pobs, bread soaked in milk, half diluted with water; women who have no milk in their breasts because they are undernourished. And you, fed on nothing but the best . . .' He jerked his head towards the beefsteak on his wife's plate. 'You deny your child what is hers by right!'

'I thought you had no time for undernourished women,' Libby said sweetly, seeing in her mind's eye Tom Silver holding Carrie's hand. 'I thought that women who couldn't pay your fees didn't even exist for you, Harry.'

He left the room angrily, hurt and bewildered. Libby pushed her own tray from her and, turning her head into the lace-edged pillows, wept like a child.

When, all unsuspecting, Carrie called that afternoon, still wearing the becoming costume with her hair curling over the brim of the tiny hat and her eyes shining as if a candle had been lit behind them, Libby, without preamble, said what she was bursting to say.

'Harry told me you were with Tom Silver this morning.'

Carrie blushed a deep rosy red. 'Yes. I told him about the baby, Libby, and he sent his kind regards.' She was so full of a strange sweet feeling that in her innocence she said entirely the wrong thing. 'He wants to see me again, Libby, and I think he means it. He's such a strange man, isn't he? He doesn't seem to have a thought in his head for himself. He's the sort of man who will kill himself worrying about other people. And he's had such a sad life. Did you know his wife was killed during the war, when he was in France at the front?'

Libby's breasts were throbbing, making her want to tear off

the tight binder. She could feel the wetness as the milk soaked through the layers of material, and she could still see Nurse Tomkin's look of disgust as the baby had refused to suck at the rubber teat of the bottle.

'Did he tell you he once asked me to go away with him?' Libby's voice was high through her physical discomfort. 'Did he tell you how he asked me to go into the house and pack my things? "I'll wait ten minutes," he said. Has he asked you to do the same?'

Carrie's head drooped low as all the bright promise of the morning disappeared. 'I didn't realize you had known him that well,' she said slowly. 'You never told me. Why didn't you, Libby?'

'I did try to warn you.' Libby winced and slid farther down in the bed. 'Tom Silver is an ambitious man, Carrie. He has proved that by getting himself onto the council so quickly. And that's only the first step. Westminster is where Mr Silver has set his sights, and if to get there means climbing on the shoulders of one of the town's most prominent families, then he will do just that.'

'But he – he didn't strike me as . . . I thought he . . .' Carrie's voice was a whisper.

'You or me. What does it matter?' Libby reached for a grape from the bunch at the side of her bed. 'To a man with his sights set high, one twin is as good as the other. He even mistook you for me the first time you met.'

Carrie's head drooped even farther, and Libby saw a single tear drop onto the folded gloves on her sister's lap.

'It's funny really, if you think about it,' she said, spitting a grape pip neatly into a cupped hand. 'I thought after your Mungo episode you'd be more worldly-wise.' Then, the damage done, her dark eyes softened as she looked with genuine fondness at her twin's bowed head. 'Have some grapes, love,' she said. 'And don't look so distressed; there are plenty more fish in the sea.'

'Like Roger Fish?' Carrie's expression was hard and un-Carrie-like as she made the feeble joke.

And as they laughed together, as they had always laughed together, Libby refused to see that her sister's eyes were now as bleak as moorland stones.

Twelve

The middle classes, Tom remembered wryly, as he rang the door bell set high in the big front door at Westerley, did not call uninvited. They telephoned or wrote a letter first to make sure it was convenient. He smoothed his wet hair away from his forehead and waited, surprised to find that his heartbeats had quickened. All he needed was a nosegay in one hand and a box of chocolates in the other, and the poem he had been struggling to write in his pocket.

It was a dark November evening, with the fields surrounding Westerley wreathed in damp, clinging mist. His jacket was beaded with droplets as if he had walked through a shower of rain. He must be mad, he told himself. He rang the bell again, then wished he hadn't as the door opened. Carrie was standing there, dressed in something long, blue and flowing, looking even more beautiful than he remembered.

'Mr Silver! Tom!' Her voice was high as she stared at him in amazement. 'Come in! Oh, what a dreadful night! You look so cold.'

Leading the way into the big lounge, she told him to sit down in a wing chair at right angles to the fire roaring up the wide chimney and throwing out a heat that made his face burn. 'Mother is upstairs, and Mrs Edwards has gone to the pictures, but I'll get you a hot drink. Or would you perhaps like something stronger?'

'A cup of tea would be very welcome.' Tom's eyes took in the large room, the thick carpet, the heavy mahogany furniture, the chintz-covered chesterfield and the long velvet curtains shutting out the winter.

'You were going to bed.' He nodded at Carrie's housecoat

and beaded slippers. 'I've come at an inconvenient time. You haven't been ill, have you?'

'I often wear this thing after dinner,' Carrie explained gently, realizing with a pang of tenderness that he thought she was wearing her dressing gown. 'You just sit there and get warm. I won't be a minute.'

Then, with flushed face and hands that surprised her by their trembling, she stood in the kitchen willing the kettle to boil.

When Tom was balancing a fluted cup and saucer on a bony knee, he suddenly said, 'My late wife's mother died last week.'

Carrie, confused, mumbled regrets and wondered what he was leading up to.

He took a sip of the tea, then put the cup carefully back in its saucer. 'No, don't say anything. She was old and tired and her time had come. But one of the last things she did was to ask the owner of her house if I might be allowed to take it on. The rent is five shillings a week, but it has two up and two down, and an outside lavatory in a tiny yard. A palace compared to the place I've been living in.' He grinned. 'So you see sitting before you a man with his own house. 'Would you say that makes me into a man worth knowing, Carrie?'

'Where is it?' Carrie looked away from the unspoken message in his dark eyes.

He told her and she saw, in her mind's eye, the district with its warren of short streets, and endless rows of chimney pots, the doors opening straight onto the pavement. She nodded. 'It's up by the infirmary, isn't it?'

'It's nearly a hundred years old.' Tom sat forward in his chair, the cup and saucer tilting so precariously that she got up and brought a small table and placed it in front of him.

'There. I should have done that before. Won't you mind living alone?'

She thought he was going to take her hand so she moved quickly back to her own chair, picked up her cup and then set it down again when she saw that it trembled in her grasp. The dark eyes never left her face.

'I've lived alone for many years and never minded till now.'

There was no mistaking the expression in his eyes, and even as her body responded Carrie was filled with resentment and

185

anger. She felt like weeping, and if she wept this would be the third time she had met this man and felt her insides dissolve into tears.

'I think I have fallen in love with you,' he said slowly. 'It's unbelievable, and yet it's true. I think I loved you from the time I found you walking down the road on the afternoon of your father's funeral.' His voice was so low she could barely catch what he was saying. 'You need a man to take care of you, Carrie. You're so lonely it makes me want to put my arms round you and hold you safe.' His glance swept the room. 'You have all this, and yet you need so much more. Am I right?'

He made no move towards her, and yet when she shrank back onto the cushions it was as if she were warding off a physical attack. When she spoke her voice startled him with its harshness.

'Are you asking me to go away with you, Tom Silver? Are you saying that you'll give me ten minutes to go upstairs and pack my things?' She lifted her chin. 'Like you asked my sister? Only, according to Libby, you waited outside in the cold for her. Now you've moved on a step and can wait by the fire.' She gave a short laugh. 'You made a mistake when you decided that one sister was as good as the other. Libby and I are twins, Mr Silver, and twins tell each other everything. Libby warned me what to expect, but even so I'm surprised at your temerity and your haste.'

Her heart was knocking wildly against her ribs. It wasn't really in her to hurt and to shock, but her feelings were no longer her own. She had thought he had just come to *see* her – that would have been enough – but now, by his impetuous talk of love, he had brought Libby's words to mind as clearly as if she were there in the room laughing at him.

'We're two people, though, Libby and I. You can't just take up with one where you left off with the other. You'll have to find some other way to further your political ambitions.'

Tom stared at her and then with a sudden movement he jumped to his feet, knocking over the little table and crashing the delicate cup and saucer onto the tiled hearth so that they smashed into smithereens. He came over to her quickly and knelt beside her.

'I'm not a gentleman, Carrie, so there's nothing to stop me

from telling you the truth. I won't imitate Douglas Fairbanks and rush from the house in a welter of misunderstandings. I want you, and I'm going to fight for you, and you must listen to me. Carrie! Look at me!.'

But she found she could not lift her head. She could only stare down at the carpet, until she felt his fingers wrenching her chin round so that she was forced to look up into his face.

'What I did to Libby was cruel and despicable, I admit it. But I didn't do it because of her money or connections. In fact, I don't really know why I did it, except that when I saw this house and remembered my own wretched room – when I thought of her doctor friend waiting for her and remembered how alone I was – I wanted to hurt her. I saw she had a thing about me, and just then I wanted to put her into an impossible position. And later I was too ashamed to get in touch with her and apologize – I was afraid of making things worse.' He paused for a moment, then went on urgently. 'Carrie, I like Libby a lot, but you must believe me when I say I never loved her, and I never seriously wanted her to come away with me – for ambition or any other reason. Please believe me, Carrie!'

He sat down beside Carrie and drew her stiff, resisting body into his arms. He could feel her gradually relaxing as he held her close. Then his hand was on her neck beneath the soft weight of her hair, and his mouth, delicate at first, trailed its sweetness down her cheeks lingering at the corners of her mouth until with a groan he pulled her close, into a kiss which deepened as her lips parted and they clung together, their bodies fusing as if they were one person.

When at last he raised his head he was seeing, not the cosy overfurnished room with its heavy drapings, the high-banked fire striking sparks off the brasses, and the silver photograph frames on the side tables, but the little back living room of the house he had just left. A room with a black fireplace with a cut steel fender, a slopstone beneath the window, in a street where women gossiped on doorsteps and children played their chanting games with a rope stretched across the cobbles.

He could never . . . he must never . . . he had so little to give, and yet as he bent his head to kiss her again and felt her response, he whispered, 'Carrie . . . oh, Carrie, my love. I love you so much. I can't let you go.'

'You must *never* let me go.' The wide sleeves of the silken wrap fell away from her bare arms as they crept round his neck, holding him even closer. 'I won't *let* you let me go.' She was half smiling, half weeping. 'I don't know you, and yet I think I'm in love too. How can that be?' Her voice came muffled from his shoulder. 'But don't put me on a pedestal, Tom. I – oh, what would you say if I told you I lost my teaching job because I was found in the arms of a fellow teacher? That he's married, and for the whole of last summer I used to meet him. In a deserted summer house.' She raised her head and he saw that her face was scarlet. 'But we didn't – that is, we never –'

'Made love properly?' He was smiling a teasing smile. 'Oh, Carrie, love. I'm not one of those men who think they have always the right to be the first. What will happen between you and me isn't written yet, but when it is it'll be on a blank page with no ghosts to look over our shoulders.'

Then he closed his eyes. What was he doing? What was he promising when he had nothing to promise? He had wanted to *see* her, that was all. The urgency of his need to see her had wiped out any practicalities; he had never intended to touch her. But holding her close he knew that he was committed to loving this lovely, lovely girl for ever.

He was so thin that Carrie could feel his bones through the tweed jacket. His lips when he kissed her were firm, not soft and fleshy as Mungo's had been. She was filled with such tenderness, such compassion for his need of her that she thought she would die of it. Carrie stirred in his arms, wanting nothing more than that the clock on the mantelpiece would stop its ticking; that time would stand still, with nothing of the outside world intruding. She was not Libby, working out ways and means. Her waiting time was over, and somehow they would find a way to be together.

Neither of them heard the door click open. At Ettie's voice Carrie looked up, staring at her mother with dream-dazed eyes.

'Mother!' Moving from the circle of Tom's arms but still holding onto his hand, Carrie looked neither guilty nor surprised. 'This is Tom Silver.'

As Tom got to his feet Ettie came forward into the room, ignoring his outstretched hand. 'I thought I heard voices . . .' She walked unsteadily to the winged chair and lowered herself into it, pulling the folds of her wrap round her knees, her face a study of disbelief and dismay. 'I don't think we have met before, Mr – Mr Silver?'

His face, Carrie saw, looked younger, more vulnerable. Gone was the teasing mockery. It was as though the past half hour had transformed him, leaving a dignity she had never seen before.

'I wish we hadn't met like this, Mrs Peel.' Gently he disengaged Carrie's clinging hand. 'I wanted to court your daughter properly, to meet her with your approval. It must seem – it must be a shock – ' He broke off as the small woman watching him clutched her heart, starting to breathe quickly so that he saw the rise and fall of the lace cascading in frills down her bodice.

'Will you please go, Mr Silver?' Ettie leaned back and closed her eyes. 'And Carrie. My tablets. They are on my bedside table. Will you fetch them, please?'

'I'm sorry,' he said again, but Ettie's face wore its shut-in waxen look, the ploy she always used when anything unpleasant occurred, the defence she had always put up when Oliver had made one of his scenes.

Carrie shook her head at Tom, moving towards the door, her eyes pleading with him to follow her.

In the hall he reached for her again. 'Is she ill?' He jerked his head towards the closed door. 'What is it? Her heart?'

Carrie put a hand to his cheek and answered him sadly. 'Mother will not face up to things.' Her voice hardened. 'My father made her like this. When she is scared she moves into illness. Oh, why did she have to come downstairs just now?'

'Will it make any difference?'

'To us?' I don't know,' she said dully.

'Carrie?' Ettie's voice floated through the closed door in a long, plaintive wail. 'Are you there?'

'Coming, Mother.'

Resolutely she put him from her. 'You must go now. I have to see to her.'

Fiercely he pulled her close for a last embrace, so close that she could feel his ribs pressing against her. 'When will I see you again?'

'Soon.'

'Tomorrow? Can I come again tomorrow?'

Then, even as he let himself out of the house, she was running upstairs. And when Tom stepped outside into the cold seeping fog of the November evening it felt as if the heavy clang of the big front door had shut out all that was warm and comfortable in his life.

Pulling up the collar of his jacket and shoving his hands deep in his pockets, Tom walked back down the winding lane with the trees on either side pointing winter-bare branches to the dark sky. He would catch the tram into town, and maybe even another tram out to the street where he now lived. Back to a house that had seemed like a palace but was now only a place to live. And he had thought . . . he had even dared to dream . . . but in that long, disquieting stare, Oliver Peel's widow had crumbled his dreams to dust.

He started to run, swinging himself aboard the tram with a recklessness that brought a shouted warning to the conductor's lips.

The tablets were washed down with a tumbler of water held in Ettie's shaking hand. Her lips had a strange blue tinge to them, and Carrie watched her anxiously.

Was she genuinely ill? She certainly looked dreadful, with her nose all pinched, and a hectic spot of scarlet burning on her cheeks. Or was that the fire? Carrie glanced at the leaping flames suspiciously. Before she left the room the fire had been deadened to a red glow, and yet now it was as though someone had put the poker to it, loosening the banked slack and the huge slab of coal, so that the flames roared upward again. Could her mother, in the middle of what appeared to be a genuine attack, have leaned forward, picked up the heavy brass-handled poker and tended the fire?

'Mother?' She took the tumbler from Ettie's hand. 'Don't you think you ought to go back upstairs? I'll follow you when I've done this.' Kneeling down she swept the shattered cup and saucer onto the brass fire shovel.

'*He* did that.' It was more of a statement than a question. The pupils of Ettie's eyes seemed to have grown, almost obliterating the blue, as she stared with pointed emphasis at

Carrie's housecoat. 'Did you know he was coming?' Was that why you helped me upstairs to my room straight after dinner, Carrie?'

'Oh, Mother!' Carrie felt her happiness dissolve. 'How can you think that?'

'How can I *not* think that?' Ettie's mouth worked itself into an ugly shape. 'It seems to me that even losing your job through – through carrying on with a man in school hours has not taught you a lesson. But I never thought you were so hard up for a man that you would allow someone of his type to make love to you. Have you no shame? No pride?'

'What do you mean, someone of his *type*?' Carrie's voice was dangerously quiet. She pulled at the tied belt of the housecoat, feeling as if her mother had caught her stark naked. 'Tom Silver is a good man. He is a councillor. He has a house of his own, and a job.' She heard herself justifying Tom's status and despised herself.

'He is common.' Ettie's face was a mask of bitterness. 'He talks in a common voice, and he wears a common suit. His hair needs cutting, and his shirt reminded me of a pyjama jacket. And he wants to *court* you. Oh, my God! What sort of an expression is that?' She glanced at the broken pieces of china on the small brass shovel still held in Carrie's hands. 'No wonder he broke them. Did he pour his tea into the saucer and blow on it first before drinking it?'

Putting down the shovel on the hearth Carrie went to the far end of the tiled fireplace and laid her head against the mantelpiece. 'Don't humiliate me, Mother. Why are you trying to hurt me?'

Ettie did not answer. Her throat was choked with fear, the fear that had caught at it when she had opened the door and seen the two lovers in each other's arms. For they *were* lovers, in the purest sense of the word. When their faces had turned towards her the surprise had been there right enough, but that was all – no guilt or shame. When he had stood up, still holding onto Carrie's hand, there had been a dignity about the tall, thin man, a steadiness in the dark eyes – and in that one moment she had known. This was the man who would take Carrie away from her. He was a working man; not a weaver with cotton fluff in his hair, nor a miner with dirt on his face,

191

but a working man all the same. He would, to use his own working-class phraseology, *court* Carrie and then take her away.

Then there would be no one in the big house but herself. No husband, no daughters, no Sarah, just herself growing older alone. The sudden pain as Ettie made the familiar gesture of clutching her heart was real this time. It was like a knife being slowly twisted beneath her ribs.

Carrie raised her head, staring down into the fire. 'I am going to marry him, Mother. He hasn't asked me yet, but when he does I am going to say yes. And no one is going to talk me out of it. Not you, not Libby. Nobody!'

The pain was doubling Ettie over, she was gasping for breath – it was filling her chest with fire, and the sound she made brought Carrie to her knees, her face a mask of shock as she saw the beads of perspiration standing out on her mother's forehead.

'I'll get Harry! Mother! Stay still. Oh, please, Mother! Don't die!'

She ran from the room, tripping over her long silken skirts in her haste. Unhooking the telephone receiver, she prayed he would be there.

'It's real!' she told the reassuring voice of her brother-in-law. 'Oh, Harry, come quickly. This time it's real!'

'She has what Harry calls a dry pleurisy.'

When Carrie went to meet Tom four days later after pleading with him on the telephone to stay away from Westerley, her heart was wrenched with a pain she had never thought she would be able to bear.

'Libby is with her now, but I can't stay. She won't have a day nurse, Tom, and she has only agreed to a night nurse because Harry insisted.' She took his arm as naturally as if they were husband and wife, and he steered her towards the same restaurant where once Libby had jumped up from the table by the window and rushed out into the street.

'It's too cold to stand talking outside, love.' He looked round at the crowded upstairs room filled with chattering women, and smiled. 'I never thought the day would come when I would join this lot on a Saturday afternoon. Do they always make this much noise?'

There were no gaps to fill, no explanations of how they knew that their relationship had progressed from a shy awareness of each other to this sweet intimacy. He felt his chest rise in a great sigh of relief as he saw his own love mirrored in her eyes. He stared down through the window to a crowded street where an early snow powdered the pavement, only to be blown away in an instant by the piercing wind.

'I can't see you for a while. Not until Mother is a lot better.' Their eyes were clinging, their hands entwined across the white tablecloth. 'And you mustn't come to the house. Harry says she must be kept calm.' Carrie closed her eyes for a moment as she felt his fingers caressing the throbbing pulse at her wrist. 'She has to sleep propped up on pillows, and she hears everything. There is no way I could ask you to the house without her knowing.'

'Was I so much of a shock to her, then?' The fingers stopped their caressing as the waitress, balancing the tray on a jutting hip, placed a teapot, milk jug, sugar bowl and two cups and saucers on the table in front of Carrie. 'Was it the shock of meeting me that made your mother ill?'

Busying herself with the tea she turned an unhappy face towards him. 'It didn't help,' she said with characteristic truthfulness. 'But she had been feeling ill for a long time, and this coughing doesn't help her heart. Mother has always been delicate.'

'And when she is better?' Tom was stirring sugar into his tea with a face set and cold. 'Will she welcome me into the family *then*, Carrie?' His dark eyes twinkled. 'You know we'll be getting married?'

Not 'Will you marry me?' Just 'We'll be getting married.' Carrie pressed her lips together in the gesture that even as a child had always meant she was hugging her happiness to herself. Conditioned by her twin's stronger personality she was content to be led, and here for the first time in her life was a man who was prepared to do the leading.

'And the next time you can get away we'll go and see the house.' Tom looked at her with love. 'Shall we say tomorrow afternoon?'

Carrie remembered that Libby and Harry were bringing the baby to show Ettie, and she smiled. 'Tomorrow afternoon,' she agreed, 'but you'll have to meet me at the end of the lane. It's too soon yet to upset Mother again. You don't mind, do you, Tom?'

But he had minded. Carrie knew that. This wasn't a man prepared to do his courting on the sly, as if they were both in their teens and avoiding the hostile reaction of a possessive parent. This wasn't Mungo willing to meet her in a secret place, their love a furtive thing to be hidden from the world.

As she hurried home, preparing herself for the inevitable questions and petulant suspicions, Carrie sent up a silent prayer of thanks that the telephone calls, the harassment from Mungo had stopped. Now she could wipe the memory of that long hot summer from her mind as if it had never existed. What lay in front of her was a future so full of shining promise that as she walked from the tram it seemed that her feet scarcely touch the ground.

'Oh, by the way, Beatrice McDermot came to see me last week.' Libby, very smart in a small fur toque matching the coat thrown casually over a chair, smiled at her sister.

Carrie turned pale. 'Mungo's wife came to see *you*? For heaven's sake, why?'

The baby was upstairs being shown off to her grandmother by a doting Harry, and the two girls were alone in the lounge, Carrie feverishly trying to get away and Libby sitting complacently in the middle of the massive chesterfield, her fingers twisting a long rope of amber beads into a knot.

'Why shouldn't she come and see me? We had met, remember? That day Harry took me to Mungo's house on an errand of mercy. To warn him that Father was on the warpath.'

Libby felt a pang of guilt as she saw the way the happiness had faded from Carrie's face. Harry had said that of course Carrie must go out, that something must be done to give his sister-in-law more freedom, and Libby had agreed. Until she had guessed where Carrie was going, whom she was meeting, and then the urge to hurt, to wound and destroy had taken over.

'There's nothing sinister about it. Heavens, Carrie, to look at your face anyone would think the woman had come to make trouble.' Libby stopped fiddling with the beads and smiled. 'It was about the boy. Edwin. His mother feels now that the time has come for him to have more schooling than she is able to give him, and she remembered that I had suggested the same. So – I've talked it over with Harry, and Mungo will drop the boy off at my house three mornings a week, then his wife will pick him up at lunchtime. I'll try to teach him to read.' She spread her hands wide. 'I *had* to find something to do, and this was a heaven-sent opportunity. I'm a trained teacher, Carrie. A *good* teacher. I'm not content merely to stay at home, like you. I'd go stark raving mad!'

Carrie let that pass. Closing the door, and closing her mind to the image of Tom waiting in the drifting winter rain outside, she tried to keep her voice low and reasonable.

'But why Mungo's son? Just when I'd thought all that was behind me, why him?' Her brown eyes clouded with anxiety. 'You must have known it was an insensitive thing to do at the very least. You must have, Libby.'

'Mrs McDermot doesn't know about you and her husband, does she?'

Carrie moved her body as if trying to avoid something. 'I pray she never knows. I don't know what Mungo told her when he lost his job, but for all his faults he wouldn't involve me. He wasn't that bad.'

'Well then?' Libby's tone considered the matter settled. 'Now you had better go if you don't want to keep him waiting. Where is it Mother thinks you're going this time?'

They stared at each other in an agony of bewildered frustration. Two identical faces; two minds with conflicting desires. Far more than ordinary sisters, the twins had power to hurt one another, but not without sharing the pain. Now, each striving for her own independence, they faced each other like jousting knights, their faces full of what, to the uninitiated, would have seemed like mutual dislike.

They met, Carrie and Tom, whenever they could snatch a few precious moments together during that long, hard winter. The unemployment figures were rising daily, the outlying factories and mines were closing down one after the other, and some of Tom's own union members were working a three-day week. His evenings were spent at one committee meeting after another, his weekends sitting at the roll-top desk in the tiny living room of his new house. He became accustomed to the regular knock at his door, heralding a neighbour with a form for him to fill in, or a query about where to apply when the rent man threatened a family with eviction. He went to a house where he saw a table spread with newspapers, and six children standing round it dipping crusts of bread into a tin of condensed milk set in the middle. He heard a widow sob on his doorstep after queueing for two hours down at the labour exchange, only to be told there was no work for her, no work of any kind. He fought with his own management to keep his men on full-time, even when he realized that short-time would soon be inevitable. Clever boys won scholarships to the grammar school and he pleaded with their parents to let them go somehow, only to discover they were forced to leave after one term to work in stop-gap jobs which brought in the few shillings needed to keep the rest of the family in bare necessities.

At one time he was almost persuaded to seek Labour nomination, but his common sense came to his rescue. He was not educated enough to put the workers' case across in a dispassionate manner, and he knew it. His temper was too short, and his reasoning too emotional.

'My place is here,' he told Carrie. 'Up here in the north we are going into the worst depression the country has ever known.'

One February evening Carrie was helping him to strip the wallpaper from the tiny front bedroom of the terraced house.

'Your mother must be well enough by now to accept the truth about us,' Tom urged her. His dark eyes twinkled. 'Why don't I come and present myself as a suitor? I'll wear my best suit and tell her that I have a job which is as permanent as any job can be at this time. I'll explain to her that I have a house, and that – most important – I intend to spend the rest of my life caring for you.'

He threw down the knife he was holding so that it dropped

with a clatter on the bare boards, took away the brush she was using to paint the old wallpaper with water, then kissed her.

'Carrie! I love you so much, and I want you so much. We are neither of us children playing at getting to know each other. You must know we can't go on like this. The neighbours must see you coming and going; even they would never believe that our relationship hasn't progressed much beyond a sweet companionship.'

He steered her towards the bed. 'Carrie – I want to marry you now. Tomorrow. Today. Not at some distant time when your mother has decided to come to terms with the thought of me.' Pulling her down beside him, he began to kiss the soft hollow of her neck, his lips tracing the pulse beating there, so that her whole body curved into his, and she sighed with pleasure.

They had been stripping the paper by the light of two candles, one set in a holder on the small cane bedside table, and the other flickering from a saucer on top of the rickety stepladder. Tom put out a hand and snuffed the nearest candle at exactly the same time as the second one died, leaving the room bathed in the soft light from the lamp standard outside in the street.

'I love you . . . love you . . .' His voice was very gentle as he began to unbutton the front of the heavy coat she had kept on in the damp chill of the little bedroom.

Carrie's voice was a whisper. 'Oh, Tom . . . this is the first time for me.' Her voice grew stronger. 'But I want to belong to you – even if – even if we can't be married for a long time. I want you to, but I can't help feeling it's wrong . . . I'm not – not a prude or anything, but suppose . . . ? Oh, Tom, I'm afraid that this might – that something – that –'

'I'll take care of you.' His hands were unfastening the buttons of her dress. 'Pull this blanket over us. I don't want you to catch cold. See, you're shivering.'

And now she was helping him, sitting up so that he could pull the dress over her head, and he was whispering as he carressed her. When he took her slowly and carefully she felt tears on her face.

After it was over they lay for a long time, entwined in a silence so deep it felt as if the world had stopped turning. Then at last Carrie tangled her fingers in his hair and he lifted his head to stare deeply into her eyes.

'That really surprised me,' she told him, and he laughed softly.

'Oh, but that was just a practice run,' he answered solemnly, and in the yellow light she saw that his own eyes were bright with tears.

He insisted on helping her to dress, grinning as his fingers fumbled with the suspenders anchoring her silk stockings.

'You won't wake in the night and wish this had never happened, will you, love?' His voice was suddenly serious. 'You won't hate me for this, will you, sweetheart?'

Her answer was to take his face in her hands and kiss him with small soft wifely kisses. 'Never. I won't be afraid again. And we *will* be married, but that'll be just a formality, because I feel married to you now.'

When they went out into the street the lamps were like oranges floating in a sea of fog. He insisted on coming with her on the tram, where they sat together, fingers closely entwined, both of them lost and floundering in a haze of love.

Thirteen

Mungo McDermot was late dropping the boy off at Libby's house that morning. Harry was already in his surgery, Nurse Tomkin was settling the baby upstairs, and Libby, fretting behind the lace curtains, frowned as she saw the droop-shouldered man turn into the gate a full twenty minutes past his usual time.

The bitterly cold February had been followed by a March beset with gale-force winds, and as a wind-blown Mungo handed over his charge, Libby's annoyance at his unpunctuality sharpened her voice. 'You're going to be late for school, Mr McDermot.'

Then, as she drew the small peak-faced boy into the hall, she gave a gasp of dismay. 'Oh, your face! What have you done to your face, Mr McDermot? Your eye looks terrible. Would you like me to ask the doctor to take a look at it? You can't go to school with a swelling like that. It needs attention.'

But Mungo was already turning away. 'I'm not going to school this morning.' He took a few wavering steps back down the path. 'I got up in the night in the dark and bumped into a door. It's nothing.'

'Well then.' Libby closed the door reluctantly and held out her hand for her pupil's overcoat, her heart aching with pity as she stared down at the small, pinched face, the eyes which she knew saw and understood everything but gave nothing away.

'She hits him,' she remembered Carrie saying. 'Mungo's wife drinks, and when she drinks too much she hits him, knowing that the boy can't hear. Sometimes he comes to school with his face all bruised.'

'We'll start where we left off yesterday,' she said, speaking

199

slowly, almost miming the words. Leading the boy into the dining room she positioned herself opposite him so that he could see every slight movement of her lips. 'What is that?' With a finger she pointed to a picture of a cat. 'C . . . cat.' Edwin's lips pouted in an exaggerated fashion, as he struggled to speak the simple word which came out as an expressionless croak.

'Well done!' Libby took his small hand in her own, holding it against her mouth as she repeated the word. 'Cat. Cat.'

Usually this procedure made the boy's intelligent eyes crinkle into amusement, but this morning his face remained solemn and set, as if part of him was walking away with his father down the path, as if somewhere in his silent world he suffered in a completely adult way for the man who allowed his wife to scream and rage and smash out at him with whatever came to hand.

Libby shuddered. How much did he know, this little boy, whose mind, she was discovering, was a prisoner in a brain never stimulated by sound? There was an adult awareness in his eyes that made her want to put her arms round him in comfort. But at the moment she was his teacher, and he was her pupil, and what mattered was the unlocking of his mind.

'Now this.' She pointed to the picture of a house, a difficult one this time, and taking his small hand in her own opened her lips to the rounded vowel, then pursed them to the consonant. 'House . . . house . . . house.'

At twelve o'clock, the time when Beatrice should have called to pick up her son, the hour came and went. Edwin lunched with Harry and Libby, sitting at the table between them, silent and stolid, picking at his food, pathetically oblivious to the conversation going on above his bowed head.

'There's something wrong.' Libby crumbled the bread on her sideplate, her appetite gone. 'I'll take him home myself. It's Nurse Tomkin's afternoon off, but she'll see to the baby if I ask her.'

'It's time Nurse went back to her own village, anyway.' Harry's red face gave nothing of his true feelings away. If the boy couldn't hear, he could see, and from the look of him he'd had his fill of grown-up battles for a while. 'You know how I feel.'

'I'll take him now.' Ignoring her husband's remark, Libby got up from the table and touching Edwin's arm propelled him towards the door.

'I'll run him back,' Harry offered, but she shook her head.

'I need to get out of the house,' she said, leaving Harry sitting at the table with a troubled expression darkening his pleasant face.

Used to silence, the small boy trotted along at her side, down the wide road, past the park, his cap pulled low over his forehead and his hands thrust deep into the pockets of his tweed overcoat. Libby's coat with its high fur collar kept her neck warm, but left her legs prey to the cold, blustery wind. The curling feather on her cloche hat blew across her face, gently stroking her lipstick, and now and again she pushed it back with an impatient hand.

When they reached the house she saw that the big front door was wide open. As Edwin turned the knob on the vestibule door and stepped inside, she stood irresolute, wanting to hand him over properly before leaving.

Feeling embarrassed and a little silly, she called out, 'Mrs McDermot? It's me, Mrs Brandwood. I've brought Edwin back. Is anyone there?'

Edwin turned a questioning face up to her as Libby, making up her mind, pushed him in front of her down the narrow lobby and into the living room at the back of the house. 'Mrs McDermot?' she called out again, then the words tailed away into an awful silence as she stared down at the man lying face downwards on the carpet, a pool of blood seeping from a gash on his head and running down his white starched collar.

The silence was broken horribly by the low gutteral sounds coming from Edwin's mouth. Harsh, animal-like noises, all his careful tuition forgotten as he communicated in the only way he knew.

Before Libby could move he was down on his knees, his fingers bloodied as they touched his father's hair, his face a mask of horror as he stared over to where his mother crouched in a corner, her fat face working convulsively, a breadknife clutched in her hand.

Beatrice McDermot was drunk. As the woman pulled herself up slowly by the edge of a chair, Libby moved to pull the boy away from the still figure on the floor. 'Upstairs!' She mouthed the word, her face on a level with Edwin's staring eyes. 'Go upstairs! Now!'

Then as he obeyed, Libby ran back down the lobby, her legs turned to water, to throw herself into the surprised arms of a sober-coated man letting himself out of the house next door.

'Have you got a telephone?' She gripped the lapels of his coat, staring wildly into the astonished face beneath the bowler hat. 'Yes? Oh, thank God! Telephone for the police! Quickly! There's been a murder next door.'

She wanted to run. All she wanted to do was to run as fast as she could, away from the street, to put as much distance as possible between her and the scene she had left. But there was the boy . . . With her hands held to her trembling mouth Libby recalled the sodden, drunken expression on Beatrice McDermot's bloated face, the insane gloating in the small eyes as she had advanced towards her son with the knife held in her hand.

With her heart beating like a tomtom, choking her throat with its pounding, Libby forced herself to turn and go back into the house, hearing the ruby-red panels of glass in the vestibule door shiver in protest as it swung to behind her.

With a small sigh of thankfulness she saw that Beatrice was still in the living room, too stupefied by drink to climb the stairs after her son.

'Give that knife to me!' Libby advanced towards her, her teacher's voice ringing out so clear that even in her terror its calmness surprised her. 'Mrs McDermot! Give that knife to me. Now! At once!'

The fat jowls quivered, and the small eyes, sunk into cushions of fat, narrowed into evil slits, but the knife dropped to the floor.

Keeping her eyes on the swaying, whimpering woman, Libby picked up the knife and put it on the sideboard. 'Now we will wait for the police to come,' she said. Beatrice slid to the floor again, wailing and weeping, rocking herself backwards and forwards, her short arms folded round her body. Libby stood quite still, willing away the next ten minutes, the longest minutes she had ever experienced.

When Libby heard a car draw up outside she closed her eyes

for a moment in a fervent prayer of thanks. Now it was all over. The police would take the wailing woman away; they would take the man that had been her husband away, and Libby could go home. And she would take the boy with her. Harry would know what to do next. Oh, Harry . . . At that moment she knew she would have given anything to see his square-set body coming through the door, his face full of concern as he held out his arms to her.

'*She* did it!' Libby's eyes flew wide as Beatrice struggled to her feet and faced the two policemen coming in through the door, one in uniform and the other in plain clothes. 'She's been carrying on with my husband, and when I threatened to tell *her* husband she went for me with a knife.' She pointed to the knife on the sideboard. 'There it is!' She took an unsteady step forwards. 'It was me she went for, but he got in the way.'

Libby shook her head from side to side. It wasn't possible that the drunken woman could be saying such things. Beatrice was paralytic with drink. For the past fifteen minutes she had been moaning incoherently to herself, crouched on the floor, and yet now her voice held the ring of truth as she pointed to Mungo's body.

Then, before anyone could move, Beatrice lurched across and with the toe of her shoe turned her husband's dead body over so that his face, the eyes wide open, the skin a dirty grey, presented itself to them in all its horror.

'See!' Beatrice pounced. 'Here's her photograph! She was trying to snatch it from him when I found them together. See! See for yourself!'

And as Libby looked, she saw Carrie's face staring at her from the photograph held in Beatrice's outstretched hand. Carrie, before her hair had been cut, smiling into the camera, wearing the white blouse she had pin-tucked herself, her dark eyes steady in the sweet serenity of her face.

'See for yourself!' Beatrice said, then was sick on the carpet.

When they put her into a cell down at the police station Libby couldn't believe it was happening to her. When she heard Beatrice shouting obscenely she asked about the boy and was told that he was being taken care of. When she was told that they were trying to contact her husband but without success, she put her head down in her hands and wept, imagining Harry going about his business, making his prolonged afternoon calls in blissful ignorance of what was happening.

When they brought her into an interview room an hour later and she saw Carrie standing there, Libby went straight into her sister's arms, all antagonism forgotten as they clung together. Two halves of one, as united as if the shadow of Tom Silver had never come between them.

'It's all right, love. Everything will be all right.' Carrie smoothed Libby's hair away from her forehead. 'When Nurse Tomkin couldn't find Harry she telephoned me. There's nothing to be afraid of. Hush, hush . . . don't cry.'

When the plain clothes man coughed discreetly by the door and they moved apart, he asked Carrie to go through into the next room. 'I'll call you in when I'm ready,' he said. 'Just wait till you're told, lass. Right?'

Libby stood with bowed head as they brought Beatrice in. A cleaned-up though still sour-smelling Beatrice, defiance flaring from her eyes, and only the quivering of her chins betraying her agitation.

'Are you sure that this is the woman who you say was having an affair with your husband, the deceased?' The policeman placed the photograph in the middle of the table. 'This woman?' He pointed to Libby. 'This same woman as on this photograph?'

Beatrice nodded firmly. 'See for yourself. What can't speak can't lie, can it? It's her all right.'

The detective constable made a sign to the uniformed man standing by the door, then as Carrie came in he motioned her to stand beside Libby.

'Now.' He spoke firmly. 'Now, Mrs McDermot. Are you still sure that the lady you accused is the one in the photograph? That *she* was the one who went for your husband with the knife this morning?' His voice whispered, silken soft. 'Because this lady here,' he pointed to Carrie, 'has told me that *she* was the one friendly with your husband and *her* alibi this morning is as tight as a sealed drum.' He motioned to the sisters to stand even closer. 'Now, make up your mind, Mrs McDermot. Do you still stick to your statement?'

Beatrice's mouth stayed open in a wide startled 'O' of amazement. Blinking, she stared as if she could not believe the evidence of her eyes. Identical faces, identical hair, noses, eyes . . . She stared first at the photograph, then at the two faces staring at her silently. She staggered, the sickness rising thick in her throat again, then before her fuddled brain could react coherently, the detective barked at her, '*You* killed your husband, Mrs McDermot! You found him looking at the photograph, and in a frenzy of jealousy you went for the knife and you killed him. You've been attacking him for years. Isn't that true? Isn't it? Well?'

Before Beatrice could reach the sisters, her arms were pinioned behind her by the policeman standing by the door, but he was too late to stop the spit shooting from her mouth straight into Libby's face.

'Yes, I killed him!' she screamed. 'He was a *nothing!* A weak bundle of nowt! He wasn't a man! He wasn't even man enough to fight for his country. I *hated* him. He wasn't even man to give me a proper son. He deserved to die! I wished he'd died more slowly, but oh no, one slash and he went.' She fought like a maniac as the policeman dragged her away. 'He didn't even put up a fight for himself! He just stood there and let me do it – just stood there, egging me on!'

It was a long time before her cries died away, and even when they had stopped both Libby and Carrie knew that they would be hearing them for a long time to come.

When the detective said they could go, they walked away together as if they were one person, leaving him scratching his head and staring after them, scarcely believing the evidence of his own eyes.

Fourteen

'There's a man at the door says he wants to see Miss Carrie.'

Mrs Edwards, wearing a flour-spattered apron, looked flustered. It wasn't her place to answer the door but what with the new girl being off with the flu, the morning help having gone home and something serious going on in the lounge, she didn't know whether she was coming or going. Added to which, her deafness had stopped her from hearing the caller's name properly.

Harry jumped to his feet at the sight of her anxious face. 'I'll see to it, Mrs Edwards.' He turned and nodded at the three worried faces. 'If it's a reporter I'll send him packing. We have nothing to say to the papers, not now or ever.'

He was back in less than a minute with Tom Silver, a grim-faced Tom who, going straight to Carrie, took both her hands in his own.

'They gave me the brief details to set up at work.' His eyes searched hers. 'It merely said that Mungo McDermot had been murdered and his wife is helping the police with their inquiries. But there are rumours, and when I heard them I just put my coat on and came straight out.' He shook her hands gently. 'Carrie, love, you mustn't set foot out of the house. I know what the press can be like when they scent a mystery.'

Then for the first time he seemed to be aware that there were others in the room. 'Mrs Peel.' He nodded politely in Ettie's direction, still keeping hold of Carrie. 'I apologize for barging in like this, but I couldn't stay away.' He gave Libby a cursory glance and a brief nod. 'Libby . . .' Then he held out a hand to Harry. 'You must be Dr Brandwood? My name is Silver, Tom Silver.'

'Glad to know you.'

Harry shook the outstretched hand, pumping it up and down, his innate good manners not quite good enough to conceal the flash of interest in his eyes. So *this* was the man Libby had been so scornful about. The man she was convinced was after the Peel money. Well, well . . . Tom Silver might not be old-school-tie material, but neither was he a flat-capped moron. Quite presentable really, Harry decided.

'Oh, Tom.' Carrie drew him down to sit beside her on the chesterfield. 'I'm so glad you've come. Everything has been so dreadful.' She caught hold of his jacket sleeve. 'It was Libby who found the body, not me.' Then in a low voice, never taking her eyes from his face, she told Tom the whole story. 'We were going to have the boy brought here but the police told Harry that one of Mungo's wife's sisters had already been and taken him away. Libby thinks this will have undone all the progress she was making with his speech. She wouldn't be surprised if he never tried to speak again. For a child to see his father . . . oh, Tom, Mungo's wife is *insane*. He used to tell me she was, but I thought he was exaggerating, and now Libby is involved, and it's all my fault – oh, Tom . . .'

As though they were entirely alone, Tom took her in his arms, holding her head, stroking her hair, whispering, groping in his pocket for a handkerchief, and then drying her eyes as tenderly as if she were a child.

Libby watched them closely, seeing, with a painful sense of loss, the love of two people belonging together as if they were indeed one person.

'Harry!' Her voice was harsh and abrupt. 'Now that Mr Silver is here I think we can go.' She reached for the fur-trimmed coat lying across the back of a chair, holding it out for Harry to help her on with it. '*You* will have patients waiting, and I have the baby to see to. Mother? You are sure you don't want to come back with us? Mr Silver will see that Carrie is all right, I'm sure of that.'

'I think I'll go upstairs and lie down for a while.' Ettie, too, got up from her seat by the fire and held out a wavering hand to Harry. 'Perhaps you will see me to my room, Harry? My head is aching and my back hurts.' She took a few tottering steps towards the door, sliding out as usual from a situation she found intolerable. 'Ask Mrs Edwards to have something sent up to me on a tray, will you, Carrie?'

Embarrassed but obedient, Harry took her arm. Libby drew on her gloves. 'You know where I am if you need me, Carrie.' The door closed behind them.

'Ah, well . . .' Tom's dark eyes held for a moment their customary twinkle. 'No one could exactly say that I'm welcome round here, but what does that matter?' He traced the outline of Carrie's mouth with a finger. 'This will blow over, love. Whatever comes out in the paper, the public have short memories.' He smiled at her with love. 'Today's news is tomorrow's fish-and-chip wrapping. Always has been and always will be. Right?' He tightened his arms round her. 'And when your mother's settled in her bed I'm going up to talk to her. No, don't say anything. I'm not going to slink from the house this time like an intruder. Your mother can't collapse on me twice on the trot. Even your brother-in-law might suspect that she might be malingering this time.'

Suddenly he was very serious. 'You have to make up your mind, love. You should have come for me before you went along down to the police station. My office is only a minute away, for heaven's sake. You must understand that from now on we face things together.' He hugged her tightly. 'Even murders, love. You're never going to need to face any kind of trouble alone. Never. You understand?'

'But it was Libby who suffered, not me.' Carrie shook her head. 'Not me. She might have been killed, Tom. She went back into that house alone to protect the boy, and never even said that the photograph wasn't of her. She was so brave. Far braver than I would have been.'

'Rubbish!' Tom held her away from him, looking deep into her troubled eyes. 'Your sister will always be able to stand on her own two feet; she's made that way. She might *look* like you . . .' He grinned. 'And seeing you together for the first time gave *me* a bit of a turn, I might tell you. But I know how completely different you are.' He took a deep breath. 'Now! Do you think your mother will be decently in bed and ready for me to go and see her? Because that's exactly what I'm going to do, and if she faints I'll just wait till she comes round, then tell her we're getting married all the same. Ready?'

'Alone!' he whispered, as Carrie let him into the big front bedroom where Ettie lay against her pillows, a handkerchief soaked in eau de Cologne pressed to her forehead. 'You go back downstairs, and leave this to me. Right?'

He walked to the foot of the bed and stood there, his chin up in a gesture that, had the frail woman in the bed known it, spoke more of shyness and reserve than defiance.

'I would like a word, Mrs Peel,' he said.

Ettie's eyes were closed behind the scented handkerchief, but her mind was working feverishly. Like Libby, she had seen the love that shimmered between this man and her daughter, and seeing it had known for certain this time that she had lost.

'I am not very well, Mr Silver.' There was a plaintive pleading in her voice. 'This terrible business has upset me dreadfully. And now I would like to sleep.'

Tom stood his ground. He felt completely out of place in a room like this, with its thick carpet and the billowing satin eiderdown on the bed. There was a fire burning in the grate, and he wondered what this tiny woman would say if she knew that it was the first time he had ever *seen* a fire in a bedroom? Down his street babies were born in unheated bedrooms, put to sleep in drawers lined with newspaper and tatty blankets. There were chamber pots underneath the beds instead of a bathroom down the landing, candles set in saucers, and coats on the bed in the middle of winter when ice formed on the inside of the windows.

He cleared his throat. 'Mrs Peel, I want to marry your Carrie.' He found he was gripping the mahogany bed-end. 'I know I might not seem much cop to you, but I have a job, I have a house, and I will cherish Carrie for the rest of my life.' He raised his voice without meaning to. 'As long as I'm there I won't let the wind blow too hard on her, Mrs Peel. She will only have to ask, and if it's in my power then I will give her whatever she wants. I'll be faithful to her; when she's sick then I'll nurse her, and when she's happy then I'll be happy too. I haven't known much joy in my life, Mrs Peel; I was left without mother or father when I was sixteen, but I managed somehow, fending for myself and serving my time to get myself a steady job. I've been married before, Mrs Peel, to a young

209

lass who got blown to bits in an explosion at the munitions factory out Darwen way. I was in France at the time, at the front line, Mrs Peel – I didn't even get home for the funeral. She was a nice young lass, my wife, and her mother and me, we liked each other a lot.' He coughed. 'I would like to think that you and me might get on fine, Mrs Peel. We have a lot in common, after all, you loving Carrie and me loving her as well. I would like it fine if you came to see us a lot. Not that our house would be anything like this, but you'd be right welcome, Mrs Peel.'

He took a necessary breath. 'I know you can hear me, Mrs Peel, underneath that hankie, and I haven't finished yet. Not by a long chalk. I want you to know that my politics come in a different colour from what yours do, and although I haven't been to church for a long time, if I *did* go it would be to Chapel where the prayers aren't all set out in a book, but spoken from the heart, in the way I'm speaking to you. And another thing. When we're married, Carrie and me, I'm not that proud that I won't let her buy some of her own clothes, if that's what she wants, but everything else, Mrs Peel, *everything else*, I provide. I promise you this – as God's my judge, and oh aye, I believe in Him all right – I'll make her a good husband, and what's more I'll look after you. You being Carrie's mother makes you my responsibility as well. When Carrie's babies come they won't have a nurse to see to them, but they'll be *your* grandchildren, and if any of them take after you then I'll be well satisfied. You're a bonny woman, Mrs Peel.' He came round the bed and gently lifted the handkerchief from Ettie's face. 'So you can come out from under there and stop that play-acting. All right then, Mrs Peel?'

The tablets administered by Harry were taking effect. Ettie felt drowsy and warm, and the earnest face bending over the bed seemed to have fuzzy features, and a smile that was lop-sided in its gentleness. Her eyelids were as heavy as if pennies had been laid on them, and when she spoke her voice came muffled on the very edge of sleep.

'I heard you all right, Mr Silver,' she said. 'And what you said sounded like poetry. Do you know that?' Her smile wavered. 'Do you know how long it is since anyone told me I was a bonny woman?' Her hand came up and Tom clasped it in his firm grasp. 'My husband wasn't a man for pretty speeches . . .' Her head moved from side to side slowly. 'And though I'll regret it in the morning when I wake up, I feel, right this minute, that you might be just the man Carrie needs.' She tried to lift herself up on an elbow but fell back. 'You're a nice young man, Mr Silver. A very nice young man, *and* kind. And do you know something?' The drug was making her as maudlin as if she had drunk half a bottle of whisky, and realizing this, Tom smiled.

'Yes, Mrs Peel?'

'I think you and I might be friends some day . . . I do. I really do. But I wish you'd have your hair trimmed a bit. You can talk like a poet, but you don't have to *look* like one. Do you, Mr Silver?'

'She was *flirting* with you!' Carrie, coming into the room and overhearing the last few words, turned to Tom in amazement as they went back down the wide staircase together. 'It's no wonder women fall in love with you.' When they were back in the sitting room, she reached up and pulled his face down to hers, holding him still between the palms of her hands. 'Oh, Tom. If you and Mother are going to get on so well, why don't you come and live at Westerley after we're married? She'll be so lonely when I'm gone, and the house is so big. We wouldn't be in each other's pockets all the time.'

'You don't mean that?' Gently Tom disengaged her hands and put her from him. 'You said that without thinking, didn't you?'

'No. I mean it.' Carrie's face was flushed. 'When I thought that you and Mother were going to be – well, not exactly seeing eye to eye, there was no question of it. But now . . . oh, Tom, think what it would mean to Mother having a man about the house, and think what it would mean to me to be able to keep an eye on her all the time. She'll take to her bed permanently when she's all alone. She will. I *know* her, remember.'

'Carrie!' Walking over to the fire, Tom pushed a piece of coal into position with his shoe. 'How old is your mother, love?'

'What has that got to do with it?'

'How old is she?'

Fifty-nine. No, fifty-eight. She'll be fifty-nine in September. She was thirty-four when we – Libby and I – were born. Why?'

'Then she isn't an old woman. Not by a long chalk.' Tom put out a hand to draw Carrie to him, but at the look in her eyes he drew it back.

'She's a sick woman, Tom.' Indignation flushed Carrie's face to pink. 'She's been an invalid ever since I can remember. It was having us – twins – and then later Willie being killed. It's understandable.'

'Rubbish!' Tom kicked at the coals again. 'I know women who lost their sons in the war and kept straight on standing at their looms. I know women who have babies, one after the other, and still go out scrubbing right to the moment of birth. There's nothing wrong with your mother but what goes on in her mind, and that's unhappiness. She wants to be needed, love. Can't you see?'

'And me asking you to live here doesn't mean I'm thinking about her?' Carrie stood erect, both hands clenched by her sides. 'Isn't that caring?'

'Caring for someone isn't the same as letting them think you need them.' He dismissed her last words with a wave of his hand. 'That mother of yours hasn't been needed for a long, long time. Not by your father, nor by you and Libby. It's staring at you from her face, love. The blank loneliness of never being needed. I know!'

'You seem to know a lot about her in a short time.'

'Yes, as a matter of fact I do.'

'And you won't even consider coming to live here?'

'Not for a minute.' He grinned, then saw at once the grin was a mistake. 'Carrie, love. Can you see me being waited on by a maid in a pinny? Can you see me letting that woman who let me in call me "sir"? If she came in now to see to the fire I'd snatch the coal shovel from her. I'd be ashamed to let a servant do for me.'

'So you think Mrs Edwards is downtrodden, do you?' Carrie felt the sting of tears behind her eyelids. The events of the morning were making her edgy and prickly. Tom was being unreasonable. They were quarrelling for the first time, at least

212

she was quarrelling. *He* was merely stating what he thought to be the facts, and expecting her to agree. She waited with eyes narrowed for what he would say next, and when he said nothing she burst out childishly, 'All right then! Go into the kitchen! Go right now and ask Mrs Edwards if she feels in any way like a slave. Ask her where she would be if it wasn't for us. And if she won't tell you, then I will. In the workhouse, that's where! She hasn't got any family or any money, and she's practically stone deaf. So where would people like her be if it wasn't for people like me and my kind, Tom Silver? You think the whole population should be equal. But they will never be equal, because that's the way it has always been. Ask Mrs Edwards to take my mother's place and she would die of boredom in a week. Ask my mother to take Mrs Edwards's place and she'd be dead of overwork in a week.'

'And yet I'm expecting you to make that transition?' At last Tom felt his own temper rise. He glanced at the clock. 'I have to go to a meeting tonight so I must go now. Maybe rushing here wasn't such a good idea after all.'

Watching him go Carrie frowned and bit her lip. Tom would spend the rest of his life fiercely upholding what he felt to be right. She reminded herself that his sometimes unbending attitude had lost him his job once. Was it possible that the same attitude could help him to walk away from his love? She had a sudden picture in her mind of her life as it had been before he came into it, and she took a step forward, ready to throw herself into his arms and tell him that she would live with him in a tent if need be. Anywhere, as long as they were together.

But, as if warding her off, Tom put the width of the door between them and spoke to her through the opening. 'Think well on it, Carrie. Go upstairs when your mother has had her sleep and talk to her. *She* knows and understands how I feel. She'll tell you that happiness doesn't always come wrapped up in expensive paper. You think deeply about it all, Carrie. Then let me know.'

His fear was as great as hers, if she had only realized it. When he left the house, taking the steps down to the drive two at a time, Tom was already doubting some of the things he had said to her. Was he being fair? He was speaking that very evening on the subject of class privilege, but here he was proposing to step over it with no regard for the implications. Oh, Carrie . . . Carrie, love. Tom swung himself onto the tram platform just as the conductor rang the bell, his face a mask of worry above his high starched collar.

'Mother seems almost resigned to the idea of me marrying Tom.'

Carrie sat with Libby in the nursery watching Nurse Tomkin feeding the baby. It never occurred to her not to talk family business in front of the little woman carefully holding the feeding bottle at the right angle. Besides, Nurse Tomkin wasn't exactly a servant, more like one of the family now. Those strange, short-sighted eyes behind the whirlpool lenses seemed to miss nothing.

Carrie smiled at her sister. 'I don't know what Tom said to Mother, but he obviously charmed her yesterday. You were wrong about him wanting to move into Westerley, Libby. He wouldn't hear of it.'

Libby was feeling very fragile that morning. Harry, in spite of his obvious concern for her, had berated her soundly on her rudeness to Tom Silver.

'Those two will marry,' he had said, 'in spite of whatever you or your mother might say. I thought it was very touching the way the chap went straight to Carrie when he came in. It was as though no one else existed. He won't be intimidated, that one.'

There was a great weight of misery in Libby's chest. Last night she had wanted Harry to make love to her. She had wanted him to take her fiercely, even cruelly, but ever considerate he had kissed her a chaste goodnight and actually tucked her in before going down to write a letter to the *Lancet* on the high incidence of heart attacks in the town. He had a theory that it might have something to do with the lack of lime in the drinking water, and though he was only skirting round the idea he hoped his tentative probings might interest someone able to follow them up in a more practical way.

'Oh, Harry . . .' Libby had cried into her pillow. 'Why don't you *make* me love you?' Then she had stared wide-eyed at the ceiling. 'And what will I do now that Edwin will no longer be coming to the house for lessons?'

Now she stared at her baby, bald except for a fringe of hair straggling down into the nape of its fat neck. Maybe Harry was right and she should send Nurse Tomkin back to her village. She moved in her chair with the old restlessness, her dark eyes looking for something that wasn't there, searching for the stimulation, the excitement so necessary to her existence.

'Mother could come and live here.' She spoke without thinking, then shook her head. 'But Mother will never leave Westerley. She'll grow old quickly and die soon, and there's nothing we can do about it.' She sighed. 'Oh, why did Willie have to go and get himself killed? He would be married now and the natural heir to Westerley and the mill, and Mother would live the rest of her life surrounded by Willie's children.' She pushed at her fringe so that the calf-lick stood up in an untidy spike. 'That bloody awful war. Its consequences never end for some, do they?'

Nurse Tomkin sat the baby up and started to wind her. The small eyes were narrowed into slits as she wrestled with what passed for her conscience. The promise she had made to Sarah Batt she had kept, but now . . . well, all things being equal, maybe she could . . . Settling the baby back on her other arm she thrust the rubber teat into its wildly groping mouth.

'Sarah Batt's mother died a month or so back,' she said, as if telling the news to the baby.

Immediately two faces, identical in their expressions of concern, turned towards her.

'Oh, poor Sarah!' Carrie spoke first. 'What will happen to her? The cottage was only rented to them as long as Mrs Batt lived. Isn't that right?'

Nurse Tomkin nodded. 'Yes, that's right.' She prized the teat from the baby's mouth to stop the milk from being gulped too quickly. 'I saw Sarah when I went back last weekend. She's in a right mess. She was going out scrubbing at one of the big houses, but now they are cutting down on staff she's got the sack.' She sniffed. 'It's all these mills closing, and the mines paying the miners next to nothing. The women come out from the town and take our jobs. For less money,' she added bitterly.

'So Sarah is without a job?' Libby exchanged a glance with Carrie, a glance which the little woman noted with satisfaction – so far so good.

'Yes. Before long she'll be without a roof to her head, and she can't go for a living-in job because of the boy.' The grey head dropped over the tilted bottle. 'He's a right larnt-up one, that lad. Too big for his boots, if you ask me, but a clever scholar, they say.' She waited, holding her breath. Well, she hadn't broken no promise yet, had she?

'So there would be nothing to stop Sarah coming back to Westerley?' Libby's voice was eager, her lethargy forgotten now that there was something she could organize.

'There's still her son.' Carrie sat forward, clasping her hands round her knees. 'But Mother wouldn't mind having Sarah's son living with her. Not if it meant getting Sarah back. Would she?'

'But why hasn't Sarah got in touch?' Libby frowned. 'She knows how upset Mother was when she left. I used to think that Sarah meant more to her than we did.'

'Pride.' Carrie nodded. 'You know what Sarah was like, how she would flare up if we tried to talk about her boy.'

'Hiding her shame,' Libby broke in quickly. 'As if that mattered now, after all this time.'

'So we'll write. Now. Today.'

'Can she read?'

'Oh, heavens, Libby, her son will read the letter to her.'

So fascinated was Nurse Tomkin at the turn of the conversation that she was allowing the baby to suck at an empty bottle. Listening to those two was like listening to one person speaking. Two minds perfectly attuned, and she had said practically nothing, given nothing away.

'Sarah is past thinking straight, if you don't mind me interrupting,' she said. 'That lad of hers grows out of his britches faster than a stick of rhubarb growing from a muck heap. His mother is going without, if you ask me.'

'Without food?' Carrie was horrified.

Nurse Tomkin nodded. 'If I was you, Mrs Brandwood,' she focussed her myopic gaze on Libby, 'I would get the doctor to drive you out there this Sunday.' She hoisted the baby onto her shoulder and rubbed its back in a circular motion. '*I'll* be here to see to the baby.'

'But it's your weekend off,' Libby protested, not too vehemently.

'I don't mind.' Nurse Tomkin closed her eyes to hide the glitter of triumph at the way she had managed things. 'Why not take your mother with you, Mrs Brandwood? The country is lovely just now. It would do her good to get out of the house; this business yesterday must have upset her a lot.'

She smiled to herself as the two sisters immediately got up and clammed their mouths tight shut. Their reticence didn't bother Nurse Tomkin. She had been the one to answer the telephone when the police rang, hadn't she? And she had already found out enough to be going on with. She would ferret out the whole truth one way or another, and for the time being she had done her good deed.

It rained hard on Sunday, but they still drove out to the country. From the car window Ettie watched the rain falling on the fields and the little gardens fronting the stone cottages.

'Are you sure we ought to be interfering like this?'

She asked the question to Libby's back, but Libby was, as Carrie would have said, 'on the warpath'.

'We are doing the *right thing*,' she said firmly.

But when Sarah, painfully thin and tired-looking, opened the door to them, Ettie forgot her misgivings immediately.

'Sarah? May we come in? I have something I want to ask you. It's a favour, a very great favour.' She glanced up at the grey sky. 'We are getting wet, dear. It won't take a minute. May we come in?'

The little back room of the cottage was so small, the ceiling so low, that when they all sat down Ettie had the feeling that the walls were closing in on them. She smiled at Sarah. 'Don't look so scared, dear. We heard about your mother, and we are sorry, so very sorry.'

Sarah nodded. Her mouth was hanging half open, giving her a look of utter stupidity. It was all far worse than Libby had expected it would be. The whole atmosphere smelled of poverty, and Harry was shifting in his chair, obviously wishing he was miles away. So with her usual lack of finesse,

217

Libby came straight to the point.

'Carrie is getting married, so Mother needs you, Sarah. It would make us all very happy if you came back. With your son, of course,' she added. 'Westerley is more than big enough, and we all feel it would be a very suitable arrangement, especially as Nurse Tomkin told us you are under notice to leave this cottage.'

'Well, Sarah?' Ettie leaned forward. 'What do you say? Will you at least think it over, dear?' Then, getting no response from the still figure, she added, 'We don't want to upset you, Sarah. What's troubling you so much, my dear? You must at least try to tell us. We have come because we want to help.'

For a long moment no one moved or spoke. Suddenly the back door opened and a young boy hurtled into the room, socks slipping down over muddy boots, thin jacket black with rain, blue eyes sparkling with mischief. As he hesitated, snatching his cap from his head, a shaft of sunlight broke through the clouds, transforming his barley-pale hair to a halo of gold.

Libby gasped in astonishment. Ettie jumped to her feet, clutching both hands together in front of her chest, swaying as the colour drained from her cheeks to leave her face a strange chalky white.

'Go upstairs to your room, son!' Sarah's voice shattered the uncanny silence, rough with despair so terrible that it might have been a voice speaking from the grave.

'But Mam. . . ?'

Bewildered by the ring of faces, most of all by the sight of the small elderly lady rocking herself backwards and forwards as if she was barmy, Patrick stood his ground. 'I was just going to . . .'

'Upstairs!' Sarah was on her feet advancing towards him. 'These – these people will be going soon.'

'Oh, God, dear, dear God . . .'

Patrick stepped back as the moaning woman held out both her arms. With his blue eyes searching first one strange face then another, he said, 'Are you all right, Mam? What's happened? I'd rather stop down here with you.'

'Patrick!' Sarah's voice was a sharp as the crack of a whip. 'Upstairs! You and me will talk later. Do as you're told!'

Stumbling in his muddy boots, half defiant and more than a little afraid, Patrick did as he was told, running up the uncarpeted stairs then closing the door of his room with a loud crash.

The sound coincided with Ettie's release from her half-paralysed state of shock. Going over to Sarah, she took her by the shoulders and shook her with a force one would hardly have believed she was capable of.

'That boy is Willie! Oh, dear God in heaven, that child is Willie's son! He is my Willie as a little boy. Sarah! Your son is my grandson. *Isn't* he?'

'No! No, Mrs Peel! He's not. He's not!'

Sarah's pathetic, almost hysterical denial was sliced away by a downward sweep of Libby's hand as the teacher in her took over. In a firm, no-nonsense voice, she stated briskly, 'Of course he is Willie's son, Sarah. He's the living image of the brother I once had. It was like seeing Willie come to life again. So let's sit down and talk about it calmly.'

'Yes. Calm down, Sarah, and you too, Mother. This isn't doing you any good.'

At the sound of Harry's quiet tones, Sarah dropped down into her chair, setting it rocking furiously. When she spoke her voice was still full of despair.

'I knew there'd be no keeping it from you once you set eyes on him. That's why I kept him away from you all these years!'

With her face wrenched out of shape, she turned to Ettie. 'Oh, Mrs Peel, forgive me.' Tears rolled from the blue eyes. 'Willie never loved me, never really *loved* me, but it happened when he came home on that last leave. I was too frightened to tell you. Mr Peel would have killed me for being a bad girl with his son in his house, an' it wasn't like that. It wasn't!' She took a deep breath. 'Willie never told you how it was out there in the trenches in France, Mrs Peel, because he knew you couldn't have borne to listen. But he told *me*. An' it was terrible! Willie wanted to spare you, but *I* listened, an' I comforted him, as best I could, Mrs Peel.'

'My grandson . . .' Ettie began to speak as if she were quite alone, as if not a single word of Sarah's pathetic confession had penetrated her understanding. 'All this time, and I didn't know. That lovely, lovely boy, my Willie's son, and I never knew!'

219

'But you can't have 'im! He's *mine!*' Sarah gave a shout of anguish. 'Since me mother died, he's all I've got!' She was looking directly at Libby now. 'You think because you've a lot of money you can just come here and – and –'

'Sarah!' Ettie, all pretence at pride gone, went to kneel down on the cut-rug by the rocking chair. Libby opened her mouth to say something, but Harry silenced her with a look.

'It's all Nurse Tomkin's fault,' Sarah muttered. 'She went back on her word. After she'd promised she went back on her word.'

'Nurse Tomkin said *nothing.*' Ettie's normally soft voice rang with conviction. 'Until that boy came through the door not one of us here today even guessed. Oh, Sarah! Listen to me, dear. Mr Peel is *dead.* It's me, Mrs Peel, you are dealing with now, not my husband.'

Kneeling up straight she tried to pull the stiff unyielding young woman into her arms. 'Think, Sarah. You would be coming to me as the daughter-in-law I never had, and Patrick . . . oh, my dear, I could give him so much. The best schools, the finest education money could buy.'

Sarah's face peaked into lines of obstinacy. 'But he'll pass his scholarship, Mrs Peel. My son is clever. He won't need no money to pay for his education. He'll win his own way.'

'But what about his clothes, his shoes, and his books?' Libby could contain herself no longer. 'It takes more than brains to keep a boy at a grammar school, Sarah.'

'You'll take him from me, Miss Libby!' Sarah was shouting now. 'I know you! Once you get a hold of him he won't be mine no longer.'

'Don't be silly,' Libby said, then opened her eyes wide as Harry pulled her to her feet.

'This is between Sarah and your mother,' he said firmly. 'We'll go outside and wait in the car. Coming, Libby?'

When they had gone Sarah looked into Ettie's upturned face and saw that the older woman had scarcely noted their departure. Her whole soul was in her pleading eyes. It was no longer mistress and servant; now they were merely two women meeting on common ground.

Taking both of Sarah's hands in her own, Ettie said gently, '*You* are Patrick's mother, dear. You would have first say in everything concerning him.' Tenderly she shook the work-worn hands. 'You trust *me*, don't you?'

Sarah nodded, biting hard at her bottom lip. 'Oh, yes. You was always good to me, Mrs Peel.'

'Well then, dear?'

It was as though Ettie had stopped breathing as she waited for Sarah's answer. She knelt there, small and dignified, her face still a chalky white and her eyes never leaving Sarah's face. Sarah wavered.

'And you wouldn't change his name or nothing? There wouldn't be no solicitor's papers making him over to the Peels or anything?'

Ettie shook her head. 'My house would be home for both of you, for as long as you wanted to stay — that's all,' she promised. 'This I swear to you.'

For a long moment the only sound in the tiny room was the sudden shifting of a log on the leaping fire. Then getting up from her chair and going to the foot of the stairs, Sarah called out, 'Patrick? Come down here. That's a good boy.'

When Ettie joined Libby and Harry in the car her face was transfigured by a blinding joy that was almost tangible.

'Let's go home. I have a lot to do,' Ettie said, her smile like a blessing.

Fifteen

'Now we can all be happy,' Carrie said, holding hands with Tom. Her eyes filled with mischief. 'Oh, Tom, it's just like the ending of a book where everyone walks off into the sunset.'

Tom grinned down at her, humouring her, loving her with such transparent devotion that Libby had to turn away. She ached to be tinged with the same kind of happiness, but there was always this feeling of restlessness, this disappointment, this certainty that somehow her life had taken a wrong turning.

She watched Harry talking to Tom Silver, easily, freely, and it came to her that if only Tom could have stayed as a dream-like shadowy lover in the background of her life, then her feelings for Harry would have been intensified. Fidgeting with the long rope of beads hanging down the front of her waistless dress, Libby frowned at the irrationality of this idea even as she accepted its truth.

She ached for Harry to look at her in the way Tom was staring at Carrie, and yet, if he had, she knew she would have met the look with indifference.

What was *wrong* with her?

The wedding took place at four o'clock on a Saturday afternoon in May. There were no church bells ringing, no choir-boys in red surplices singing 'O Perfect Love'.

Carrie's dress was Macclesfield silk, Libby's Chinese shantung, and they both wore hats shaped like the bells on a sprig of lily of the valley. Sarah's straw hat was decorated by what looked like a field of poppies, daisies and cornflowers, and,

222

accompanied by Patrick in a neat grey suit, she was almost as radiant as the bride.

Back at Westerley for the quiet family reception, Patrick was placed by Ettie's side at the big table in the dining room, a table set with cold ham, salads, and a huge joint of underdone beef.

Carrie managed to have a quiet word with Sarah. 'We're lucky to have such a good Catholic college in the town, aren't we? Mother tells me Patrick has settled in so well his masters are already talking about his future. Has *he* any ideas of his own about what he wants to be?'

'An officer in the army,' Sarah said at once, then her round face went pink with pleasure. 'Oh, Miss Carrie, Patrick can't hear enough about his father, and Mrs Peel is only too happy to oblige. They spend hours, the two of them, poring over old photographs.' She bit her lip. 'I did wrong not telling him the truth, but then you see, I never realized how . . .' she struggled to find the right word, 'how uncomplete he felt not knowing.'

Carrie patted her arm. 'Well, one thing is certain, Sarah. There'll never be another war in Patrick's lifetime. Not after the last one.'

'Yes, that's a blessing.' Sarah crossed herself furtively over the bodice of her crêpe-de-Chine two-piece. 'That would be something I couldn't bear.' Then she sat up straight as Harry began his well-rehearsed speech. 'Ssh,' she said to no one in particular.

The telephone rang just as the speech ended, and Ettie's new maid, a young weaver from the mill, beckoned importantly from the doorway.

'It's for you. Doctor,' she announced, and with an apologetic glance in his wife's direction Harry walked quickly into the hall.

'Oh, no!' Libby gave a deep sigh. 'You'd think his patients would leave him alone, just for today.'

But when Harry came back into the room his expression was grim.

'There's been an accident at Crowhead colliery, a roof fall a long way out with ten men trapped.' He looked straight at Libby. 'I have to go, love.'

Then he turned to Ettie. 'I'm truly sorry, but I'll have to

223

leave right this minute. I have things to collect from the surgery.'

'I'm coming with you.' Libby moved towards him. 'We have put upon Nurse Tomkin's good nature long enough as it is.' Her smile was brilliant. 'I was going to say "be happy", but I don't think either Carrie or Tom needs that advice.'

Before Harry had turned the car out of the drive, she turned to him in exasperation.

'Why you, Harry? That colliery is five miles away. Why pick on you, for heaven's sake?'

Harry pressed his foot down hard on the accelerator. 'They are going to need all the help they can get, by the sound of it. It's two hours' walking to this particular coal face, apparently, and with so many trapped men who might need medical attention on the spot, and me being on call –' He glanced sideways at Libby. 'You could have stayed on at the party, though.'

'They didn't need me.' Beneath the flower-pot hat her face was set and bleak. 'Mother has Patrick, and Carrie has Tom. I almost felt it was a double celebration, didn't you?'

Harry collected what he needed and rushed out of the house with his bag. She followed him to the door. Smiling at her, he turned to wave, and as he slid behind the wheel she saw that his wedding posy, a white carnation, was still fixed in his buttonhole. A sudden premonition caught at her breath.

'Take care!' Libby's words were lost in the sound of the car's engine, leaving her to go slowly into the house and close the door behind her.

At nine o'clock, when he had been away for over three hours, she went up to the nursery to tell Nurse Tomkin that she would see to the baby, should she wake up and demand a bottle. Like her mother before her, Libby's baby slept in snatches, ignoring set rules and going her own way.

Libby looked down at the small sleeping face. 'I must have something to do,' she explained.

Nurse Tomkin's eyes glittered behind her spectacles. 'I once saw a man hurt real bad. He was a fitter though, not a miner. There was a valve needed opening so they put a plank over the cage to the shaft wall. He fell off it, and they brought what was left of him up in a bag.' She sniffed. 'Nobody knows the conditions those men have to work under. It's no wonder they came out on strike, and for what? I've heard it rains like the clappers down some pits, and do you know what they pay them extra for getting soaked? A shilling a day! I ask you!'

Listening to her, Libby felt the blood drain from her face. She shook her head. 'But the doctor won't have to go down. The rescue party will have their own doctor. If my husband is needed at all it will be at the surface.'

At eleven o'clock, with the baby content after an extra bottle, Libby went to the window of the front bedroom, lifted the curtain and stared down into the quiet road.

She had not heard the rain, but now the pavements were shining black and a soft wind sighed in the trees. Too uneasy to undress, she wandered downstairs, moved the guard away from the dying fire, then built it up again with coal from the brass scuttle in the hearth.

Harry had said it was almost two hours' walk to the coal face where the men lay trapped . . . Libby shuddered as she watched the flames begin to lick round the shiny nuggets. At the time of the strike she had read how the miners worked on their knees, and sometimes lying flat on their stomachs, with sixty tubs to fill before they reached anything approaching a living wage. At the time she had been horrified; now it came back to her with a fresh shock.

No wonder Tom Silver felt as he did . . . and yet . . . it was *Harry* who was actually risking his life for the miners, not Tom. Libby looked at the clock on the mantelpiece ticking the slow minutes away. Leaning her head back she closed her eyes. Her thoughts were leading her down avenues she had never explored before. Unlike Tom Silver, Harry had no platform on which to stand and shout the odds. All Harry did was go about his daily routine, soothing the sick and closing the eyes of the dead.

She slept for a while, then started up when she thought she heard a car outside. But there was nothing but the silent avenue with its trees waving dark branches against the night sky. Back by the fire she sat motionless for another hour, then went to sit in the darkened nursery, falling asleep, waking, then falling asleep again until a grey finger of light touched the window.

225

'Is the doctor not back yet?' Even as the baby gave her first experimental cry, Nurse Tomkin came through the door with her grey hair straggling round her shoulders, a brown woollen dressing gown hugged tightly to her squat figure.

'Something has happened to him.' Libby's eyes were bleak with a feverish worry. 'I knew something terrible was going to happen at the wedding tea when everyone was so happy. When the telephone rang I knew I was right. It doesn't pay to be too happy. Being too happy is asking for trouble.'

If Nurse Tomkin had known Libby as a child, then as a young unmarried woman, she would have known this was the old dramatic, fanciful Libby talking, but even so, the nurse knew there was no point in arguing with her when she was in this mood. So when Libby said she was going to ring for a taxi and go out to the colliery, she merely nodded. But when she was alone once again with the baby, Nurse Tomkin voiced her thoughts out loud to herself.

'She's feared for him now she thinks she might be losing him. There's some who need a bit of a shake-up before they realize which side their bread's buttered on.'

They let Libby through the gate and into the colliery yard when she told them who she was. Walking over to the pit head she joined a small knot of women standing quietly in the falling rain.

'They've got nine of them up, love.' A woman with a hard face gentled into resignation moved her hand from beneath a grey fringed shawl and laid it for a moment on Libby's arm. 'The one left down there has a pick through his body. It had to come out, and when the doctor went down there was a second fall, and now they're trapped good and proper. Three of them – the poor bugger with the steel inside him, the doctor and the manager.' She nodded. 'Oh, aye, the manager's down there for all he's supposed to be a hard nut.'

Libby felt sick; she could have been sick right there. She knew the doctor was Harry. She had known even before she came, but she went to ask just the same, and as she ran across the yard to the office she saw, lying on the cobblestones, the white carnation, muddied and flattened, trampled by rushing

226

feet. She saw herself in her bell-shaped wedding hat slotting it into Harry's lapel, and she remembered how she had turned her face away so that his kiss had landed on her cheek instead of her lips.

'Oh, Harry . . .' She wanted to scream out her terror. She wanted to demand that the rescue party, still in their sweat and pit clothes, take her down with them. But knowing that would be impossible, she stumbled away to stand with the women, her beige coat with its ermine collar a sharp contrast to their sombre clothing.

'Usually it's the single men they send down.' The woman who had touched Libby's arm began to speak as if their conversation had never been interrupted. 'But they're all family men, all three of them.'

'The doctor is my husband. We have a baby, a little girl.' Libby felt the bile rise in her throat again.

'It's my son-in-law down there,' the woman confided. 'My daughter is near her time, so I made her stop at home.' She stared straight ahead, seeing nothing. 'There's nowt we can do, anyroad.' Suddenly her voice rose to a startling angry wail. 'Why couldn't they have fetched him up with the pick still in him? Why?'

'Because they knows best, love.'

A woman standing behind spoke up, her voice roughed with compassion. 'There's nowt you can do but wait, Mrs Parker. She's had it all before,' she whispered to Libby. 'Her husband was killed on the job three years back.'

'Oh, dear God. Oh, no!' Libby moved closer and touched the grey shawl. 'There's a car waiting for me. Would you like to go and sit inside it? You are wet through, Mrs Parker. Please let me take you to the car.'

'I'm stopping where I am.' The woman spoke without moving her head. 'I want to see him when they bring him out. For my daughter's sake it's the least I can do.'

Libby nodded, understanding at once. It had been a cold wet night for May, and now it was a cold wet morning. The fur at her neck was already uncomfortably sodden, and she could feel droplets running down her back. She glanced down at the women's feet sturdily clad in clogs, then at her own shoes with their thin soles, the soft cream leather patched with damp.

227

There was no more talking, no weeping, just a quiet standing there, keeping out of the way of the men rushing backwards and forwards. The ambulance was waiting, doors open, red blankets piled on stretchers, the driver's face impassive beneath his peaked cap.

'Are you by yourself, Mrs Brandwood?' A man in a trilby hat came and spoke softly to her. 'Will you come into the office and wait there?'

'I'm stopping where I am.' Unconsciously Libby echoed the words of the woman by her side. 'But thank you. Thank you just the same.'

'The cage is coming up!' It was a great sigh, and as Libby felt herself urged forward, she saw them coming out. Black-faced men with eyes picked out in the coal dust on their faces. As they trailed away dejectedly towards the office, she felt her own shoulders slump in sympathy.

She could taste the wine in her mouth, sour and nasty, the wine she had drunk at Carrie's wedding. She wanted to be sick, but knew she couldn't give way with the women crowding her in. If they could stand it, then so could she.

Like an echo from the past, she heard Tom Silver's teasing voice: 'Finding out for yourself how the peasants think and feel?'

Libby frowned and bit hard at her lip. She had been so sure she was in the right, that time down on the market place at the beginning of the strike. She remembered how she had seen Harry striding towards her, his face set into lines of uncharacteristic anger, and she remembered how she had taunted him for his lack of feeling.

'Oh, Harry . . .' Even as she went on standing there, her face set into a stony mask, she was screaming his name aloud somewhere deep inside her.

When the sky lightened and the rain softened to a raw drizzle, she saw the cage descend yet again, and found she was praying as she had never prayed before. 'Oh, God! Let Harry be alive. Even if he's hurt, let him live long enough for me to tell him I'm sorry. Don't let this be my punishment for not loving him enough.' If Harry died, she told herself fiercely, the one thing she would never be able to put from her mind would be the memory of his hurt face as she had turned away from his

228

kiss. She stared across the yard to where the carnation still lay, a dirty white mark on the greasy cobblestones.

Loneliness swamped her.

At seven o'clock she sensed that Carrie was there. Turning round she saw her twin coming across the yard with Tom Silver, and the next minute she was being held in Carrie's arms.

Now at last she could give way, but not until Carrie had led her away with Tom following close behind. Sobbing, Libby told them, sparing them nothing.

'Harry is trapped down there. It's a long way out, and there was a second fall. They are trying to get through, but I think I heard one of the men say something about *gas*.' She stared straight at Tom and saw her own despair mirrored in his dark eyes. 'Oh, Tom . . . what will they do if they can't get them out? Harry won't be left buried deep in the dark, will he? Not Harry. He was – he is always so *clean*.'

She was close to hysteria now. 'I can't bear to think about him all black and cold and wet. Oh, Carrie, he's still wearing his wedding suit.'

Over her head Carrie and Tom exchanged meaning glances.

'Come home with us, lass. It may be a long time yet, and there's nothing to be gained by you staying. Come home with us.'

Libby's refusal was immediate. 'No! No! I have to wait. I have to be here when they bring him out. Even if it takes for ever, and even if he – if he's dead, I have to be here, waiting for him.'

She looked at Carrie and her new husband as if seeing them properly for the first time. 'This is your honeymoon. Today is your first day together in your new house. You must go back.' She nodded towards the women standing solidly together, waiting impassively, silently for what must be. 'I'm with *them*. I'll be all right.'

'Do you think I'd leave you?' Carrie's voice was a passionate cry. 'How can you think for one minute that I would leave you to bear this alone? Oh, Libby . . . Libby, love . . .'

Tom followed more slowly as they moved back towards the group of women. 'Two halves of one,' he told himself wryly.

229

The thought touched him deeply so that when he looked up at the grey clouds, moving swiftly now, he found he was blinking tears from his eyes. It had been a strange wedding night, with his bride tossing and turning beside him, waking suddenly to sit up and call her twin's name aloud.

Now, as a watery sun tried to break through the clouds, he took his place by the two sisters, accepting their closeness and somehow glorying in it.

It was after another two long hours of waiting that the second rescue party came up from the mine.

'They've got through to them!' The murmur spread like a sigh through the knot of watching women. 'Thank God. They will have them up soon. You can always tell by the way they look.'

'Aye, it's something on their faces.'

Another hour went by, then the first stretcher came out, with the unconscious pit manager lying on it.

'He's lost a leg.'

The women pressed forward, one of them shaking the arm of a rescuer. 'Is it true?'

The news was conveyed in a low voice: 'He says the doctor took the leg off down there. It was the only way they could get him free.'

Carrie felt her sister stiffen. 'That means Harry could be alive! Oh, Carrie, he *has* to be alive. Please, please God, let him be alive!'

But the face of the man on the next stretcher was covered with a blanket, and his body lay twisted into a grotesque shape.

'That's Jack.'

The little woman in the grey shawl buried her face in her hands. 'Them's his boots. Oh, God, how I can tell me daughter I don't rightly know!' Her eyes hardened. 'I could tell her that the Lord giveth and the Lord taketh away, but I doubt that will give her much comfort. She'll know the baby will just be another mouth to feed with no man bringing in his wage of a Friday. So I won't say it. I won't say it . . .'

She was led away by a neighbour just as the third stretcher

was brought out. With a great cry Libby broke free from Carrie's restraining arm and rushed forward.

'Stand clear, missus!'

The ambulance men moved into action, but ignoring them, Libby bent over the stretcher to kiss the dirt-ingrained face above the swaddling blanket. The thick brown hair was matted with coal dust, and an ugly gash clotted with dried blood gave Harry's face a strange twisted expression.

'Harry!' Libby whispered his name at first, then her voice rose to a scream. 'Harry! Open your eyes Oh, Harry, darling, darling love, open your eyes and speak to me! It's me, Libby. Harry? I love you!' She raised a piteous face to one of the rescue party standing close by. 'He won't die, will he? He's not hurt badly enough to die, is he?'

Hands pulled at her, trying to drag her away, but with the strength of a madwoman she resisted. With all semblance of control gone, Libby tried to pull the unconscious man up into her arms.

'Now then, love.' A rescue worker moved Libby round to face him. 'The doctor is alive, lass. He's a bloody hero. His foot's broken with us having to drag him out at the last, but he'll live.'

The miner's exhausted face was touched with grief for the loss of his workmate, but with infinite patience he appealed to Tom. 'Get her away, lad. The sooner the doctor's seen to at the hospital the better.' He lowered his voice. 'His foot needs looking at right away.'

But it was Carrie who led Libby gently away, and Tom who told the driver of the waiting car to follow the ambulance to the hospital. Tenderly he helped the sisters into the back of the car, his heart aching at the sight of the two identical faces, both tear-streaked, pale and drawn in their shared anguish.

'When I thought he might have been killed I wanted to die. Oh, Carrie . . . if Harry had died then I would have wanted to die with him. Oh, how could I have loved him so much, and never known it? How?'

'Harry never doubted that you loved him.' Carrie's voice was soft with understanding. 'You are the joy of his life. You must know that.'

'Oh, yes, I do.'

Tom found he was having to blink back the tears from his own eyes as Libby whispered, 'Oh, Carrie. I thought I wanted – oh, I didn't know *what* it was I wanted. I had Harry and the baby, and yet . . . And now God has given me another chance. I don't deserve it, but He has given me another chance.'

Then, as the car swung out of the pit yard in the wake of the speeding ambulance, Tom turned round and saw the sisters clinging together, comforting and soothing as they would always comfort and soothe each other.

'See, girls. The sun is beginning to shine,' he said softly.

On the following pages are details of Arrow books that will be of interest.

MAGGIE CRAIG

Marie Joseph

From the natural successor to Catherine Cookson

At the turn of the century, the north of England was a hard, bleak world. A world where the only things in plenty were work and poverty – where joy and love were words in someone else's book. A world where men were resigned and women oppressed. It was here that Maggie Craig was born.

Strong-willed and spirited, as rebellious as she was beautiful, Maggie Craig flew in the face of the harshness of her life – and found a man she truly loved. But that passion was to cost her dearly all her life . . .

£1.50

A LEAF IN THE WIND

Marie Joseph

She was hardship's child – born to struggle and to serve.

He was fortune's favourite – born to flourish and be served.

They lived worlds apart. Jenny was the girl from the cat-meat shop, born into squalor and defeat. Paul Tunstall was a soldier and a gentleman, arrogant and charming, with his silver-light eyes and boyish smile. And yet from the moment they met there was a spark between them – and their separate lives of pain and loneliness seemed to beckon to each other.

But should she succumb to that plea in his eyes, to that longing in herself? Should she cross the line of class, the boundaries of propriety? Dare Jenny risk all to lose herself to love?

£1.50

CAPRICE

Sara Hylton

She had been as unpredictable, as enchantingly exotic and as exuberantly alive as her name. Caprice had been Thorn Lytton's beloved – but now she was just his memory . . .

It was not only Thorn Lytton who lived haunted by the memory of Caprice: it had driven his wife, Elsa, mad; it had stricken his grieving mother with silence; it had turned their sumptuous home, Milverton, into a dark museum of bitter secrets and twisted loves.

To Milverton comes Carla, destitute and orphaned, to make her living and find a home. Instead, she finds herself menaced by phantoms from the past, caught in a maelstrom of emotions, entangled in a mystery that may cost her her life – and hopelessly in love with a man whose heart died with another woman.

'I thoroughly enjoyed *Caprice*' *Victoria Holt*

£1.60

ELIZA STANHOPE

Joanna Trollope

Wilful and unconventional, Eliza Stanhope despises the marriage of her cousin and childhood companion, Julia, to rich, self-satisfied Richard Beaumont. Richard is certainly the dullest man in Hampshire and even Julia mocked him before she calculated the advantages his fortune would bring.

But when Richard's charming, younger brother, Francis, returns home from war, bringing with him his delightful fellow officer, Pelham Howell, Eliza sees some potential in the marriage. Soon she finds herself facing the bewildering and challenging demands of first love . . .

Joanna Trollope – a descendant of one of the great masters of the English novel, Anthony Trollope – has written a brilliantly creative story that puts her among the front rank of historical novelists.

'Joanna Trollope writes dazzlingly . . . a highly accomplished novel' *Newsagent and Bookshop*

£1.50

SISTERS

Claire Rayner

Everybody knew the Morris sisters. Rich, talented and envied, they were the toast of London. But their wealth concealed a background of poverty and hardship. And their success was built on a gnawing secret guilt.

Hester would sacrifice anything or anyone to her career in television. . . . Hildegarde uses her icy beauty to manipulate her way to the top of the fashion world. . . Bonnie holds the key to her sisters' fate and her own happiness.

A story that sweeps from the gloom of wartime Hackney to the glamour of Chelsea in the sixties, *Sisters* is a compelling novel of revenge, greed and family jealousy.

£1·25

BESTSELLING FICTION FROM ARROW

All these books are available from your bookshop or news-agent or you can order them direct. Just tick the titles you want and complete the form below.

THE DEFECTOR	Evelyn Anthony	£1.75
THE HISTORY MAN	Malcolm Bradbury	£1.60
1985	Anthony Burgess	£1.50
THE BILLION DOLLAR KILLING	Paul Erdman	£1.75
THE YEAR OF THE FRENCH	Thomas Flanagan	£2.50
EMMA SPARROW	Marie Joseph	£1.50
COCKPIT	Jerzy Kosinski	£1.60
CITY OF THE DEAD	Herbert Lieberman	£1.60
STRUMPET CITY	James Plunkett	£2.50
TO GLORY WE STEER	Alexander Kent	£1.75
TORPEDO RUN	Douglas Reeman	£1.50
THE BEST MAN TO DIE	Ruth Rendell	£1.25
SCENT OF FEAR	Margaret Yorke	£1.25
2001: A SPACE ODYSSEY	Arthur C. Clarke	£1.50
	Postage	
	Total	

ARROW BOOKS, BOOKSERVICE BY POST, PO BOX 29, DOUGLAS, ISLE OF MAN, BRITISH ISLES

Please enclose a cheque or postal order made out to Arrow Books Limited for the amount due including 10p per book for postage and packing for orders within the UK and 12p for overseas orders.

Please print clearly

NAME ....

ADDRESS ....

....

Whilst every effort is made to keep prices down and to keep popular books in print, Arrow Books cannot guarantee that prices will be the same as those advertised here or that the books will be available.